Curse
of
the Evil
Librarian

Michelle Knudsen

CANDLEWICK PRESS

Copyright © 2019 by Michelle Knudsen

First edition 2019

Library of Congress Catalog Card Number 2018963114
ISBN 978-0-7636-9427-2

19 20 21 22 23 24 LSC 10 9 8 7 6 5 4 3 2 1

Printed in Crawfordsville, IN, U.S.A.

This book was typeset in Chaparral Pro.

Candlewick Press
99 Dover Street
Somerville, Massachusetts 02144

visit us at www.candlewick.com

For Jenny Weiss —
I'm really glad you're my friend.

Chapter | 01

Italian class is like one of those cliché horror-movie villains who just refuses to die.

You think you're done, that the awfulness is over, that everything is finally going to be okay. You think that it's time for you and the other survivors — exhausted, bloodied, but still standing, if only barely — to share a moment of relief or grateful tears or maybe even some shaky laughs. Maybe you'll all go out for pizza or something and talk about how lucky you are to be alive. But — *nope!* — suddenly the hellscape is before you once again, the monster back for one final attempt to drag you kicking and screaming into an early grave, all of your happy visions of the future dissolving into tattered, broken, hopeless dreams.

Okay, it's possible that analogy got a little bit away from me.

I suppose it's not really *quite* that bad. And it's entirely my own fault that I'm sitting here right now. I could have left Italian behind with my junior year, but did I? No. No, instead I signed up for *AP Italian,* which was completely voluntary, which means, to be clear, that I could have *not* signed up for it. Somewhere in an alternate universe there is an alternate Cyn blissfully napping in study hall right now or taking an extra elective or going out for coffee, thinking about how nice it is that her days in Italian are *finito.*

Sometimes I make really questionable decisions.

Not always, though. I look to my left, where my lovely boyfriend, Ryan Halsey, is sitting, still so completely worth staring at, and also still my *boyfriend,* and I congratulate myself on the decisions that led to this happy result. Well, to be fair, there were plenty of questionable decisions involved in there along the way. But the main decision, to fall in love with Ryan, was truly outstanding, and so let's just think about that one, okay?

I also stand by my decision to save Annie from her demonic would-be abductor/husband and evil former librarian, Mr. Gabriel. Both the first time, last fall, and then again this past summer at camp. She is also here, sitting to my right. One of the few good things about how Signorina Benedetti runs her classroom is that she lets us sit wherever we want, just like actual college students supposedly do.

And really, other than forty-five minutes of advanced Italian three times a week under the firm, merciless, and often incomprehensible hand of Signorina Benedetti, things are actually pretty great right now.

The main great thing, of course, is that we — Annie, Ryan, Leticia, Diane, William, Peter, and me — are all still here and alive. In case you have forgotten, there was a lot of almost-dying over the past several months. (There was also some actual dying, by other people, but I'm trying to focus on the positive at the moment.)

Also great: no one has broken up since the summer! Ryan, as I have mentioned, is still my lovely boyfriend. William is still Annie's lovely boyfriend, and Leticia and Diane are still each other's lovely girlfriends. We are all deliriously besotted.

So we are back at school for our senior year, there is lots of love going on, and no one has been killed or damaged by demons for just over two months now. In fact, there have been no demons at all since we saw the last of Mr. Gabriel and his horrible little brother at camp over the summer. Well, except for Peter, who is, of course, one of the rare non-evil demons. And who is lovely in his own way. Ways. Shut up. And he's not actually here; he's at some other high school, pretending to be a normal if especially attractive human boy who just happens to have amazing musical-theater writing and composing skills. But he checks in from time to time. Which is not confusing or distracting to me at all.

Another super great thing is that Mr. Henry has announced the musical for this fall, and it is *Les Misérables*. Which has me all excited because *the barricade,* and has Ryan all excited because *Javert,* and has Mr. Henry all excited because apparently he's always wanted to do this show and this is the first time all the stars have aligned or whatever and he has the budget and the resources and everything else necessary to achieve this lifelong dream. Which we are all very happy to be a part of. Because we love Mr. Henry, and this will be the last show we ever get to do together. And also we love *Les Misérables*.

We just found out this morning, and so Ryan and I are especially not very focused on Italian at the moment.

Javert is the role that Ryan has wanted to play pretty much since birth. He loves *Les Misérables* even more than *The Scarlet Pimpernel*, and trust me, that's really saying something. I've already caught him singing "Stars" under his breath twice since the period started.

As for me, I am busily drawing little preliminary sketches of what the barricade might look like for our show. Mr. Henry has already named me tech director again, so I can get started right away. Ryan has to wait until this Friday's auditions, and then callbacks, to really know the part is his, but of course there's no question he's going to get it. And then we'll be able to work on the show together, which we haven't done since *Sweeney* last year. But this time we'll be *together*-together the whole time, and I'll get to watch him at rehearsal possessively instead of longingly, and we'll get to experience the magic of the show coalescing side by side, which is pretty much the most romantic thing I can think of.

Once upon a time, I would be getting very nervous right about now. Nervous that everything is a little too good, and that surely something terrible is about to happen and screw everything up.

But not this time. This time yours truly is going to trust all of this goodness with her whole heart and not be afraid.

Because we have all suffered a great deal to get to this point, and we deserve every bit of this happiness. I'm not going to ruin it by thinking about unpleasant possibilities. Like, for example, about how easy it seems to be for demons to intrude into our lives on a fairly regular basis, or about that last trip I still need to make to the demon world to fulfill my deal with the demon queen. Besides, she seems to have things pretty well in hand down there, and Mr. Gabriel is locked up tight under her watchful eyes and teeth and stingers and other parts, and so there's no reason she'd need to call on me and my special demon-resistant "super-roach" power (yay for flattering demon names for things) anytime soon. There is no reason to fear anything demon related at all.

The bell rings and we can all stop pretending to pay attention. Well, except Annie, who may possibly have actually been paying attention.

Ryan practically leaps out of his chair with all the excited energy he's been holding in check. "I can't believe auditions are this Friday. He could have given us more time."

"Why do you need more time? You know what you're going to sing. You've got all week to practice. And you know the part is yours, anyway." I place a calming hand on his thigh. "Relax!"

"I can't relax! I'm too excited! Come here and distract me." He pulls me up into a deliciously tight embrace, as though he's trying to absorb me by osmosis. But not in a creepy way. My mouth is slightly smushed against his chest, but I don't mind. It's hard to talk at times like this anyway, when I am temporarily overwhelmed by all the nice, warm feelings involved in the hugging. Ryan is very good at making me think happy thoughts. And feel happy feelings. Happy, warm, tingly, exciting feelings.

I hug him a little tighter. And then a lot tighter.

"Hey," he says, laughing. "Careful, or you're going to get us detention. Again."

"Worth it," I murmur against him. I am aware that my hands have started wandering outside the school-approved hugging zone, but I don't care.

"Well, yes," he agrees, "but it would be better *not* to get detention, and then you can come over after school instead of both of us having to sit and stare wistfully at each other across the room while Mrs. Manning glares at us for an hour and a half."

He makes a good point. I put my hands back where they belong. They are sad, but I tell them we will make up for it later.

There is brief good-bye-for-now kissing and then we go to our separate classrooms. I have AP English with Annie and Leticia, which is generally a good time. But now that I'm not distracted by my warm, tingly Ryan-feelings, I find myself thinking again about how Old Cyn would totally be feeling anxious right now, worrying that we can't trust the good times, that we are all just being lulled into a false sense of security by the cruel and tricksy universe.

But that's dumb, I remind myself. Old Cyn is crazy. Everything is awesome!

I walk to class with Annie and smile very brightly and non-anxiously at Leticia, who gives Annie a *what is wrong with our dear Cyn?* kind of look that makes us all laugh, and soon enough I forget to think about all the things that aren't going to go wrong and remember that things are really as awesome as I knew they were.

After school, Ryan drives the two of us to his house. We listen to the complete symphonic recording of *Les Mis,* singing along, and I love that Ryan doesn't care how thoroughly I cannot sing. My enthusiasm more than makes up for my lack of musical talent, I believe. I shut up for all the Javert parts, though, because *oh, my God* I love listening to Ryan sing. Especially roles that he particularly loves, like this one. He starts off kind of just fooling around but he can't help it, within a couple of lines he's completely into it, eyes closed, hands outstretched dramatically, voice full and strong and powerful and amazing.

It's adorable that he's worried about whether he'll get the part. He's perfect.

We stop singing after Javert's suicide, because I have to kiss him, and then there is a lot of that for a while. Kissing Ryan still makes my whole brain turn into a lovely sort of mush. I am vaguely aware that the music from the rest of the show is continuing to play in the background, but mostly I am just aware of Ryan and myself and the parts of us that are touching and how electric every part of me feels when we do this and there's no sense of time or place or anything, just the kissing and being in love and absolutely nothing else.

I barely have any brain left at all by the time I make my way home.

* * *

When I arrive, there is a letter waiting from Peter.

Peter writes me letters now. It is a thing that he does. A very Peter kind of thing.

The whole Peter subject is still kind of a touchy one. Because of the way that I kissed him that one time. And I get it — of course I do. Ryan feels about Peter the way I feel about Jules, who is luckily far away and is only a summer-camp issue. I know Ryan is in touch with her, which is fine, of course, because they are Just Friends and they should totally be in touch whenever they want. As long as I don't have to see her or hear about her and Ryan lets me sort of pretend that she doesn't exist.

Peter, on the other hand, is only about an hour away. I have no doubt that his selection of high school was very deliberate: far enough that I couldn't really object on any reasonable grounds, but close enough for him to be able to make a nuisance of himself. Well, a potential nuisance, anyway. To be fair, he has not once shown up or interfered in our lives or otherwise abused his relatively close proximity. But he likes to remind us that he's there. A lot.

And the way that he does this is by sending me letters.

I told him from the very beginning that I show them all to Ryan, because I am not keeping anything from Ryan on that front. (Except, of course, for the dreams I still have about Peter, which do not count. I don't discuss those with anyone. Not even Annie. There are some things a girl just has to keep for herself. *To* herself, I mean. To herself. And it's not like I dream about him on purpose. Or that I would ever really do any of those things with him. Never mind what things. Leave

8

me alone.) Unfortunately, this only makes Peter push things even further in the letters, because he likes to mess with Ryan. I think I have convinced Ryan that this is the case, and that if Peter were writing just to me, the letters would not be nearly so . . . provocative.

I don't think Peter can feed (demonically) on any drama he might create between us from so far away, but I suspect it gives him great pleasure to try.

My mother hands me the letter when I walk in. She is wearing one of those *I'm trying not to have any kind of expression* expressions that drive me up the wall.

"That's your camp friend, right?" she asks. She asks this every time.

"Yes."

"And you're sure he just —"

"*Yes*, Mom. He just wants to be friends. Ryan knows that Peter writes to me. We talk about theater and stuff. There is nothing shady happening here. Not that it is any of your business."

"Okay, okay," she says, retreating back into her office. But she pauses in the doorway. "It's just . . . you know . . . he writes you *letters*. It's so old-fashioned and romantic."

"Peter's an old-fashioned kind of guy. But they're not romantic. Trust me."

I head to my room and close the door. Then I sit on my bed and look at the letter.

My name and address are, as usual, written in Peter's ridiculously elegant hand, with little flourishes on all the uppercase letters. The return address is ever so slightly darker, as though he were pressing just a little harder on the pen, as if to subtly call my attention to his location and how not-so-very-far away it is. This may seem a far-fetched interpretation, but I suspect I am correct.

With a sigh, I tear it open and begin reading.

My dearest Cynthia, it begins. The letters of my name are even more perfect than all of the other letters. As though he wrote them very slowly and deliberately.

I sigh again and read on.

After the usual opening pleasantries, he updates me on his current projects — the amazing material he submitted to the drama teacher was well received, and his one-act musical is currently in rehearsals. He promises to send tickets if I would like to attend. He shares his latest thoughts and plans about what he might do after graduation, where he might want to travel, where he might decide to go to college.

I know that he tells me all of these things because I'm the only one who really understands how important his hard-won faux-human life is to him, and how much he went through to get it. And I like hearing it, because I care about him and want him to be happy. And I owe him, because he helped us fight Mr. Gabriel and his horrible brother. Even though it was technically kind of Peter's fault that we had to fight them in the first place. Well, second place. But it wasn't on purpose. And without his help and the help of the demon queen (aka Ms. Královna, which was her temporary human name last fall and still the only name we actually have to call her), we never would have succeeded in driving Mr. Gabriel into captivity.

And during that whole camp struggle, Peter's one true friend and human helper/companion-person died trying to save my life. (RIP Hector.) And so now Peter is pretty much alone in the human world, and I am the only one he can really talk to without having to hide who and what he is. And so it is fine that he writes to me, and fine that he wants to keep me up-to-date on all the exciting things happening that he always wanted to have happen.

But somehow the sight of his handwriting, the feel of the paper in my hand, everything that is so completely *Peter* about both the form and content of his communication always puts me back in that moment at camp when Ryan had abandoned me and Peter was the only one still standing by me, until he wasn't standing, he was kneeling, and then he was kissing me, and then I was kissing him back.

I don't want Peter. I don't. I want Ryan. I *love* Ryan. And I stopped that terrible, incredible kiss very shortly after it started, and it never happened again. Despite several offers of a repeat performance on Peter's part.

But I can still remember how much I liked it. And there is a tiny traitorous part of me that wants to do it again.

It is seriously only a tiny part. Like probably just a single cell. Maybe just an electron or something. And if I could locate it and cut it out of my body, I totally would. Because I hate that reminder of my (brief! very, very brief!) betrayal, and I hate the way that part of me still gets excited when one of Peter's letters arrives in the mail.

As always, I hope this missive finds you well. Please give my best to Ryan. Unless you guys broke up. Did you break up? Don't forget to tell me if you break up. Remember, I am only an hour away. I can be there anytime you need me.

He always says something along those lines. He does it to irritate Ryan, of course. And asking him to stop would only make it worse, so I just ignore him.

I tuck the letter into my bag to present to Ryan in the morning. Full disclosure. No more secrets.

I feel a tiny electron-size twinge somewhere deep inside me.

Almost entirely no more secrets.

I sigh again and head downstairs to see what the story is with dinner.

Ryan grimaces through the letter in the morning. When he gets to the end he turns it over and goes back to the beginning.

"Stop," I tell him, grabbing for the letter. "You don't' need to read it again."

He pulls it out of my reach. "I can read it again if I want to."

"But why do you want to?"

He shrugs and keeps reading.

I had hoped he'd start to get used to the stupid letters and not take them so seriously. Because it's nonsense, all the flirty stuff. Which I keep pointing out. And a rational person would maybe laugh and brush it off. But Ryan is scouring each finely penned word, searching for secret messages and hidden meanings. Or so I assume. He won't actually say.

"Peter letter?" Annie asks, dropping to the floor beside me. We are sitting on the floor of the band wing, waiting for homeroom to start.

Ryan makes a grumpy sound.

"Yes," I translate.

"Ooh, let me see! I love looking at his penmanship."

Ryan rolls his eyes. But he hands over the letter.

Annie reads and admires while I pet Ryan's arm soothingly. William arrives and sits beside Annie, tucking an arm around her and reading over her shoulder. Leticia and Diane show up soon after, and the letter is passed around some more, and everyone expresses happiness about all the things that are going so well for Peter. Except Ryan, who just says "hmph" a lot.

Finally the bell rings for homeroom and everyone begins to disperse. Ryan gives me an extra kiss to show me he's not really *that* grumpy before he heads off down the hall. I link arms with Annie and head for the stairway, still feeling the aftershocks of Ryan-kissing and also just generally feeling happy and good and safe and not even a tiny bit worried about anything possibly happening to screw up all the things that are going so well.

Everything is going to be fine.

Chapter | 02

In what seems like two seconds, it is Friday. Auditions. Ryan has gotten over his initial nervous excitement and is now just the regular kind of excited. I have listened to him sing "Stars" about five million times this week so far, but I can't wait to hear him sing it again, onstage, while Mr. Henry sits in his favorite seat and jots down all kinds of positive notes on his legal pad.

I sit through a bunch of other auditions first, though. I'm in my own favorite seat with Ryan's stuff piled in the seat next to me; he's off in a stairwell somewhere, warming up. All of the usual suspects seem to be here, plus a few new faces who might be freshmen or transfers or else aspiring theater kids who only just got their nerve up to try out. A show like *Les Mis* will do that sometimes. One of the unfamiliar girls is really good — a potential Éponine, maybe. I can see Mr. Henry making his impressed face as he scribbles away.

When Mr. Henry calls Ryan, my beautiful boyfriend bounds up the steps with his usual otherworldly grace and stands confidently in the center of the stage. I love seeing him up there. It's like glimpsing some rare wild creature in its natural habitat, where it is perfectly at home. Ryan onstage is a reflection of a world that makes sense. Given our recent nonsensical demonic experiences, I am particularly hungry for things that make sense right now. Everything in its proper place. Ryan center stage. Demons safely confined to the demon world. Mr. Henry in fourth-row-left-aisle. Everything as it should be.

The intro music begins, and then Ryan is singing. And he's so good. Of course. I tear my adoring and possessive gaze away to glance at Mr. Henry, who is nodding and smiling and jotting as expected. Ryan finishes his section and thanks Mr. Henry and Mr. Iverson (the accompanist) and then bounds back down the steps and up the aisle and shoves his stuff over so he can drop into the seat beside me.

"You were great," I whisper, squeezing his hand. "In the bag."

"Thanks." He squeezes my hand back. "And thanks for listening to me practice all week. It really helped."

"You didn't need help. But you're welcome."

We stop talking as the next name is called. It's one of the new people; a boy this time. Jeff something. He's freckly with reddish-blond hair, which for some reason makes me think he's going for Marius, but when Mr. Iverson starts playing, it's the familiar opening to "Stars" again. Jeff looks a little nervous as he waits for his entrance. He must be a transfer student; I definitely haven't seen him around, and he looks too old to be a freshman.

Then he starts singing, and I find myself staring open-mouthed.

His voice is like . . . velvet. It's deep and strong and smooth as anything and all traces of his initial nervousness vanish as soon as he starts to sing. Ryan is staring beside me with the same shocked expression, and so is Mr. Henry. So is Mr. Iverson, who knows the music well enough at this point to be able to turn to stare and still keep playing.

I can feel Ryan's deepening dismay like a physical presence, taking up more and more space as the song continues. When Jeff gets to the stopping point, Mr. Iverson plays several extra bars before his fingers remember to stop moving.

There is a moment of utter silence, and then Mr. Henry coughs. "Thank you, um" — he checks his notes — "Jeff. Very nice. Thank you."

Jeff thanks him back and leaves the stage. Ryan is still staring at the empty space where Jeff had been standing. With visible effort, he blinks and turns to look at me. His face is pale and shaken and there is an underlying panic that makes me want to weep.

"Where the hell did he come from?" Ryan whispers finally. "Who is he?"

I shrug helplessly. "Transfer, I guess? I've never seen him before." I hesitate and then say it, because someone has to. "He's really good."

Ryan barks a very unamused laugh. "Yeah. No shit." He

leans back in his seat, staring at the stage again, and adds, somewhat contradictorily, "Shit."

Someone else is called in, and we stop talking again. I don't take my eyes off Ryan, though. He looks . . . bad. This is bad. This is wrong. Javert is *his* part. I thought that was understood. I thought the universe was on board with that. The universe was not supposed to send this Jeff guy with his velvety voice and fake-nervous expression and part-stealing aspirations. I want to believe that it doesn't matter, that Mr. Henry will cast Ryan no matter what, but . . . well, that is the downside of Mr. Henry having a heart of gold. If he thinks Jeff is the better guy for the part, he'll give it to him. Even if it breaks his golden heart to do it.

"I have to . . . I'll . . ." Ryan doesn't bother to finish making his excuse; he just pushes up from his seat and walks quickly out the rear door of the auditorium. My immediate impulse is to follow him, but it's pretty clear that he wants to be alone right now. I sink back into my seat and look up at the stage, where someone has started to sing "Castle on a Cloud," which is the one song from this show that I actually kind of despise. I glance again at Mr. Henry. He seems distracted, not really jotting so much as absently tapping his pen against the paper. I don't like how unhappy he looks right now.

This doesn't mean anything, I tell myself firmly. Sure, okay, this Jeff guy will get a callback for Javert. So will Ryan. And Ryan will just have to crush him at callbacks, and then everything will be fine. Ryan is amazing. He can do it. He just . . . he'd just gotten complacent, maybe, relaxed into knowing he was the best singer in our school. And so now he has to remind everyone how awesome he is. So okay, that's what he'll do. No problem.

As the auditions continue, I keep sneaking hopeful glances at the auditorium doors.

But Ryan doesn't come back for a very long time.

In fact, technically, Ryan never comes back. Not on his own. I have to go and find him.

Luckily, I know his favorite haunts by now, and where he's most likely to go when he's upset. As expected, he's in the seldom-used far east stairwell, sitting on the bottom step on the basement level. There's not even a doorway down here to get into the basement proper; it's just a weird vertical dead end, like the contractors forgot what they were doing and built this area by accident.

I sit down beside him. He doesn't look at me.

"Hey," I say.

"Hey," he says back.

We sit in silence for a few minutes.

"Okay," I say finally. "So you've got some competition. That's okay. It's unexpected, but it's okay. You'll both get called back, and you will kick his ass. You know you will. You were born to play Javert."

He sighs. "I sure used to think so."

"Ryan, come on. You can't let this guy get to you."

He shakes his head. He's still not looking at me. "It's not . . . it's not just him. I mean, yes, at the moment, it's *largely* just him, but . . . I think he was sort of a wake-up call. And I don't like what I'm waking up to, Cyn."

"What are you talking about?"

Now he looks at me, and I'm shocked by the anguish I can see in his eyes. My Ryan is usually pretty goddamn resilient. I thought he'd have shaken this Jeff guy off by now and already be looking forward to their inevitable callback confrontation. But he's not. Not even close, apparently.

"I think maybe camp and high school spoiled me, you know? I thought . . . I thought I was really good. I mean *really* good."

"You *are* —"

"No," he says, cutting me off. "I'm pretty good. I mean, I know that. I'm good for high school, and I'm even good for theater camp. But I let myself think that meant I was *really* good, like professional-level good. And then this guy . . ." He runs a hand through his hair. "Jesus, Cyn. That's what professional-level good looks like. I'm not — I'm not there. Not like that."

"This is crazy talk." I reach over and take his hand. "You're just not over the surprise of having competition yet. He's good, yes. But so are you. And I think . . . I think maybe you just relaxed for a while, you know? Because you could. And now you have to step it up a bit. But you can, and you will."

He just shakes his head again.

"Okay, listen. How many recordings of *Les Misérables* do you own?"

"What does that — ?"

"How many?"

"Well—I don't know. Original London, original Broadway, complete symphonic, twenty-fifth anniversary concert, twenty-fifth anniversary U.K. tour, several foreign language versions . . ."

"Okay, and how many different actors play Javert in those?"

"Well, lots. I mean they're mostly all different, except for symphonic and tenth anniversary, which are both Philip Quast, but—"

"So you're saying there are at least several great actors who can play that role professionally."

"Well, of course. I mean there are lots of Javerts who aren't even on any of the recordings . . ." He trails off, narrowing his eyes at me. "I see what you're doing. But it's not the same thing."

"Oh, okay. So you're saying that because this Jeff guy is good, you suddenly aren't, but that same logic doesn't hold in any other circumstances? This is special Ryan-Jeff logic that the rest of the world can't possibly understand?"

"Cut it out. You know that's not what I mean."

"I'm trying to show you how ridiculous you're being."

"I'm not! I'm just—I'm just saying that he made me think. About how much I'd been taking for granted. I thought . . . God, Cyn, I thought I'd get into every college theater program I applied for. I imagined you and me sitting around with all our acceptance letters, eating snacks and discussing the pros and cons of all of our many options."

My heart melts a little at this, because OMG. "You did?"

"Yes, I did. And I bet we'll still get to do that for you,

because you're amazing, and you *will* get into every program you apply to. But . . . but I kind of just realized that I might not. That I almost certainly will not. That there are tons of guys like me out there, big fish in little ponds, dreaming their stupid impossible dreams. Shit, Cyn, I'm not even a triple threat. My dancing sucks. I should probably rethink that business degree my dad keeps not-so-subtly randomly mentioning over dinner all the time now."

He leans over and rests his sad head on my shoulder. I squeeze his hand harder.

"Don't you dare," I say softly. "Don't you dare let this one setback derail you from all of your hopes and plans. Or me from mine. *I* am still looking forward to sitting around together weighing the merits of all our many program options. I am already planning out the snacks in my head. You are not allowed to introduce that happy daydream to me and simultaneously kill it with your negative self-talk and melodramatic storm clouds of doom. You had better damn well at least *try* to beat this guy before you give up, Ryan Halsey."

He's quiet a moment, taking this in. His head is still on my shoulder. I wait, still holding his hand.

"Will there be really good snacks?" he asks finally. "I mean, like Oreos?"

"There will be amazing snacks. The best snacks that exist in this universe or any other. Including Oreos. But not Double Stuf."

"Well, no, of course not. Those things totally screw up the cream-to-cookie ratio."

I take a breath. "This is why I love you."

"Because we see eye to eye on Oreos?"

"Well, there are some other reasons, too. But that one's pretty high up there. Good cookie appreciation is important."

"Damn straight." He lifts his head and turns to look at me. His eyes are clearer now. "Have I mentioned lately that you are the best girlfriend ever?"

"Nope. You are way overdue, in fact."

He gives me one of his slow, delicious lopsided smiles and leans toward me. "Best. Girlfriend. Ever." He punctuates each word with a kiss.

I grin back at him helplessly, because that is what happens when he kisses me, but eventually I manage an awkward throat-clearing sound and an offhand "Don't you forget it." It wouldn't do to let him know how completely he can still turn me into pudding whenever he makes the tiniest effort.

We emerge from the basement level and go to collect our stuff from the auditorium before the custodians toss it all in the lost and found. By the time we get to Ryan's car, he seems almost back to his old self. We pick up some take-out Thai food and grab a mini pack of Oreos from the convenience store next door and then sit in a corner of the parking lot, sharing noodles and listening to one of my favorite musical-theater mixes on my phone.

Afterward, when nothing is left but a few stray Oreo crumbs, we sit quietly in the dark for a while.

"It will be okay," I say. "You'll see. We are going to have the best senior year ever. We've earned it. Nothing is going to take that away from us."

Ryan strokes the inside of my arm with his finger. "Who

am I to argue with the wise and beautiful Cynthia Rothschild?" he asks. "If you say it, it must be true."

"Ha," I say, since we both know I have been less than truthful on more than one notable occasion. But his compliment is appreciated all the same. Also, the inner-arm stroking is making it hard to think straight. "It is true. I refuse to let anything go wrong this year. Everything is going to be perfect."

"*You're* perfect."

"You're ridiculous." But I'm not fooling anyone. I love it when he says things like that.

"I'm not," he says seriously. He reaches over and touches my face, his eyes suddenly burning into mine. "I love you, Cyn. You know that, right?"

My heart swells ludicrously inside my chest. It's not the first time he's said it; we've both said it plenty of times by now. But it still gets me. Every time. And having him so close, his hand on my cheek, his eyes so serious and intense and focused entirely on me . . .

I discover I have to make another of those awkward throat-clearing sounds before I can speak.

"I love you, too. Now stop talking and kiss me."

He doesn't need to be asked twice. This is yet another of the things I love about him. I would tell him that, but we are busy now.

We stay out about as late as any of our parents will tolerate, and then Ryan drops me off at my front door. Well, first he pulls over, and then I kiss him good night, and then there is more kissing, because *Ryan*. He makes my heart happy. And all my other parts, too. I am only able to get out of the car by silently reminding myself that I will get to see him again tomorrow night.

My parents are already in bed; when I close the door behind me, my dad calls down, "That you, Cyn? How were auditions?"

"Great," I call back. "Ryan was awesome."

"Glad to hear it. Don't stay up too late drawing set designs, okay?"

I roll my eyes, even though no one is there to see it. "Good night, Dad!"

"Good night, honey!"

I lock up and make my way upstairs. Ryan was all smiles by the time I got out of the car, and not only because of all the making out. I think he's going to be okay. I know the Jeff thing was a shock, but he just needed to regroup. And have snacks. And be reminded how amazing his girlfriend is.

I meant what I told him about this year being perfect. We *have* earned it. The events of last fall and the beginning of the summer were really terrible, and while it's not like I've forgotten — there are some things you can never forget — it's time we put it all behind us. And he'll see that his fears about the future are groundless, too. Once he gets his confidence back, once he gets this part and remembers how truly amazing he is, he'll set his horizons back where they belong.

I smile again thinking about what Ryan said about his vision of us sitting around together and planning our futures. I'm not naive; I know we can't necessarily plan on going to the same school. But it *could* happen. We're both looking for great theater programs, after all. And anyway, the part that gets me is that he was thinking about us doing that, looking ahead together to see what the future might bring. What options we have, and what we might decide to do. Together.

Things have been great since we got past the difficulties during that first session at camp over the summer. Really great. Really, really, really great. But I've been trying not to let myself think too far ahead, since I know that, no matter what we might want, everything might change come graduation. I know that everyone might go off in different directions and that some directions are very far apart from one another. Some directions are opposite directions, even. Anything could happen.

But also, *anything could happen.* And the fact that Ryan was sitting around, thinking about us thinking about our futures . . . it makes me want to let myself think about our future more than I'd been letting myself thus far. Not too much, I'm not going to go crazy . . . but I might let a daydream or two of same-direction college plans slip in there from time to time.

Who am I to tell Ryan not to give up on his dreams if I'm not willing to give myself a few extra ones of my own?

Chapter | 03

Monday morning the callback list is posted on the lighting-booth door. (Mr. Henry always sneaks it up there like a thief in the night and then hides the rest of the morning in his office so he can avoid the angry and the disappointed as long as possible.) Ryan has promised to wait for me so we can go look at it together, and so as soon as I start up the front walkway toward the school he pounces on me and grabs my hand and practically drags me up the stairs and down the hall to the hallowed location. We wait impatiently for the several people in front of us to finish looking and walk away either elated or deflated, and then we step forward together and scan for Ryan's name.

It's there, of course, under Javert, as we knew it would be. And Jeff's name is there, too, as we knew it would be.

"*I vill destroy him,*" Ryan whispers in some kind of

pseudo-Dracula-sounding accent, and I put my arm around his waist.

"Duh," I say.

He kisses my forehead and then we look at the rest of the list. That unfamiliar girl I noticed at auditions did get a callback for Éponine, and Danielle, who played Johanna in *Sweeney Todd*, got a callback for Cosette, which is also as we knew it would be. I like that Javert doesn't have a romance of any kind going on, and so I don't have to think about what girl Ryan might have to pretend to be in love with. All he has to do is seethe with vengeance and struggle with existential questions about the nature of good and evil and his place in the universe and whether or not mercy can coexist with justice.

Callbacks are set for Friday. That gives Ryan the rest of the week to get his best bass-baritone game on.

"I booked three rehearsals with my voice teacher," he tells me as we walk back down to the band wing to wait for the bell for homeroom. "I'm not taking any chances."

"Good. If I have to watch that Jeff guy play Javert, I will never forgive you."

Ryan laughs, and the bright and airy sound of it is both a joy and a relief. The fear and panic of Friday afternoon seem to have vanished completely. He is back to being confident and slightly contemptuous of all challengers to his musical-theater throne, and while in general I don't advocate contemptuousness nor find it at all an attractive quality, in this particular circumstance I will take it and be happy, thank you very much.

Several of Ryan's friends give him various forms of shoulder punches and fist bumps when he gives them the news, and

Jorge actually hugs him, because Jorge is his best friend and really gets how important this is.

Annie also hugs him, and then hugs me, and then hugs Leticia and Diane, who themselves just give Ryan *we told you so* looks over Annie's curly, happy, hugging head. William arrives and also accepts his hug from Annie, and then congratulates Ryan when he learns what all the hugging is actually about.

The bell rings and Annie tells me she'll see me later as she dashes off to get a few last pre-homeroom minutes with William. Ryan gives me an extra-long, extra-confident kiss before heading off down the hall, and my heart is full of light as I make my own way in the other direction. I don't even have to remind myself that this year is going to be awesome, because it's so obviously apparent. Sure, things got a little off-kilter on Friday, but the universe has now righted itself and I am certain once again that everything is going to be fine. Whatever stupid tiny part of me keeps bracing for disaster is, well, *stupid,* and it will see that it deserves nothing but to cower in shame and embarrassment as the rest of us go on to enjoy the wonderful and magical senior year that we deserve.

Smiling the smile of the fearlessly happy, secure in my good feelings, I push the door open to the stairway, and I start up the steps toward the third floor.

I am so securely feeling good that when the hand suddenly grabs my shoulder from behind, I'm barely even alarmed.

But then I turn.

And I see that it is Aaron.

And that he is covered in blood.

And I know that my stupid tiny fearful part was right after

all, *dammit,* and everything is about to go horribly, horribly wrong.

"*Aaron?* What—?" He shouldn't be here. Someone else could walk into the stairway at any second.

I can't stop staring at all the blood.

"Cyn. You've got to—my mistress, she's—" He suddenly whips his head around to look back over his shoulder, and that is when I notice the flames and the smoke visible in the tiny window of demon realm that I can see behind him.

"Aaron, just . . . just slow down. What's *wrong*? What happened?"

He turns back to me, and the panic on his face makes me want to throw up or run away or both. I've never seen him like this. Aaron is a person who willingly became a demon's consort. Aaron is a person who *loves demons,* who enthusiastically went to live among them, who thrives on all the horrible things that come with the demon world and who is apparently very much enjoying his own slow metamorphosis into a more demony version of himself with random fish-themed appendages and things. I cannot even begin to think of what might be so bad that even *Aaron* is terrified.

But then I know, even before he says the words.

"He's loose. He—"

I don't wait to hear the rest. I fly up the stairs and race to Annie's homeroom.

I don't stop to think as I burst through the door.

"Can I help you?" the teacher begins, but I talk right over her.

"Sorry — it's an emergency."

Annie's face went white as soon as I came in. I grab her hand and drag her back out into the hall with me over the teacher's increasingly loud and unhappy objections. I don't stop until we come to an empty classroom and I pull us both inside.

"Cyn, what?"

I grab her by the shoulders and stare into her eyes. "Are you okay? Are you — do you feel okay? Is everything . . . ?" I don't ask what I want to ask: *Is Mr. Gabriel already back inside your head? Is he making you think you're in love with him again?*

She shakes me off. "I felt fine until you came barging into my homeroom with that look on your face. What happened? Talk to me!"

"I just saw Aaron in the stairway."

"Aaron?"

I realize I am stalling.

"Mr. Gabriel got out."

Annie's face goes to some new level of pale far beyond what it already was. She is nearly translucent. She backs into a chair and sits heavily down.

"Are you sure? How . . . ?"

I shake my head. "I don't know. I didn't stay for the details. As soon as he said it I came to find you, to make sure —"

"I'm fine," Annie says. She's not *fine*, obviously, but she is at least still here and not under any apparent demon mesmerization. I don't think Mr. Gabriel could trick her in the same way he did the first time, not now that she knows what he is, but she's not immune like I am. He could still get to her somehow.

But not if I can help it.

I grab her hand again. "Hold still. I'm going to share my protection with you." *You should have been doing this already,* I scold myself silently. *You should have known this would happen, you should have kept her protected from the second you knew you could do it.* But I know Annie wouldn't have allowed it. You can't live your whole life bracing for the worst.

Except . . . clearly we should have been doing just that, because . . . because . . .

I turn off my brain and close my eyes and focus on trying to extend my special protection to Annie in the way I did at camp that time, making it so Mr. Gabriel couldn't take over any of my friends' bodies like he so horribly took over William's for a few unbearable minutes. Annie lets me. She might not want to live in fear, but she's no dummy.

"I feel it," she says as I open my eyes again. "Can you do everyone else, too? Do you . . . have enough? I still don't really understand how it works."

"Join the club," I mutter. I should have been learning more about it. I should have been figuring out how to use it more effectively. How to use it to protect everyone I care about when danger inevitably came around again.

How to use it as a weapon.

But I didn't. I wanted to believe that I wouldn't need to. And now I'm caught unprepared.

Again.

"Do you know where William's homeroom is?"

Of course she does, and we stand outside the door beckoning until he makes an excuse to his teacher and comes out to join us.

"This isn't alarming at all," William says to no one in particular as we whisk him frantically around the corner and out of sight of the classroom.

Annie explains while I grab his hand and repeat the sharing procedure. William looks shaken, his former good humor gone, and I don't blame him — as Annie's boyfriend, he knows he's a potential target for Mr. Gabriel.

"It'll be okay," Annie tells him earnestly. He nods in response, but his face as he turns back toward his homeroom looks anything but reassured.

Diane is the next closest, and then Leticia. By the time we're done with them, homeroom is just about over. I send Annie back to her room — she'd left her books behind when I abducted her — and continue on alone to find Ryan.

The bell rings just as I arrive, and I wait outside the door for him to come out. But he does not come out. After the last of the other kids file into the hall, I lean inside but the room is empty.

The tight little ball of panic I had just barely been managing to keep under control begins to grow painfully inside me.

You should have come for him first.

But I couldn't have. Annie was obviously the one I had to check on first. She's the one Mr. Gabriel wants more than anything. He hates the rest of us, sure, especially me, but of course Annie would be his first priority. It never occurred to me that he might —

Stop it.

Ryan could still be fine. He might have some perfectly normal reason for not being in homeroom.

I know he has math first period, so I swing by his classroom to see if he's there. But I don't expect to find him, and I don't. The ball of panic in my belly has swollen into something bulging and awful and alive. I imagine it filled with bloated panic beetles, all of them ready to punch through its paper-thin panic membrane and crawl eagerly throughout my body, leaving oozing trails of panic slime in their wake.

I take a breath and try to make myself stop imagining horrible things and focus on what to do next.

He might still be fine. He really might still be fine. But I'm having trouble putting any faith in that idea.

Resolutely, I turn and head for the library.

At the end of the summer, mostly as a joke, or at least slightly as a joke, or maybe not as a joke at all but only our desperate attempt to reclaim some sense of sanity and control, we agreed to make the school library the rendezvous point if there was ever an in-school emergency of the demon-related variety. It seemed both easy to remember and perfectly safe, since the new librarian who took over after Mr. Gabriel left transferred from another school and has a legitimate personal life and work history (we checked) and is absolutely not a demon.

Entering the library still gives me the creeps, though.

I force myself to walk calmly through the doors so as not to alarm Mrs. Davenforth (Mr. Gabriel's human successor), but I needn't have worried; she's apparently busy with something elsewhere. One of her library monitors is sitting at the circulation desk. He gives me a cursory glance and then goes back to reading whatever book he's got open in front of him. I have to admit that Mr. Gabriel ran a far tighter ship when he was the librarian. But the monitor's lack of interest in library visitors suits me just fine at the moment, and I start walking between the bookshelves, looking for Ryan.

I find him sitting in one of the reading chairs at the very back. I enjoy one nanosecond of relief that he's here, but I know better than to relax. The panic beetles are tracing complex lines and figures somewhere in my abdomen now. I feel them readying themselves for the moment when the panic is fully unleashed. They seem to sense it will be very soon.

"Ryan?" I ask softly. He is sitting very still. He doesn't look up when I speak. He is holding his left hand in his right, palm up, and seems very engrossed by whatever he sees there.

I walk over and kneel beside his chair. He closes his hand into a fist before I can get a look at it.

"I was hoping you'd think to come here," he says. He's still not looking at me.

"Ryan, what happened? Did . . . did you see Aaron?" Maybe Aaron went to find Ryan after I ran away from him in the stairway. That's a thing that could have happened. It would explain why Ryan decided to come here. How he knew there was an emergency. But not so much the thing with his hand.

"Aaron? No. I — I saw Mr. Gabriel."

The panic beetles rejoice. I swallow hard and try not to let them out.

"You saw him? He was here?"

"Not . . . not here, exactly." He shakes his head. "I'm not sure. I was about to go into homeroom and then I remembered I'd left my math textbook in my locker. So I went back but when I opened it, it wasn't my locker inside, it was . . . it was like that scene in the original *Ghostbusters* when Sigourney Weaver opens the fridge and instead of milk and salami in there it's the Gatekeeper and the Keymaster prancing around. Only in this case it was Mr. Gabriel." He pauses, then adds, "He wasn't prancing around, though; he was just standing there. Like he'd been waiting for me."

I want to reach over and make him open his hand, but I'm afraid to move.

"What did he do?"

"He laughed, mostly. He was kind of blurry, but I could hear him laughing. And then he stopped laughing and he reached out of the locker and did . . . something. . . ."

I swallow again. It feels like the beetles are crawling up my throat now.

"Ryan, please let me see your hand."

Both of his hands clench tighter for a second, but then he opens his left hand and shows it to me.

There's an angry red welt in the center of his palm. It's about the size of a quarter, but with rough, uneven edges, and the skin there looks raw and delicate and painful. The color is dark and crimson and terrifying.

"It's kind of pulsing," he says. "What do you think it is?"

"I don't know," I say honestly. But whatever it is, it can't be good. "I'm going to try something," I tell him. I close my eyes and try to share my protection with him. *A little late,* the panic beetles whisper, but I tell them to shut up. Maybe I can cancel out whatever Mr. Gabriel did to him. I know I can do more with my power than just use it as passive resistance. I just . . . don't really know how.

At least I'm getting better at the whole voluntary-sharing procedure by this point. It's not hard at all to take hold of my power and push it gently outward toward Ryan. But whatever Mr. Gabriel did to his hand doesn't seem to be affected by my ability. There's no change; the dark-red mark remains just as scary looking as before.

It *is* too late. Mr. Gabriel got to him first.

I give up and open my eyes. "Oh, Ryan. I'm so sorry. I should have . . ."

I trail off, because there is no good way to finish that sentence. I had to go for Annie first. I see Ryan struggling with wanting to tell me he understands but also totally not understanding. Because right now he has some crazy pulsing demon wound in the center of his left palm, and there is no way that that is any kind of okay. And it's my fault, because Mr. Gabriel would only come at Ryan to get to me.

Yes, I know, Ryan would already be dead if I hadn't stopped Mr. Gabriel in the first place. But . . . it's hard to feel like that matters now. All I know is that my boyfriend is in danger. And I should have known this would happen. I should have been prepared to stop it.

"Does it hurt?" I ask.

"Not . . . exactly. It feels pretty weird, though."

We fall silent again. I want to feel shocked and appalled that we are facing demonic catastrophe once more, but somehow I can't muster the appropriate emotional energy. And I'm not shocked, of course. Not really. I'd been waiting for this ever since Aaron told us that they were going to keep Mr. Gabriel alive. I knew he wasn't going to stay imprisoned forever. And I knew he wasn't done with us yet.

Aaron. "Crap. We need to talk to Aaron. I just left him there — he was in pretty bad shape."

"What else did he tell you other than that Mr. Gabriel was out?"

"Not much. Something about his mistress, but he never said all the words. He was a mess, Ryan. Covered in blood, and so *scared* . . . also everything behind him seemed to be on fire."

Ryan stares down at the reading-area carpet. "This sounds pretty bad, huh?"

"Yeah."

More silence. The bad kind, where there are things that should be being said but aren't. I take a breath.

"I think we need to call Peter."

Ryan takes a breath of his own. "Yeah. Yeah, I know."

There is so much unhappiness in those words.

Well, he may not like it, but Peter's our best resource at this moment. And I am not going to screw around when Mr. Gabriel has already begun moving against us.

I get out my phone.

Peter answers on the first ring. "Did you break up?"

The sound I make in response to this is part laugh and part

sigh and part scream. Ryan stares at me but I can't even begin to explain. "Not a good time for your nonsense," I tell Peter. "Something very bad is happening. Can you come?"

"Is it Mr. Gabriel?" His voice is immediately serious. "Never mind; of course it is. He's the only reason you'd be calling me. I'll be there in a minute."

"But aren't you an hour —"

I can almost hear him rolling his eyes. "By car, sure. But you do remember I'm a demon, right?"

Before I can answer, there's a flash of light and Peter is standing before us.

The library monitor, suddenly and inconveniently deciding to do his job, sticks his head around the bookshelves to peer at us. "Hey, no cell phones in the library, you guys." He looks at us suspiciously, no doubt wondering how Peter got in without him noticing.

"Sorry, won't happen again," Ryan tells him. He glances at me and I stick my phone back in my bag. Then he turns back to the kid. "Now go away, please."

"What are you doing back here? Does Mrs. Davenforth — ?"

"Study group," Peter says with peculiar articulation. "We have permission."

"Oh!" the monitor kid says, instantly full of cheer and free of suspicion. "Sorry to have disturbed you, then. Let me know if you need anything! I'll just be back at the circ desk." He smiles brightly at all of us, lingering a few extra seconds on Peter, and then retreats back out of sight.

"Did you — ?" Ryan begins.

"Yup," Peter says. "Now tell me what's going on."

We tell him the very little that we know. When we mention Ryan's hand, Peter steps forward and grabs Ryan's wrist.

"Hey!" Ryan protests.

"Quiet." Peter stares solemnly at Ryan's palm for several very long seconds. "This is really not good."

"What is it?" I ask him.

Peter blows out a long, slow breath. He lets go of Ryan's wrist and doesn't seem to notice the way Ryan wipes it against his jeans as though to scrape off whatever Peter-germs it might have caught during that brief contact.

"It's . . . a curse. That's probably the best word for it. A mark of demon magic that's been, um, embedded and set to ignite."

"*Ignite?*" Ryan asks in alarm.

"Not literally. Well, probably not."

"Great," Ryan mutters, staring at his palm again.

"Okay," I say. "Okay, so how do we remove it? What do we do?"

Peter looks at me, and my heart breaks a little at the expression on his face.

"Only Mr. Gabriel can undo it," he says. "I'm so sorry, Cyn."

The panic beetles are ecstatic, but I refuse to acknowledge them. "There must be some way to . . ." I trail off as he shakes his head.

"There's not. This is an ultimatum. He chose Ryan because he knows you'll do anything for him. And unlike Annie, he's expendable, at least as far as Mr. Gabriel is concerned. You have to go down there. If you don't, if you don't go down and find out what his terms are for undoing the curse, then whatever bad thing he's implanted in your boyfriend's hand is eventually going to fulfill its evil purpose in a drastic and horrible way."

"Down where?" Ryan asks. He knows, though. We all know.

"He's not going to deal with you up here," Peter says, answering Ryan's question but only looking at me. "You have to go to him."

The stupid (but clearly not so stupid after all) tiny fearful part of me is feeling entirely vindicated right now. There is a big feeling of *I told you so* coming from deep inside my soul. I give myself one short moment to indulge in silent outrage at the incredible unfairness, to feel complete and utter fury that Mr. Gabriel is doing this to me, to us, yet again.

And then I make all the vindicated and outraged and also really, really sad parts of me shut up, and I try to prepare myself for what is going to come next. Because of course Peter (and therefore Mr. Gabriel) is right, and I will do whatever it takes to save Ryan.

Which means I have to go back to the demon world. Much sooner than I'd hoped. And under far worse circumstances than I ever expected.

I am sure it goes without saying how much this totally, totally sucks.

Chapter | 04

"Screw that," Ryan says. "You're not going down there, Cyn. We'll . . . we'll figure out something. . . ."

"I'm telling you," Peter says, "there's nothing you can do except to find out what Mr. Gabriel wants."

Ryan squints up at him. "Yeah, well, I don't entirely trust your motives on this, sorry."

Peter opens his mouth to give some angry and indignant reply, but I don't have any patience for this right now.

"Stop it," I tell them. "Just . . . everyone shut up a minute."

Miraculously, they do as I say.

Which leaves me alone with my thoughts and the teeming multitudes of panic beetles churning away in my guts.

Practical. I need to be practical. I have to go, that's accepted, okay. I mean, not okay, obviously, it's the opposite of okay, but since it appears to be nonnegotiable, I have to suck it up and move on. Which is not so easy as I'm trying to make it sound, but whatever. *Just . . . just keep going, Cyn.*

Do I have any chance of going down there and coming back up alive again?

I don't know.

What would help increase my odds of survival?

Peter.

Even if he's not the super-strong fighting kind of demon like Mr. Gabriel and his brother and Principal Kingston and Ms. Královna and pretty much all the other demons I have encountered thus far, he's still a demon. He knows things about the demon world, and about other demons, and . . . and also I really just don't want to go down there alone. Especially when it appears I won't even have Aaron or the queen around to be at least vaguely on my side when I do.

Aaron! Right. I turn to Peter. "Can you try to contact Aaron? If I have to go down there, I want to try to get a better sense of what the hell is going on before I do."

"I can try," he says. "If it's as bad as it seems, he might be hard to find."

"Cyn," Ryan says. "You can't . . ."

"I have to. You know that. I can't just sit here and wait to see what horrible thing Mr. Gabriel is going to do to you."

"But it's a setup! I mean, this"—he waves his hand around—"is designed to get you to go down and put yourself in his hands or claws or whatever. You can't just walk right into his trap!"

"Yes, I can. I'll go down, and I'll see what the situation

is, and then . . . and then I'll figure out how to save you and not die."

He glares at me. "You're so irritating sometimes. Do you know that?"

"Yeah, well, you knew what you were getting into when you decided to date me, mister."

"Fine. Then I'm coming with you."

I blink at him, momentarily without a comeback. It's true that I desperately don't want to go alone, but Ryan will be defenseless down there.

But then, if Mr. Gabriel wanted to kill him, he probably could have just done it instead of planting whatever slow-burning curse he decided to go with instead.

But then, there are like a million other demons who don't have a secret plan involving threatening Ryan to get me to do what they want, and they might kill him just for fun.

But . . .

But . . .

But I need Peter to come with me, if he'll do it. And there's no way I can refuse Ryan's offer and then take Peter. Ryan would never forgive me.

Why do boys always have to make things even more complicated than they already are?

Speaking of which, Peter has apparently decided that the best response to Ryan's declaration is derisive laughter.

"What are you talking about?" he asks when he finishes laughing. "You won't be any help to her down there. It's the *demon world*. It is full of *demons*. What are you going to do, sing at them?"

Ryan is standing; I'm not sure when that happened exactly, but he is now at full height and making every use of the few inches he has on Peter. He takes a step toward him, the better position from which to look down at his adversary.

"I don't know," Ryan says in a frosty, controlled tone that I have rarely heard him use before. "But if you think I'm going to just sit up here cowering in fear while my girlfriend goes off to the demon world alone to try to save me, you're even stupider than I thought."

"Oh, okay, so you'll go down there and cower in fear instead? Good plan."

"At least I'll be there! At least I can try to help her! Unlike some pretend-human guys I could point to."

"Actually," I break in, not wanting to let this go on any further. Both boys turn slowly to look at me. There is an uncomfortable silence.

"You can't be serious," Ryan says, understanding what I am about to say.

Peter says nothing. He has grown very quiet and thoughtful as he watches my face.

"Ryan," I say gently, "I think it's pretty safe to say that we need all the help we can get. If Peter is willing, we need to bring him with us."

I turn to Peter, who still hasn't said anything. I can see that he is struggling with wanting to show up (or at least match) Ryan in the bravery department, while also wanting to never have to go back to the demon world ever, ever again.

"I *know*, I know the last thing you want is to return after you worked so hard to escape," I tell him in the same gentle voice. "But surely it's in your own best interest to help us put down Mr. Gabriel for good, right? The demon queen is the one who granted you your freedom. If Mr. Gabriel comes into power, couldn't he take it away?"

Peter looks very unhappy as he reflects on the sense in what I am saying.

Ryan looks very unhappy, too.

I decide one more little push is in order. For both of them.

"We could really use your help, Peter," I say quietly. And then, shamelessly: "*I* could really use your help." And then, with just the right amount of reluctance: "But, I mean, if you can't, of course I understand. Maybe there's some way you can help from up here."

Ryan folds his arms across his chest, his mouth twisting up into a smirk.

Peter glares at Ryan, then looks at me. I hate asking him to do this, but I don't feel like I really have a choice. As he pointed out, I'll do whatever it takes to save Ryan. And Mr. Gabriel probably really will come after Peter once he's done with the rest of us. He's not likely to have forgotten the role Peter played in his defeat over the summer.

"He has no idea what any of this really means, Cyn," Peter says, gesturing at Ryan. "He can't even imagine what it's going to be like."

"Well, apparently he's about to find out. Do you really want to send us down there alone and unprotected?"

Peter makes a frustrated sound deep in his throat. "But I can't protect you! You know I don't have that kind of strength. I'm not that kind of demon."

Ryan starts to say something snarky (I can tell the tone just by his quick intake of breath), but I hold out a hand to silence him and take a step closer to Peter. "Then be the kind of demon that you are. The non-evil kind, remember? The kind who has friends and people he cares about."

"I don't care about Ryan."

Ryan huffs a laugh behind me. I don't turn around. I just keep looking at Peter.

"All right," he says finally. "But just to be clear, I'm doing this for you, Cyn. Not for him."

"Fine. And Peter . . . thank you."

Peter gazes at me for another long moment, then abruptly looks away. "Well, first things first. Let's see if we can reach Aaron. I'm going to go convince our friend at the desk there that he has pressing business out in the hall, keeping everyone else out of the library for a while."

"Check for Mrs. Davenforth, too," I tell him. "She might be in the back office."

He gives me a thumbs-up as he walks away.

I turn to see Ryan looking at me with a guarded expression. "I suppose I can't be annoyed about you flirting with him if you're doing it to save my life," he says.

"I wasn't flirting! I was . . . um . . ."

"Playing on his affections?"

"No, that's not —"

"Shamelessly manipulating —"

"Hey! Enough, all right? Trying to save you, remember?"

He sighs. "Yeah." He looks down at his palm again.

Dammit.

I walk over and put my arms around him. "I'm so sorry, Ryan. If it weren't for me, you'd never have been dragged into all this demon stuff in the first place."

"Sure, but then think of all the fun I'd have missed out on."

"Yeah, tons of fun," I say morosely.

"Hey," he says, giving me a squeeze. "If it weren't for you, Mr. Gabriel would have killed everyone in the whole school last year. Including me."

"That's true."

"I'm sure you'll figure out how to save me again. I'm not worried."

I laugh, despite everything. "I will try to be worthy of your confidence."

Peter returns, clapping his hands briskly. "All right, cuddle-bunnies. Ready to do this?"

I reluctantly extract myself from Ryan's embrace. The three of us spend a few minutes dragging the furniture out of the way to make a clear workspace, and then Peter gets to work on the containment circle. I can see the trace of demonic energy he's using to draw it. Ryan can't, but he's familiar with this procedure from when we watched Peter summon Aaron at camp over the summer. Which suddenly seems like a million years ago.

When he's done, Peter sits down and closes his eyes. We wait anxiously. Ryan reaches over and silently takes my hand in his non-cursed one.

Nothing happens.

Peter opens his eyes and frowns.

"No luck?" I ask.

"Let me . . . let me try again."

We wait. Still nothing.

"Damn." He looks up at us. "I can't find him."

"I don't understand," Ryan says. "I thought summoning a demon — or, well, an Aaron — was, you know, like some kind of compulsion. That he had to appear when you called him."

"Not exactly," Peter says, and I am pleased to see that they are both being civil to each other again. "It's only like that when the summoner is stronger than the summonee, or if you have some sort of special talisman or other helpful device."

"Aaron is stronger than you?" I ask, surprised. "He's not even a real demon."

"No, but his association with the demon queen gives him certain special advantages. Her protection, even in small doses, is pretty significant. Among other things, it makes him harder to summon against his will."

"But he wanted to talk to me. Why would he resist now?"

"Based on what you saw last time, he's probably running from someone. If he's trying to hide, letting himself be summoned would expose him. I think we're going to have to wait until he's ready to try again to come to us."

Dammit. Waiting feels like the last thing we should be doing.

"However . . ." Peter looks suddenly thoughtful. "Ryan has given me an idea."

He closes his eyes again, then opens them and looks at us. Again. "Whatever happens, just play along, okay? I'm going to have to, uh, do a little performing."

We nod and wait to see what he's going to do.

This time when he closes his eyes, his expression changes to something harder and darker than I've ever seen on him before. He breathes in and out once, slowly, and then his outline starts to rearrange itself. He doesn't fully transform into his demon form, but he somehow becomes a bit more horse- and dragon-like, and his enormous demon-antlers stretch up and outward from his head. He seems to concentrate for a moment, and then suddenly a figure appears in the middle of the circle.

It's not Aaron. It's not anyone or anything I've ever seen before. It's . . . a very tiny demon.

It looks around, clearly terrified. It's about the size of a cat, and seems to be sort of half reptile, half ball of fluff. When it sees Peter, it throws itself facedown on the reading-area carpet, tiny arms stretched out in supplication.

"Great One!" it squeaks.

"Cower before me, insignificant worm!" Peter bellows in a voice that sounds nothing like his usual playful tenor. Ryan and I both take an involuntary step backward.

"Wh-what is your bidding, O Master? I live only to serve —"

"You lie! You have forgotten me in my absence!"

"No!" The tiny demon tries to press itself even farther into the library floor. "No, Great One! I faithfully await your return!"

I want to look at Ryan to see what he is making of this exchange, but I cannot tear my eyes away from the tiny demon. It clearly worships Peter as some kind of god.

"Prove your faithfulness, worthless one! Tell me what you know of what has happened to the demon queen."

"O yes, Master!" The demonling seems thrilled with this request, bouncing slightly against the floor in its enthusiasm to answer. "I can tell you much, for I have seen with my own eyes! Her rival—the John Gabriel who was captured—has escaped. He has damaged the beautiful queen and fled away to safety. There was a great battle, and many terrible demons fought and died! The capital writhes in flames, and there is glorious confusion and alarm!"

"Does the queen still live?"

"Yes, Great One! But she is gravely injured, and may yet die. Her consort flits about, seeking assistance, but most refuse to take sides until the outcome is more clear."

"And the John Gabriel—who helped him escape?"

"Those same demons who saved his life essence after he lost the battle for the throne. His loyal supporters who still want him to be king." Suddenly the demon lets out a high-pitched, near-hysterical peal of laughter. "They brought him an amulet to make him strong! One to fill with the souls of his enemies to use their strength as his own. But the John Gabriel could not wait—he slew all but a few of his supporters and used their souls instead. Now he is stronger than he has ever been before! But he still has not regained his physical form. That is all that prevents him from ending the queen and taking her reign for himself."

There is a moment of near silence in which Ryan and I barely breathe and the tiny demon gasps and trembles in the center of the circle. Then Peter says, "You have pleased me, tiny one. I may call on you again. You will earn much favor if you have more to tell me at that time. Especially more regarding this amulet."

"Yes! Yes, Great One!" the tiny demon squeaks in apparent ecstasy. "I will find out all I can! You will see! I am your most faithful servant!"

"Go then, faithful one," Peter says, and the tiny demon vanishes.

Peter exhales heavily, then returns to his human shape.

"So, who was that?" I ask, finally.

"Old friend," Peter says. "I used to kind of look out for him, when I was still in the demon world."

"An old friend who calls you 'Great One'?"

Peter gives me an annoyed look. "You must understand by now that things work differently down there. 'Friend' doesn't mean the same thing in the demon world as it does up here. There isn't a whole lot of goodwill and generosity of spirit. Only power and protection and exchanges of favors." He makes a sad face, then adds, a little wistfully, "I think he really missed me. Poor little guy."

"So what was all that about the amulet?" Ryan asks.

Yes. Important question.

"I have heard of such things from time to time," Peter says slowly. "Items of great power, used to amplify or increase a demon's strength or talents. It explains a lot. Like how Mr. Gabriel was able to punch through to our world and plant his curse." His expression is grim. "It's definitely not good news. Items like that are rare. Their creation is one of the few things that counts as true criminal activity in the demon world, because of how they can upset the balance of power. Kings and queens aren't generally fans of things that can give others the strength to unseat them. They were outlawed to prevent precisely what Mr. Gabriel is trying to do right now."

"But he still doesn't have a body, right?" I ask.

"Right, but that's less limiting in the demon world than you might think. I mean in the short term, anyway. He's still got most of his abilities. And if he's really even stronger than he was before . . ."

"So . . . okay, just trying to get all this straight," Ryan says. "His loyal friends, who saved him from dying all the way in the first place, broke him out of wherever the queen had him locked up, and they gave him this powerful amulet, and then he killed them and . . . and fed them to it?"

"Yes, pretty much. Most of them, anyway."

"And so now he's super strong, but still has no body. But that isn't really holding him back from doing major damage to the queen or hiding out in people's lockers to put horrible curses on them."

"Well, to fight the queen, he would need some kind of physical form. But he may have borrowed one of his supporters' bodies for that. Or else his supporters damaged her on their way to free him. That seems more likely, actually."

"Okay, but regardless," I break in, "he is now free and super powerful and dangerous. And I am supposed to go have a chat with him to find out what he wants in exchange for not killing my boyfriend, and also, *how the hell did the queen let him get loose when everyone swore to us that that would never, ever happen?*" I realize I have screamed this last part when I notice how Ryan and Peter are both staring at me. I sit down shakily in one of the chairs.

"Oh, God," I say in a much, much smaller voice. "I can't believe I have to go back down there." I put my face in my hands to prevent the panic beetles from spilling out of my eyes.

Ryan and Peter are both at my side in an instant. My face is still in my hands, but I can totally picture the awkward moment when they look at each other and then Peter backs off and Ryan sinks down beside me.

"You don't have to go," Ryan says. "I'll go. Or . . . Peter and I will go."

"Wait, what?" Peter asks.

But I'm already shaking my head. "He doesn't want you. He wants me. He wants revenge, and he also probably wants to use my power for something." I take a breath and look up at him. "But thank you for offering. God, I wish I could take you up on it. Except, you know, I wouldn't."

"Yeah," Ryan says. "I know."

"But, hey, we'll all go together! It will be like a road trip. Except, you know, in hell."

Ryan puts his hands on either side of my face and looks deeply into my eyes. "You're about to completely lose it, aren't you?"

"Possibly," I agree. "This is just really not how I envisioned today going, you know?"

"Yeah," Ryan says. "Trust me, I know." He lets go of my face so he can stare at his palm again.

There is a sudden displacement of air in the room, and then Aaron is standing in the containment circle.

"Aaron!" Ryan, Peter, and I all shout in unison.

He winces. "Shh! Not so loud." He looks just as awful and blood covered as I remember.

I stand up and lunge toward him. Peter grabs my arm and yanks me back before I can cross the circle's edge. Which I guess is a good thing. Except that I really want to throttle Aaron, I have suddenly realized. I want to lock my hands around his throat and squeeze as hard as I can. I want to hurt him in some deep and significant way for not preventing this catastrophe from occurring.

"What *happened*?" I growl at him. "How did he get out? This is exactly what you promised us would not be possible!"

"Oh, so *now* you want to talk to me," Aaron grumbles.

"Do not try my patience right now, Aaron. Besides, weren't you about to beg me to help you? Isn't your beloved mistress at death's door at this very moment?"

"She is *not* at death's door!" Aaron shouts. "She's going to be fine! She —"

"Aaron," Peter breaks in gently. He releases my arm and takes a step closer to the circle. "Tell us what happened."

Aaron looks at Peter, and all his bravado seems to dissipate at once. He sinks to the floor, his voice cracking as he speaks. "It's my fault. I didn't . . . I didn't realize. . . ."

Peter sits down on the floor on the outside of the circle across from Aaron. Ryan steps up beside me, but we both remain silent. It seems clear that Peter is the guy for this job.

"He was safe. We had him contained in so many layers of protection that there should have been no way anyone could get him out. But then . . . I got distracted."

"But you weren't responsible for keeping him contained, surely . . . ?"

"No." Aaron shakes his head. "No, of course not. But there was this demon — they come sometimes, you know, to talk to me. Because they're curious about humans, or because they want to see about trading favors with someone so close to the queen, and usually it's fine. I can see what they're after and decide whether to deal with them or not. But this one . . ." He stops and shakes his head again. "I got so caught up, I forgot to pay attention. And I had no idea he was one of Mr. Gabriel's. He got inside my head. I mean he literally got inside my head. I'd let my defenses down, and he . . . well, he got in. And I knew all the things about how Mr. Gabriel was contained, of course. She trusted me with that information. She trusted me and I didn't keep it safe and now she's . . ." He stops and looks up at me with wide, desperate eyes. "Please. Please. You have to help her."

"Mr. Gabriel was here," Peter says. "Do you know that? He marked Ryan with some kind of time bomb to get Cyn to go down and deal."

"Of course he did." Aaron turns toward me again. "He wants your help, too. But you can't. If you give him what he wants, he'll kill us all."

"If I don't give him what he wants, he'll kill Ryan."

"Better him than all of us," Aaron says. He looks apologetically at Ryan. "Sorry, but you know it's true. The needs of the many . . ."

"Yeah, yeah." Ryan waves this away. "What can you do to actually be helpful?"

Aaron turns suddenly and looks over his shoulder.

Then he vanishes.

"That wasn't really what I meant," Ryan says.

There's a kind of rushing, roaring sound, and then the circle so recently vacated by Aaron is filled with a mass of teeth and tentacles and evil-looking bloodshot eyes.

I scream before I can help myself and fall back hard against the floor. Ryan rushes over to me while Peter shouts "Crap! Crap!" and finally does something to close the containment circle. The demon disappears in a flash of magic energy.

"Sorry," Peter gasps. "Sorry! My fault!"

"Yeah," I say, still trying to catch my breath. "Please don't let that happen again."

Ryan helps me up and we all grab chairs.

Then we all sit in silence for a few moments.

"So," Ryan says finally. "The demon world is going to be, like, full of those things, isn't it? I mean that thing that showed up after Aaron. Somehow I hadn't really been thinking about that part."

"Well," Peter says, "you won't be wading through them like grass in a field. I mean, they have lives and stuff. Most of them will be busy doing other things."

"Just not the ones who want to kill us for Mr. Gabriel," Ryan says.

"Right. Although since he killed a lot of those demons already, there shouldn't be too many of those. So that's something. But we'll need to be on the lookout for other random demons who might just happen to notice us and want to kill us for no reason in particular. And also for anyone who's not currently a supporter of Mr. Gabriel but who sees which way the wind is blowing and now thinks they might be able to curry favor with him by doing bad things to us. And —"

"Stop," Ryan says. "Please."

"Okay," I say. "So how do we even get there? If Mr. Gabriel really wants me to come, shouldn't he have, you know, sent a car, or something?"

"I can get us there," Peter says reluctantly.

"Great," I say. Although, of course, it's not great. It sucks. I don't want to go back. But there is no sense thinking about what I want and don't want. I know what I have to do. "Do you need to do anything to prepare, or can we go anytime?"

"We can go anytime."

"Great," I say again. (It's still not actually great.) "Then can you please go and use your demony influence to get Annie, William, Leticia, and Diane out of their classes without any teachers making a fuss and bring them here? Then we can fill them in before we hit the road. I can't leave them in the dark about this. I promised I wouldn't."

Peter nods and heads out. Ryan looks at me.

"So we're going right away, huh?"

"What would be the point in waiting?"

"To, you know, put off the time when we have to go to a terrible, scary place."

I smile at him. "I wish we could. But that thing on your hand is already spreading."

"What?" He stares down at his palm again.

"I saw it when you helped me up before. Tiny red line stretching toward your wrist."

"Well, crap."

"Yeah."

To avoid having to think or talk any further about what's happening or what we're about to do, and since we seem to be done with the demon summoning for the time being, Ryan and I move the furniture back into its original position. Before long, we hear the library doors open, followed by footsteps and voices. Peter and the others appear from around the bookshelves.

"Peter already told us the whole story on the way here," Leticia says.

Annie comes over and stands in front of me, crossing her arms. "We're coming with you."

Chapter | 05

Everyone is looking at me. I consider my options carefully.

Annie has her stubborn face on. They all do, actually. Well, except Ryan and Peter, who have their curious faces on instead as they wait to see what I will do. My first impulse is to ask Peter to give them all some kind of temporary paralysis so that we can make our escape without any further argument or interference. But that would not be very diplomatic of me.

"I don't think that's really the best idea," I say finally.

"That's too bad," Annie says. "You can't make us stay behind."

"Well, actually I'm pretty sure I can. I mean, if I ask Peter nicely not to bring you with us when we go."

She raises her eyebrows. "Then we'll start looking into ways of following on our own. Aaron's old bookstore is still there. We could go and do research and start experimenting wildly with dark magic and arcane practices that we don't even begin to understand."

"Annie, that would be really stupid. And you know it."

"So don't put me in a position where I have to do that."

I look around at the others in exasperation. "Are you all insane? Why would you possibly want to come? I don't even want to come! I'm only going because I have to."

Annie hasn't moved. "You only have to because of me. If I had never gotten involved with Mr. Gabriel in the first place, you would never have had to do any of this."

"But that wasn't your fault. He brainwashed you!"

"Guys," Diane breaks in, "none of that really matters. That's all in the past. What matters is what we can do right now. And we want to help you, Cyn."

I shake my head. "It won't be like it was at camp. That was just two demons. And only one of them had an actual body. And we were ready, and we had a plan. . . . This time . . . this time there is no plan. We're going because if we don't, then Ryan will die, and then Mr. Gabriel will probably do some other terrible thing to try to get me down there."

"Which is exactly why you need all the help you can get!" Annie insists.

"Annie, he's going to *be* there. We are going to talk to him. Do you really want to be present for that?"

Her expression goes a little twitchy, but she still doesn't look away. "Of course not. I don't want to see him. I don't want to go anywhere near where he is. But I don't want to sit up here pretending everything is normal while you're down there without me. And maybe I can help! I know him better than anyone else does. I mean, yes, it was mostly lies and supernatural coercion, but"—her tongue seems to stumble over itself, and now she does look away—"but not all of it."

I look at Leticia, feeling a little desperate. "And you? What's your excuse?"

She shrugs. "We're your friends."

I sit down and put my face in my hands again.

"This is what I think," I hear Ryan say. I raise my head again so I can see him. "I think I get to decide on this one, because I'm the one with the horrible demon curse embedded in his hand. And I think only Cyn, Peter, and I should go. Annie, I understand why you want to come, I really do, but think about it. What if bringing you down there turns out to play directly into Mr. Gabriel's plans? What if we can't stop him from grabbing you? Let us go and figure out what he wants."

"But we know what he wants," Annie says. "He wants me. And he wants to be the king of the demons."

William puts an arm around her. "Annie, maybe you should listen to them."

She looks mournfully at him. "I thought you were going to be supportive!"

He looks pretty mournful himself, but he stands his ground. "I understand why you want to help. I do. But this doesn't sound like the best way to do it. What they're saying makes sense. This guy is serious bad news; you've told me that yourself. It doesn't sound like a good idea to walk willingly back into his life. Afterlife. Whatever."

"But I can't just sit here doing nothing!"

"I think you can," William says. "At least just for right now. Wait until they find out a little more information. Maybe you'll be able to help later in some specific way. Some really important, valuable way. You don't need to go rushing in right this second and maybe blow your chance."

"Yes," Ryan says, shooting William a grateful glance. "If Mr. Gabriel still wants you, then bringing you down to him is the last thing we should do. If nothing else, as long as you're not there, you're a potential bargaining chip. I mean not *really,* obviously — but if he thinks there's a chance we'd give you up somehow, it would give us time to try to figure something out."

"He also wants revenge, though," Diane says. "What if when you show up he just kills all three of you on the spot?"

"I don't think that will happen," Peter says. "He needs Cyn for something. Something only someone with her ability can do. Otherwise he wouldn't have bothered with the mark on Ryan's palm. He would have just killed him, to punish her. If he had strength and freedom enough to cast the curse spell, I think he could have cast a deadlier one."

Something just occurred to me. "Wait. Ryan, you said you saw Mr. Gabriel through the portal. But if he's still only in spirit form, how — ?"

"It was just a projection," Peter explains. "He could make it look like anything. And he would have wanted Ryan to recognize him, so he could tell you what happened."

Leticia raises her hand. I realize she's the only one who hasn't been super vocal about coming with us. "Can I ask a question? Even if you're right that Mr. Gabriel needs Cyn's power for something, so that's why he's not just killing everyone right away — we're all clear that he's going to try to do that eventually, right? That once he gets whatever he wants, he will at that point start killing everyone Cyn cares about?"

"Not if we can stop him," I say.

No one looks especially confident about that potentiality. I'm sure I don't, either.

"And why exactly do you have to go down there right now without any time to think or plan?" Leticia continues. "Can't you, like, at least get some weapons or something?"

I open my mouth to explain why that's not possible. And then I realize that I have no idea why it's not. This all feels so urgent, has felt so urgent since the second I saw Ryan's hand, but is it really? Could we take a little more time? I turn to look inquiringly at Peter.

"The kind of weapons we could get up here wouldn't be any help," Peter says. "And we do have to hurry. I don't know exactly what Mr. Gabriel's curse will do to Ryan, but I do know that placing that mark was like lighting a fuse. The clock is ticking."

"Okay!" Ryan says abruptly. "Enough talking. I stand by my resolution that I get to decide who goes, and I have decided. Now let's please just get this over with."

"Okay," I say, standing up.

"Okay," says Leticia.

Diane twists her mouth to the side, but then nods. "Not okay," she says. "But I guess I accept it."

"All right," Annie says reluctantly. Beside her, William looks extremely relieved. "I mean, it's not, but . . . okay. But tell us the second you get back. The *exact* second. Promise?"

"Promise." I take her hands. "We'll be okay. And somehow we'll figure out how to deal with this whole situation and all come out alive on the other side."

I give my phone to Annie and ask her to cover for me with my mom if necessary, and Ryan quickly texts Jorge to cover for him as well. (I don't know what excuse he gives, since Jorge doesn't know about the demons, but I trust Ryan to manage his own affairs.) Then there are several seconds of hugging and brave faces, and then Peter, Ryan, and I shoo everyone else out of the library. Annie looks back from the doorway, and for a second I'm afraid she's not going to leave after all, but then she lets William pull her out into the hall, and the door closes behind her.

Peter begins to construct some new kind of energy shape on the carpet. Luckily it seems to be smaller this time, so we don't have to move the furniture again.

"So," Ryan says to me. "There's really no plan?"

"Nope. Not yet, anyway. Think of it as improv."

"You refused to take improv with us at camp, remember?"

"Yeah, but you love it. I'm counting on you to be inspired and brilliant in the moment."

Peter finishes drawing and walks over to us. "Ready?"

"God, no," I say. "How is this going to work, anyway? Will we have to hold our breath?"

They both look at me strangely.

"When I went with Aaron that last time we had to hold our breath!"

"Uh . . . well, not this time," Peter says. "But it might get a little cold."

I realize we are now, finally, about to depart. The panic beetles surge back with a vengeance. Peter presses a hand against each of our backs and there's a flash of light and then suddenly it's as though all the warmth in the universe has evaporated. Ryan grabs on to me and I crush myself against him, trying to protect at least some part of myself from the unbearable cold. Frigid wind tears at us from all directions, seeming to want to rip into our flesh and pull us apart with icy teeth. I keep my eyes tightly closed, my frozen fingertips clenching the fabric of Ryan's shirt.

And then all at once the rushing of the wind explodes into a cacophony of horrible sounds at the same instant that the unbearable cold is replaced by unbearable heat. I tear my face away from Ryan's chest to look around wildly, one arm thrown up in a useless attempt to shield my face from the searing, ash-filled air.

Everything is on fire.

Black and orange flames rage through the darkness around us. From varying distances, animal-like howls and violent crashing and breaking sounds cut through the constant roaring and burning. I only have a second to try to take any of this in, however, before Peter shoves me forward. I turn to see him gesturing urgently toward the closest dark alley, which shifts in appearance from a dirty corridor between two gutted buildings, to a large crack in some kind of black rock formation, to what might be the shadowy undergrowth between two impossibly tall trees. Ryan seems too overwhelmed to move on his own. As I watch, Peter grabs him and begins running, half dragging Ryan along beside him. I follow at their heels.

And then something huge and dark and terrifying suddenly reaches out and snatches Ryan away into the blackness.

There is a split second where I am frozen in shock and disbelief and then he begins to scream and then his scream is abruptly cut off and by then I am racing into the blackness after him. I barely register Peter's cry of objection behind me.

The shadows close in until the light from the fires is strangely muted. I can still see enough, however, to make out the shape of my boyfriend struggling in the clutches of some hideous, giant, twisted thing. My first thought is simply relief that he's still alive. But that could clearly change at any second.

I throw myself forward, trying to reach him, cursing my stupid roach-power for not being any good against physical attacks. Ryan is still thrashing in the demon's grip; slender tendrils of long, flat, tentacle-like appendages are wrapped around him, including one covering his mouth, which explains the cut-off screaming. The demon's other, much larger appendages are also reaching toward Ryan, seeming to fight with one another to see which is going to be the one to drag him into the gaping open mouth. They don't bother with me; I guess the demon isn't especially worried about prey that's actually trying to get closer. Ryan turns and seems to see me but I'm not sure if he really does — his eyes are so wide and terrified. He might not be altogether aligned with reality right now.

Scrambling over several of the disgusting, undulating larger demon appendages, I finally get close enough to reach out and grab Ryan's ankle. I start to pull, but it's instantly obvious that I'll never be able to just yank him free. The demon is too strong. It's got him too tightly wrapped up in itself. I need to get it to let go. But I have no idea how to do that.

Something grabs my arm. I scream and try to shake it off before I realize that it's Peter.

"Help us!" I scream at him.

He pulls at me, and I have to fight to keep my grip on Ryan. What is he doing?

He pulls again, and my hand slips from Ryan's ankle. I twist around to stare at Peter.

"You can't save him!" he's yelling. "You're just going to get yourself killed!"

I kick him in the stomach, but he barely seems to feel it. I keep forgetting that even though he's not a particularly strong demon in the physical sense, he's still a lot stronger than a human.

"Let me go!"

"No!" He pulls at me again, dragging me a few more inches toward him. Away from Ryan.

"Let me *go!*" I scream again, and this time before I even know I'm doing it, I punctuate my command with a push of my demon resistance. It's something like what I did to drive Mr. Gabriel out of William's body that time at camp.

Peter stumbles backward, releasing me.

Before he can regroup I turn and start toward Ryan again. But he's higher up now; two of the appendages have beaten back the others and are together drawing Ryan closer to the waiting orifice. I start climbing desperately, but I know it's no use. I'll never get up there in time. It's going to eat him.

I'm going to have to watch it eat him. He's screaming and writhing and it's bringing him closer to its mouth and I don't — I can't —

I hear Peter's shout somewhere behind and below in the dark and I am filled with murderous rage. His fault. This is his fault. If he'd only tried to *help* me instead of pulling me away —

Then I stop, suddenly frozen by a realization. My demon resistance made Peter let go. It might not have done any actual damage, but he felt it. He felt it enough to stumble backward and lose his grip on my arm.

I slam my hands down against the demon appendage I'm currently straddling and *push* with my power as hard as I can.

The demon jerks — in surprise? pain? — and as it does so, it loosens its hold on Ryan. Despite his terror, my boyfriend is still present enough to seize the moment; he twists down and away and suddenly he's free, scrambling and sliding, racing back to me.

I grab his hand as soon as he's close enough and together we start running back toward the light of the fires, back toward where we were before. We pass Peter, who has been standing in apparent indecision or incomprehension or in-something, and we keep running. After a moment, Peter appears running beside us and then ahead of us, and I realize he's trying to lead us toward that alley he'd first indicated as our destination. We change course to follow.

Peter darts into the alley and doesn't stop until we're far enough in that the noise and heat both die down a little. He rests his hands on his thighs, breathing heavily, as Ryan and

I slump against the nearest wall and then all the way down to the ground.

For a few minutes, no one says anything. We all just try to remember how to breathe, how to have hearts that beat at something like a normal rhythm, how to not be nearly dead with panic and fear.

Finally, I'm able to turn my head to look at Ryan. "Are you okay?"

"Yeah," he whispers. His voice is hoarse from screaming. "Yeah, I think so. Jesus." He turns to look at me, eyes still too wide. "I can't believe you came back to this place voluntarily."

I shrug uncomfortably. "Well, to be fair, this visit is starting out a little rockier than the previous ones."

Suddenly I remember Peter, and how much I hate him.

I climb wearily to my feet. "You fucking asshole," I say, moving toward him. "You absolute piece of—"

"Cyn," Peter says, somewhat desperately, "I thought you were throwing your life away. I didn't know you could do what you did."

"I didn't, either. But that's no excuse. When people you care about are being attacked by horrible monsters, you fucking try to save them. That's how it works. You don't stop to think about it. You certainly don't try to stop other people from saving them."

"That's exactly what I was doing! Trying to save you!"

"Well, you can't do that when it interferes with me trying to save someone else!"

We are inches apart now, shouting into each other's faces.

"Um," Ryan says, "what are you guys talking about?"

"Peter," I say, not turning around, "tried to pull me away when I was trying to help you."

There is a brief silence, and then I hear Ryan start to push himself up against the wall. "Why does that not surprise me?"

"Ryan," Peter says, stepping to the side so he can look past me, "I thought it was a lost cause. I thought Cyn was going to die right along with you. Are you honestly saying that's what you would have wanted?"

"Are you sure?" Ryan asks, coming over to stand beside me. "Are you sure you weren't just seizing the opportunity to get me out of the way so you could have her to yourself?"

The conversation has suddenly taken a very awkward turn. I don't think I like where this is going.

"Guys—"

Peter throws back his head and laughs. It is a long, deep, scornful laugh.

"You arrogant little insect," he says, taking a step toward Ryan now. "Do you really think I need to wait for an *opportunity* to get you out of the way? I could have made you disappear anytime I wanted. I could have made it look like an accident."

"Guys, come on—"

Peter keeps going, talking over me, still moving forward. Ryan takes an involuntary step back, but his furious eyes are still fixed on Peter's.

"Do you think I haven't thought about how it could be done? I could have arranged so many things, done it so subtly that Cyn would never suspect I had anything to do with it. And who do you think she would turn to in her time of grief? Who do you think would be there to console her, to get her through the long, lonely nights —"

Ryan's hand curls into a very capable-looking fist at his side.

"Guys!" I shout, pushing between them. "Enough!"

I whirl toward Peter.

"The only reason I am not trying to scratch your eyes out right now," I say, pointing at his face, "is because you accidentally helped me figure out how to save Ryan."

I whirl back toward Ryan.

"And while I fully understand your desire to kick his ass — believe me — you need to hold it together. We need his help. W 're not going to make it through this without him."

I tactfully leave out the part about how Peter would crush him like a bug if it ever came down to a real fight.

We all stand there for a moment staring angrily at one another.

"Fine," Ryan says. He goes back to his wall and leans defiantly against it.

Peter composes himself with visible effort and then turns toward me. "Cyn," he says, "I swear. If I thought anything could have been done to save him, I would have tried."

Ryan barks out a humorless laugh, and I can see Peter forcing himself to ignore it. He keeps his eyes on me. "I really was just trying to save your life. I thought — I know how you can get, blinded by your love for your friends. You don't always seem to be able to see the danger."

I shake my head at him, but it's getting hard to maintain

my anger. "I see the danger," I say quietly. "It just doesn't matter. That's the part you don't understand."

But I am having an uncomfortable flashback to how Ryan tried to stop me from going after Annie when Mr. Gabriel stole her down to the demon world on opening night of *Sweeney Todd*. Ryan was also trying to stop me from saving someone else because he thought I was going to die. And I forgave him for that eventually. Didn't that mean I had to forgive Peter, too?

I wonder if Ryan is remembering that night as well. Probably not; boys seem to be very good at selective memory when the occasion suits them.

I sigh heavily, covering my face with my hands. Again.

"Let's — let's just focus on what we're supposed to be doing down here, okay?"

"Okay," says Peter. "But what did you do, exactly, to that demon? Do you think you could do it again?"

It's a good question. I drop my hands, considering.

"I think so. I did something like it once before — to push Mr. Gabriel out of William. I'd wondered, since then, whether there were other ways I could use my power as a kind of weapon instead of just protection. But I never . . ." *Never bothered. Never tried to practice or develop it or anything. Just closed my eyes and tried to pretend we were all going to be fine, forever.* "When I realized it had worked to make you let me go, I thought it might work on the other demon, too. I didn't think I could hurt it, but I thought if I could just distract it . . ."

Peter nods. "We should experiment. When we, uh, have time. That could be really useful."

"Agreed. Assuming we don't all die in the next half hour or whatever."

All the shouting and arguing had temporarily distracted me, but now it was sinking back in that Ryan was almost eaten by a monster within a minute of arriving in the demon world. We really could all possibly die at any second, before we ever even find out what Mr. Gabriel's demands are.

This place is the worst. I still can't really believe I'm back here again.

At least you're not alone this time, I remind myself. *And you're not weak. You've still got your resistance.*

In fact . . . I seem to have just about all of it.

My heart starts making little jerky motions inside me. Like maybe it is suddenly full of beetles.

"Peter? Can my resistance . . . I'd used some of it to protect Annie and the others, but . . ."

"Oh," he says. "Oh, man. I didn't realize . . ." He shakes his head. "I don't think it can work that way. That's why the queen needs to bring you down here when she wants to borrow it."

Which means I've left them all completely unprotected. "What if this was all a ruse to leave Annie vulnerable? What if —" *Oh, God.* "I have to go back! Peter, take us back!"

"Cyn, wait," Ryan says. He still looks ashen and shaky, and avoids looking at Peter, but he comes over to join us. "Think about it. If that's all Mr. Gabriel wanted, he could have gone for Annie first instead of going for me. He could have gotten to her before you even had a chance to share your protection. Before you even knew anything was wrong."

Peter is nodding. "He's right. I don't think you need to worry about that. At least . . . not right now."

My body is still screaming at me to *go back, go back!,* but I make myself try to calm down. What Ryan is saying makes sense. It does. I have to assume that Mr. Gabriel lured me down here for some other reason than just to get me temporarily out of the way.

"Okay," I say. "Okay. Let's . . . let's just get on with it, then. How do we find him?"

Peter goes very still. "I . . . don't think that's going to be a problem."

A very large shadow falls across the alley/crack/undergrowth. Ryan and I turn to look at what Peter apparently noticed a second before.

It is, of course, another horrible demon.

Ryan gasps beside me. I don't blame him; the thing is hideous. It's too big to fit inside the alley, but it presses its giant face to the opening and stares down at us with bright, crazy eyes. As I take in its enormous red, crunchy-looking limbs and grinning dog-bear head, I realize that I have seen this particular demon before.

"Hey, I know you," I say. "You're . . . what's-his-name's even more horrible friend. You tried to kill me the last time I was here."

The thing inches closer, looming high above us on its sharp-edged Alaskan king crab legs, smiling even more broadly. I suspect we are all wishing very much right now that Peter had taken us a bit farther down the alley before deciding to stop.

The demon swivels its head to look at each of us in turn, then begins making odd jolty motions, ducking its head down between its own legs and then twisting back up to smile brightly at us.

"It's like . . . it's like a demented dog-clown on crab stilts," Ryan whispers, staring helplessly.

"I think . . . I think it wants us to follow it," Peter says after a moment.

The demon slams its smiling face against the alley opening and thrusts one crab leg forward to point at Peter, which I think is supposed to indicate that yes, he has guessed correctly. To his great credit, Peter only flinches slightly before saying, "Well then, lead on, good sir! No reason to keep your master waiting."

I can't quite bring myself to agree. I can think of *so many reasons*.

After another head slam that sends a few crumbling bits of brick/stone/bark tumbling down near the alley's entrance and one more impossible smile expansion that threatens to split its ugly face completely in half, the demon performs a quick but complicated about-face and starts to walk away.

Ryan looks back and forth between Peter and me. "Are we really going to — ?"

"That's what we're here for, isn't it?" Peter asks. Then, before either of us can say anything else, he marches forward and out of the alley. After a second, Ryan and I follow. I grab Ryan's hand and loop his arm through mine on the way out. Nothing is going to pull him off into the shadows to eat him this time. And then we are all following the shiny red legs of the crab-demon, whom Peter quickly informs us he has decided to call Mr. Crunchy.

The fiery heat assaults us again as soon as we emerge from the alley, and within a few steps it starts to be hard to breathe. With my free hand, I pull the neck of my shirt up to cover my nose and mouth. Ryan notices and does the same. Peter doesn't seem as bothered by the burning, ashy air, at least on a physical level. He does look deeply troubled, though. As much as he hates his home world, it must still be quite a shock to see it like this.

Ryan looks around warily; I suppose he didn't get much of a chance to observe our surroundings when we first arrived. "Why is everything . . . moving?" he asks through his shirt.

Oh. Right. The shiftiness. "It does that," I tell him. "You kind of get used to it."

He gives me a very skeptical look, but says nothing.

It soon becomes clear that the good thing about following the scary demon is that the other scary demons seem to know we are spoken for, and they leave us alone. I see several watching us hungrily from various shadowy places along the way, but they never do more than watch and occasionally salivate noisily as we pass.

The bad thing is that I know every step we take is one that brings us closer to Mr. Gabriel. Which, yes, is the reason we came here, but . . . I'm not ready. I'm still reeling from the shock of learning he's free. There hasn't been time to wrap my mind around the idea of having to face him again. Especially not like this — so abruptly and without any chance to prepare.

I still have nightmares about our last encounter — ones in which we don't manage to defeat him. In my dreams I have seen all of his terrible desires played out in full. I have seen him drag Annie screaming back to the demon world; I have seen him take revenge on everyone I love; I have seen him come for me, at the last, the blood of my family and friends still fresh upon his horns and claws and face. In my dreams he is always radiant with joy as he begins the long, slow process of killing me, ripping aside my resistance like so much tissue paper, his eyes fixed on mine as he takes in my final, hopeless understanding of his victory. *You were never strong enough to stop me,* he whispers. *You never had a chance of saving anyone.* He says more, sometimes, but usually by then I am screaming too loud to hear the words.

Stop it, I tell myself firmly. I know those are lies. I *was* strong enough to stop him. I *did* stop him, dammit. I killed him! Or — I helped kill him, anyway. It's just that someone managed to snag his soul before it could finish fading away into oblivion.

I stopped him once — twice, in fact! — and I can do it again. I have to believe this is true.

We turn down a narrow pathway between darkly looming structures, and the light from the fires begins to fade until it's hard to see very far in front of us. Mr. Crunchy slows, and I know what that must mean, and I am afraid I am about to throw up all over the dark and shifty landscape. There is a building/boulder/impossible geometric shape ahead of us with a ragged opening maybe twice as wide as the alley where Mr. Crunchy had found us. It still seems way too narrow for him, but apparently it's just wide enough. He contorts himself into an astonishingly compact size to squeeze through it, then sticks his smiling head back out to make sure we understand we are to follow him inside.

One by one we climb through into the rubble-strewn interior. I manage not to throw up. I hold on to that as a small victory to savor. I will take all the victories I can get right now.

Chapter | 06

My eyes are still trying to adjust to the even-more-dark of the space we've just entered. There's a large moving patch of darkness ahead that I assume is Mr. Crunchy. I can hear the sound of his pointy limbs scraping against the floor, and the sound of Peter and Ryan breathing beside me. Everything else is quiet.

And then Mr. Gabriel speaks slowly and softly from somewhere in the blackness.

"Dear Cynthia. Words simply cannot express how delighted I am to see you once again."

The sound of his voice is like a shard of glass slicing into my brain. Even though I've been hearing it in my dreams for months, hearing it in reality is, unsurprisingly, much worse. *So* much worse. I feel myself trembling. I want desperately to be strong and brave but my legs feel like they might give out at any moment. Not ready, dammit. I'm just not ready for this.

Ryan places a hand on my lower back, steadying me. Somehow, he is handling this moment better than I am. Maybe he already used up all of his available terror by being almost eaten upon arrival. Or maybe he's just acting. Well, I may not be as talented in that department as he is, but I can sure as hell try.

"What do you want?" I ask the blackness. "And . . . where are you?" Because I still can't see him. I need to see him. I need to know where he is.

"Where am I?" Mr. Gabriel muses from the darkness. "Where indeed. It's a more complicated question than it used to be. One of the few advantages of my non-corporeal form is my ability to be almost anywhere. For example—"

Suddenly I feel his breath on the back of my neck and I scream, whirling around.

And then I feel a finger trace along my arm. I snatch my arm away, still trying as hard as I can to see him, but he's either invisible and masking his aura or he's just moving too fast for me to glimpse.

"Stop that!" I shout at him, hating the tremor I can hear in my voice.

"No," he whispers in my ear, and I jerk away again, but not before I feel something hot and wet flick against my skin.

I scream again before I can help it.

"Cyn—Cyn, what?" Ryan asks, sounding a little panicked.

"He's . . . he's here. Touching me." I shudder in revulsion and scrub furiously at my ear.

"But . . . I didn't see . . ."

"I did," says Peter. "He's gone now, though."

"Am I?" Mr. Gabriel asks.

There is a new movement in the shadows. I half expect to see Mr. Gabriel's giant-spidery little brother come high-stepping out of the black, but instead a soft light begins to beat back the darkness in the cave/abandoned shell of a building/strange formless hole we seem to be in. Ryan, Peter, and Mr. Crunchy all slowly become visible. And then part of the light seems to bend inward, intensifying, and the all-too-familiar features of Mr. Gabriel begin to assemble themselves. In seconds he is standing there, gazing back at us. He looks like the human librarian version of himself, unfairly good-looking with a disarming smile, dressed in his school uniform of jeans and a button-down shirt.

"Sorry," he says, not sounding the least bit sorry at all. "That was rather childish. I just so enjoy hearing you scream. But there will be plenty of time for that later, of course."

I want to say something clever and defiant, but I'm too busy just trying to pull myself together.

He looks around, acknowledging my companions for the first time. "I must say I didn't expect you to bring the boy-friend. And . . . the expatriate! Ah, Cynthia. You always were full of surprises."

He takes a step forward, and as he moves it becomes clear that he's not quite solid; I can just make out the shape of something behind him.

Mr. Gabriel notices me looking, and his smile twists wryly.

"Yes. Still not quite back to my old self, as you see. But I will get there. Very soon."

The something behind him appears to be a person push-ing a small cart. Or . . . not a person, exactly. A demon in person-shaped form. Its features are rough, like the lazy demons who posed as security guards during the lead-up to *Sweeney Todd*. The cart looks like something from IKEA, stained a dark faux-wood color. On top of the cart is a golden urn.

The urn is pulsing with red demon-energy.

"So is that where you are for real?" I ask, pointing at the urn. "Your essence, or whatever?"

"For now," he says. "Although, as I demonstrated, I don't have to stay in there completely."

I have to fight the urge to scrub at my ear again.

Ryan and Peter are standing silently to either side of me. Mr. Crunchy has managed to extend himself almost entirely vertically along one wall, leaving most of the space clear for the rest of us. Other than the rough-featured cart-pusher, there doesn't seem to be anyone else here.

"How nice for you. Now please remove whatever that thing is that you put in Ryan's hand."

Mr. Gabriel turns his flickery smile to Ryan. "I didn't really expect you to come with her, Sweeney. Very gallant of you. How's the hand? Does she know how much it hurts?"

"He's exaggerating," Ryan tells me quickly. "It just stings a little."

Mr. Gabriel's smile widens. "It will get worse."

"Stop screwing around and tell me what you want," I say. The fact that he's sort of just a hologram makes me feel a bit less terrified, but only a bit.

"And you," he says, ignoring me and turning to focus on

Peter. "You are a surprise, as well. I did plan to see you again, of course. When it is time to pay you back for all the trouble you caused me. But not yet."

"I'm not sure I believe you," Peter says. "How else did you think Cyn was going to get down here?"

"Oh, she's resourceful. I knew she'd find a way."

"Hello?" I break in. "Can we get to the part where you make your unreasonable demands, please? I'm missing AP Psych for this."

Mr. Gabriel sighs dramatically and turns back to me. "Always so impatient. Very well, Cynthia. What I want is your assistance in regaining my original physical form. Now that I'm not in such a rush, I find the idea of taking over someone else's body rather . . . distasteful. I want my own back."

"Isn't it bound to be kind of gross by now?" I ask him. "Decomposing in a shallow grave somewhere or whatever?"

"I don't mean my actual former body, although thank you for that lovely mental image. I mean I want to create that body anew."

"That takes a lot of power," Peter says. "I'm guessing you're not quite up to it right now."

"Yes, well, *obviously,* or else I wouldn't have needed to call upon your roachy human friend, would I?" Mr. Gabriel sounds like he's the one getting impatient now. I guess he's annoyed that we keep interrupting his little speech.

"And what am I supposed to do, exactly?"

That seems to be the right line. Mr. Gabriel smiles brightly at me.

"There is an object I require. Something that will allow me to re-create my body far more quickly than I could on my own. I need you to fetch it for me."

"Okay, well, first, I don't think so. And second, why can't you just fetch it yourself? Or send one of your minions to do it for you?" I gesture toward Mr. Crunchy, who looks pleased to have been included in the conversation.

"My physical mobility, as you have seen, is limited at the moment. And the object I want is in a place where a physical presence will be necessary. My *minions* are needed for other tasks, and even if they weren't . . . this task is one where your special ability will come in particularly handy."

"What about your powerful amulet? Why can't you use that to make yourself a new body?"

He looks at me sharply. "Heard about that, did you? How—?" He shakes his head, probably realizing there's no way I'm going to tell him. "Well. I will, in fact, be using the amulet. But there's something I need you to do for me first."

"Where *is* the amulet, anyway?" I ask, abruptly distracted. I realize he's finally about to get down to business, but suddenly the amulet is all I can think about. "I mean, you can't exactly be wearing it, since you don't have a body. Is it in the urn with you?"

"That's none of your business," Mr. Gabriel says, somewhat primly.

"Well, it *kinda* is," I say, taking a step toward the cart. I'm getting a terrifying idea. Because what if it's just *sitting* in there, right there on the cart, and someone could just walk over and—

Suddenly the blank-faced cart-demon explodes into a mass of tentacles and teeth and unidentifiable patches of fur and scales and claws. It bursts through the flickery image of Mr. Gabriel and slams me backward against a broken column of jagged stone. I cry out in surprise and pain and find myself blinking up at two tiny, malevolent eyes set above a giant mouth filled with too many teeth and at least three extra tongues.

"I said, that's none of your business," Mr. Gabriel repeats in a chillingly soft voice. "Now apologize to my associate for insulting his ability to do his job, please. Otherwise he is likely to feel a strong need to prove himself to you, and I would prefer not to have you . . . damaged . . . before you are able to complete my errand."

"Sorry," I whisper without a moment's hesitation. *Oh, God.* I stare up at those empty, enraged eyes and babble helplessly. "I'm sorry, I'm so sorry, I swear, please go back over there and I'll just stay over here far away from the cart and it will all be fine, I promise."

One of the thing's tentacles slides forward and wraps itself around my throat. My breath stops. My entire field of vision is filled with flashing teeth and writhing tentacles and those horrible, horrible eyes. Ryan makes a desperate sound from somewhere nearby, but I can't tell where he is. I can't see anything but the demon, who seems to be trying to decide whether to drive his lesson home even further. If I could speak, I would assure him that it's not necessary. Lesson learned, no going near the cart. No even thinking about going near the cart. Going near the cart is now the last thing I ever, ever want to do.

After an eternity of breathless silence, the noose around my neck loosens, and the demon draws back. It turns away and shrinks back down into its humanish shape and stands quietly in its place once more behind the cart.

Ryan rushes over to my side, now that my side is no longer blocked by a wall of horrible demon.

"Cyn! Are you okay?"

I nod and slowly sit up, not quite able to make my voice work again yet. It's amazing how easy it is to forget sometimes that all of these creatures are monsters. Especially when Mr. Gabriel is standing there yammering on in his librarian persona and acting like he's just some super-arrogant human kind of villain. Any of them could kill us with the barest effort. Even my roachy protection won't save me from a tentacle around the neck. Or a claw to the jugular or any of the countless other ways these demons could physically snuff out my life.

"Please," I say to Mr. Gabriel at last. "Please just take that thing out of Ryan's hand, and I'll do your stupid errand, okay?"

He clasps his hologram hands behind his hologram back.

"We both know that's not how this works, Cynthia. I'm not removing anything, and you're going to do exactly what I want, because if you don't, that little red line is going to travel all the way to your boyfriend's gallant heart, and then he will die in agony."

Ryan, in my peripheral vision, glances at his palm.

I root around inside myself, trying to reclaim my courage from wherever it went scurrying off to when the cart-demon attacked me. I cannot just roll over on this. I cannot. I climb back up to my feet.

"If you really need me to do this for you, then you won't let Ryan die, because you know I will *never* help you if you hurt him. So just undo your curse or whatever now, and then we'll talk."

He smiles and shakes his head.

"Unfortunately for you, I *don't* need you to do this. I *want* you to do this, because it's the fastest way for me to get the rest of what I want. If you don't do it, then it will take me longer to get my physical form back. Probably a lot longer. But I'll still get there. I don't feel like waiting, but if I have to, if you *make it* so I have to, then you'd better believe I'm going to console myself by torturing and killing all the people you love. Starting with your darling boyfriend."

I stand there, taking this in. If he's telling the truth, then I don't have much to bargain with.

I turn to Peter. "Is he telling the truth? Do you know? Can he re-create his body without my help?"

Peter nods. "Yeah, I think he can. It would take a while, but . . . yeah."

Crap.

I continue to stand there, hoping for some brilliant idea to occur to me for how to get out of this, but nothing comes. Ryan will die unless I agree. Of course, Mr. Gabriel will kill us all later anyway, even if I do what he wants. But at least that will be later, instead of now. Oh, but . . . hmm.

I take a breath. "Are we making an official deal here, Mr. Gabriel?"

I sense Peter and Ryan both going very still beside me.

"Are you agreeing to take on this task?"

"Cyn," Ryan says, "wait."

"I will take on this task if you agree to remove your curse from Ryan and to leave all of us alone forever after that. 'All of us' to include the three of us here, all of our families and friends, and especially Annie. And William."

Mr. Gabriel's face, which had been smiling good-naturedly for the last several minutes, goes dark at the mention of Annie and William.

"No. That is not the deal."

"Then what is the deal exactly?"

"You will complete the task, and I will remove the curse. That is all."

"And so then you'll get your physical body back and come right after us? I don't think so."

"If you do not agree, your boyfriend will die."

"If I do agree, my boyfriend will still die, apparently. Along with everyone else I care about. You're not giving me much incentive."

We stand there glaring at each other. I hear the creaking of Mr. Crunchy's enormous limbs as he shifts uncomfortably against the wall. Everything else is silence.

"If you agree," Mr. Gabriel says at last, "I will remove the curse from your boyfriend and promise not to harm him ever in the future."

"Cyn, no," Ryan says.

"And the rest?" I ask.

Mr. Gabriel gives me a condescending look. "You know I will not relinquish my claim on Annie. And I will not promise not to take my revenge upon you."

"Will you promise not to hurt the rest of them? Peter, Leticia, Diane, William?"

He considers this. I wait. Peter and Ryan both step close to me and start whispering urgent objections.

"Don't you dare, Cyn," Ryan says. "Don't you dare trade my safety for yours and Annie's."

"Cyn, you need to think really carefully about this," Peter says.

They continue to say things, but I'm not listening.

Instead, I'm suddenly remembering that I already made a deal for Ryan's safety a long time ago.

I can't believe I didn't think of this sooner.

"Wait a minute," I say, holding up my hands. "Everybody shut up."

I point angrily at Mr. Gabriel's flickery image. "This is all bullshit. You can't hurt Ryan. We already made a deal about that."

"What?" Ryan and Peter say together behind me.

"You promised not to hurt him. Forever. When we made that deal in the library." My eyes go squinty at him. "You're already violating that deal, in fact. How is that even possible?"

Mr. Gabriel smirks at me. "I was wondering when you'd think about that. I was kind of hoping it would take just a little longer to occur to you."

"Cyn? Will you please turn around and tell me *what the*

hell you are talking about?" Ryan's voice is not very friendly right now.

I turn around.

"Remember when I told you about the deal I made with Mr. Gabriel to get rid of all the extra demons in the school?"

"Yes . . ." His eyes are not very friendly right now, either.

I don't know why this is so hard. We're in the *demon world*, one of the demons just demonstrated exactly how little power we have here in a very painful and upsetting way, I'm trying to make a bargain for our lives, and somehow the most terrifying thing is confessing to Ryan that I still haven't actually confessed everything to him yet.

"So I didn't tell you the whole story. Part of the deal was that Mr. Gabriel wouldn't hurt or kill you or let any other demons hurt or kill you. Ever."

Ryan just looks at me for a minute, and it takes everything I have not to crumple under that gaze.

"How many times did we agree no more secrets, Cyn?"

"I know. I know! But that was such an old one . . . honestly, I just didn't remember to tell you. I swear. I mean, you can see that I almost completely forgot about it, can't you? Otherwise we wouldn't have even needed to come here, since you can't be in any danger from Mr. Gabriel." But then my eyes drop to his hand, and I am reminded again that Mr. Gabriel is already hurting him.

I whirl back around. "How are you breaking the deal? Is that whole deal thing a lie?" I whirl again, this time to glare at Peter. "Is it? Do demons not actually have to honor their bargains after all?"

Peter is looking at Mr. Gabriel thoughtfully. "It's not a lie. We do have to honor our bargains."

I turn back to Mr. Gabriel again. "So?"

"Apparently," he says at last, "dying, ah . . . releases you from all of that. Honestly, I wasn't sure about it myself until I actually placed the mark on your boyfriend. I half expected it not to work."

"But — then — how can I possibly make a deal with you now, knowing that there's nothing that holds you to it?"

"Oh, I think any deals I make now will be solid," he says. "Dying just released me from the old ones."

"Oh, you *think* so? Oh, in that case . . ." I throw up my hands. "This is ridiculous. There's no way I can trust you."

Mr. Gabriel's face darkens again and all pretense of banter suddenly disappears. He leans toward me, and even though he's not really there, I can't help taking a step backward. Only to be stopped by one of Mr. Crunchy's horrible arm-leg things, which has reached out surprisingly stealthily to prevent me from backing up any farther.

"You don't have much choice, my dear girl," he says, his eyes somehow fixing steady and determined on mine while the rest of him remains slightly flickery. "You will do as I tell you, or I will kill Ryan where he stands. And then I will start killing more of the people you care about until you comply."

I try to put the same fire behind my own glare as I force myself to take a step back toward him. "If you kill him," I say softly, "I will *never* do what you want. So if you really want me to do this thing for you, you'd better think twice about trying to bully me into action that way."

We are at another impasse of mutual glaring. It threatens to go on for quite some time, because I am out of ideas for how to proceed, and it seems that Mr. Gabriel is, too.

"I have a suggestion," Peter says suddenly.

We all turn to look at him.

"Test deal," he says.

"I'm sorry, what?" Mr. Gabriel and I say in unison.

"Test deal," Peter repeats. "Let's make a little deal right now, for something unimportant. Prove to us that you have to honor deals made going forward, and then we can go back to negotiating terms for the real thing."

I glance at Mr. Gabriel, who shrugs. "I'm game if you are," he says.

"Okay," I agree, turning back to Peter. "Tell us what you have in mind."

Chapter 07

"Let's see," Peter says. "It has to be something small, but also something that you wouldn't do unless you had to."

Everybody falls silent, thinking.

After a few minutes, Mr. Gabriel asks, "Do any of you want to be taller, or better at math, or"—he looks at me with exaggerated sympathy—"more attractive?"

"No," I say. "And those wouldn't be anything you'd care about giving to us . . . they wouldn't prove you had to honor the deal."

"We could make him inflict some kind of pain on himself," Ryan suggests.

"No," Peter says. "He'd probably like it."

And then a really perfect idea occurs to me. "Love poems," I say.

Ryan and Peter turn to squint at me in confusion.

I keep my eyes on Mr. Gabriel.

"Annie told me that you used to write her love poems. Back when you had her completely brainwashed. She said they were *so beautiful*. That no one who could write things like that could possibly be evil." I smile mercilessly at him. "Recite one."

"That's ridiculous," Mr. Gabriel says quickly. *Too* quickly. "I'm not doing that."

Peter is smiling now, too. "That seems like a perfect test to me," he says.

"Do we even know for sure that he wrote them?" Ryan asks.

"Oh, he wrote them," I say. If I had any doubt, which I don't, because he is entirely too proud to entrust such a task to anyone else, his face right now would make me absolutely certain.

Mr. Gabriel looks like he wants to stab me in the heart.

"Fine," he says, sounding as though he has to force himself to speak the word. "One poem. Of my choice."

"One love poem that you composed for Annie, and it can't be a haiku," Peter says. "Done. In exchange for what?"

"What do you mean?" I ask. "I'm not the one who has to prove I'm bound to honor a deal."

"There are two parts to any deal," Peter says. "There must be an exchange."

"You could recite a love poem to me," Ryan says, grinning at me.

"I have never written you a love poem," I tell him. "Sorry."

"You could make one up on the spot."

I want to smack him, but I also want to get this show on the road. And making up one stupid love poem wouldn't be so bad. No one would expect much of it, since it would be spontaneously composed. I could make it silly. "Fine." I turn to Mr. Gabriel. "Would you accept that?"

"No," he says. He looks at Ryan thoughtfully. "No. I think . . . I think Cynthia should have to kiss Peter." He pauses, then adds, "Again."

We all stare at him. I'd forgotten that he was, technically, in attendance when I confessed my kissing of Peter to Ryan at camp.

"No," Ryan says firmly. "Pick something else."

"Besides," I say, "I already promised that would never happen again."

"A promise is not a deal." It is Mr. Gabriel's turn to smile. "Those are my terms."

"Well, they are not *my* terms," I tell him, no longer feeling the least bit playful about any of this. *"Pick something else."*

"No." He points a flickery finger at Ryan, who suddenly screams and falls to his knees, clutching his hand. "Don't forget that until we make our new deal, I can hurt him. Do you want me to hurt him some more?"

"Stop it!" I shout at him.

His smile stretches wider. "I can also hurt you. Indirectly, at least." He gestures, and Mr. Crunchy lunges forward more quickly than I would have believed possible and slices my upper arm with the sharp edge of a crab claw.

Now it's my turn to scream. The pain is bright and hot, and there's a red line of blood beginning to drip down along my skin. I slap my left hand over it, trying to contain the bleeding.

That's enough for Ryan. "Cyn, it's okay! Just do it. Please. I . . . I know it won't mean anything."

Mr. Gabriel stops and looks at me questioningly. I'm blinking back tears, still trying not to bleed all over the place. *God, that hurt.*

Peter has been, perhaps wisely, silent this entire time. Now he says, hesitantly, "Maybe this test deal idea has gotten a little out of hand."

"No," I say. "No, we need to establish that he can be held to a bargain. Otherwise we can't trust anything he agrees to."

Mr. Gabriel's eyes are shining merrily now. "Excellent. So that is the deal. You will kiss Peter — for, let's say, forty-five seconds, eyes closed, like you mean it — and then I will recite one of the love poems I wrote for Annie. Agreed?"

I glare at him helplessly. "Agreed." I feel the skin-prickling tingle that I first experienced when I made the original deal with the demoness.

"It's okay," Ryan says to me quietly. "Just get it over with."

I nod and walk over to Peter, still holding my arm.

"No one asked how *I* feel about this arrangement," he says, trying, I think, to lighten the mood.

I give him what I hope is a scathing look, because I am not at all ready to have my mood lightened. I half expect him to sweep me into his arms in some over-the-top fake-romantic gesture, making the most of the opportunity, but he doesn't. He just stands there, waiting. Understanding, I think, how much I don't want to do this.

Don't you? a tiny electron-size voice whispers from somewhere inside me.

No, I tell it. *Not like this.*

But I agreed to this deal, and so I'd better just get it done. Peter is my friend. This kiss is only Mr. Gabriel's way of getting back at me for the poem thing. And it's just a dumb kiss, after all. Like playing spin the bottle in fifth grade in Melanie Schwimmer's basement.

"Come on, then," I mutter, leaning forward.

"So *romantic,*" Peter mutters back, rolling his eyes.

I press my lips gently against his. My plan is just to stay there, lips together, technically kissing, but there's that immediate spark of contact and I can't stop my lips from parting slightly in response. Peter feels it, too; I can tell. There's that electricity between us that has been there since the start. But he holds as still as I do, not taking it any further.

"Like you *mean* it, I said," Mr. Gabriel calls. "If you don't start actively kissing him, Cynthia, you'll have to start again."

And so I start to kiss Peter for real.

Mr. Gabriel begins counting out the long, slow seconds. I try to seem as unenthusiastic as possible, which shouldn't be hard, considering the circumstances. Except it is, because I like kissing Peter every single bit as much as I liked kissing him the first time. It's hard to keep my mind on the circumstances. It's hard to keep my mind on anything.

And now Peter is kissing *me* for real, too. Like he was just waiting for my permission, and now he's more than happy to follow my lead.

I tell myself that Ryan has probably turned away, since he wouldn't want to see this and Mr. Gabriel, thankfully, didn't think to make Ryan's close observation part of the actual deal.

I try to focus on the counting. I try to focus on anything other than the delicious softness of Peter's lips. But it gets more difficult with every passing second. I feel his hand come up and bury itself in my hair, and I know I should tell him to stop that, but I don't. I move closer. I keep kissing him.

At some point I forget to keep holding my arm. I forget almost everything but the feel of Peter's body pressed against me and his mouth and tongue and the undeniable heat that burns between us anytime we get this close. I almost don't let him pull away when he finally does, and then I realize that Mr. Gabriel has gotten to forty-five and I didn't even notice. I see that Peter knows this, and I flash him a look of shame-laced gratitude for stopping when our time was up.

"Done," I say quietly, turning back toward Mr. Gabriel. I'm not ready to look at Ryan yet. "Your turn, you bastard."

His look of gleeful satisfaction fades as we all stand facing him, waiting.

"Oh, very well," he says finally.

He closes his eyes and begins.

By the second line, I am fully regretting my choice of task for him. The poem is horrible. Worse than I ever imagined. Also, it is very long.

Soon the three of us are sitting down, hands over our ears, waiting for it to be over. The only good thing is that it seems to have totally discharged the awkward aftermath of the kiss. But that is seriously the only good thing.

Eventually, Mr. Gabriel coughs, and we realize he has finished.

"Thank God," Ryan says as we get back to our feet.

"I didn't realize there were quite so many rhymes for *bosom*," Peter murmurs.

"Well, most of them weren't actual rhymes," I point out. "He fudged a lot of them."

"True."

Mr. Gabriel glowers at us. "Satisfied?"

I look at him carefully. I suppose he could have faked the whole thing, but . . . somehow I don't think so. In addition to being awful, the poem was intensely personal. He really does think he's in love with Annie, in his own twisted, screwed-up, evil way. I don't think he could have faked the painfulness of that recital, or the shadowy look of mortification that now haunts his features.

"Yes," I say. "Are you guys?"

Ryan nods, and after a second, Peter does, too.

"Okay," I say. "So now let's make the real deal and be done with it."

"Fine," Mr. Gabriel says. He's still rather pouty. "The terms I offer are these: you will retrieve the object I require to re-create my body, and in return, I promise not to harm or kill Ryan, Peter, Leticia, Diane, and all of their families."

I'm a little disturbed that he didn't need prompting on any of the names, but I put that aside. "And William," I add.

There is a very long pause, and then: "And William," he agrees.

"And Annie's parents and siblings."

"Fine."

"And my family."

"Your family except for you."

"And you also won't order or allow any other demon to hurt or kill any of them."

"No demon will hurt or kill them at my command. I can't be responsible for more than that."

I guess that will have to do.

I look to Ryan and Peter. "Am I leaving anything out?"

Ryan is clearly still very uncomfortable with all of this, but he must realize that guarantees of safety for some of us is better than promises of death for us all. "I don't think so," he says.

Peter looks like he's trying very hard to think of something to add, but finally he shakes his head.

"All right, then. But before I *officially* accept, I want you to explain what this thing is that I'm going to get for you. I'm going to need a little more than 'retrieve the object.' What exactly *is* this object, and where do I have to go to get it?"

Mr. Gabriel narrows his eyes at me thoughtfully. Then he begins speaking, and all of his banter and nonsense is gone; it's just business now.

"My amulet, as you have noted, is very powerful. Unfortunately, it is also incomplete. There is a piece missing — a very important piece, without which I can't use the amulet to channel my power in the appropriate way."

"Wait," Peter says suddenly. I shush him. I want to hear the rest, and I don't want Mr. Gabriel to start getting all pissy about being interrupted and just end up dragging it out.

"Your task is to go to the creator of the amulet and retrieve this missing piece."

"Wait," Peter says again, and this time the dismay in his

voice finally registers. He is staring at Mr. Gabriel. "That—
that's your amulet? The one that . . ." He trails off unhelpfully.

"What?" I ask. "The one that what?"

Peter ignores me. He keeps his unhappy eyes on Mr.
Gabriel. "Is it what I think it is?"

Mr. Gabriel sighs. "I keep forgetting about you," he says.
"Yes. It's *that* amulet."

"Hey!" I say to both of them. "Share with the rest of the
class, please!"

Peter shakes his head, apparently still having trouble
accepting whatever he has suddenly figured out. "Remember
how I told you that truly powerful amulets were rare and generally not allowed, at least as far as anything is 'not allowed'
down here?"

"Yes . . ."

"So there's this one amulet that's basically the king of
amulets. I mean not in a one-ring-to-rule-them-all kind of
way, but just in being the most powerful amulet anyone has
ever known. It was so powerful that the demon who created it
was sentenced to eternal punishment for his efforts. He actually never managed to finish it before the authorities came for
him; the story is that he knew they were coming and just managed to stash the nearly complete thing somewhere before
they found him. And that he still has the missing piece with
him that would bring the amulet into its full power."

"Why did they let him keep the extra piece when they
caught him?" Ryan asks.

"Well . . . I don't . . . I don't think they *let* him, he just—"

"They didn't, like, search him or something?"

"I don't know, I wasn't there!" Peter says, rather testily. "It's just a story, anyway!"

Mr. Gabriel clears his throat. "A true story," he says. "The amulet was found, and is now in my possession. But the final piece is still locked away with its creator. Which is why Cynthia is going to find him and retrieve that missing piece and bring it back to me."

"Find him?" I ask, confused. "Don't you know where he is?"

"Oh, he knows," Peter says. "Everyone knows."

"Not *everyone*," I point out.

Mr. Gabriel starts to speak, then makes a little abortive hand gesture in the air. "It's . . . well, the name of it won't make any sense to you. But it's basically demon prison."

I turn to Peter. "What does that even mean?"

He closes his eyes for a long moment before looking at me. "Okay, so . . . you know how awful this place is? How much you hate it, and how you are never really quite able to grasp how demon society works and why we all turn on each other all the time and there don't seem to be any rules or anything?"

"Uh . . ."

"So this place he wants you to go to, it's the place where they lock up the very few demons who are so much worse than the rest of us that they can't be allowed to roam freely about."

I blink at him, taking this in.

In the meantime, Peter turns back to Mr. Gabriel. "How are we even supposed to get inside? The wards . . ."

Mr. Gabriel smiles. "Well, that's where our friend Cynthia

comes in. She'll be able to get past the wards. They're constructed of demonic energy. Which can't stop her."

"But . . . but what about Ryan and Peter?" I ask him.

He shrugs. "They can walk you to the inner boundary. After that, I'm afraid you're on your own."

My mouth opens, but for a moment nothing comes out. Because . . . because that's not *fair*. I can't do this alone. I can't.

"She'll never make it on her own," Peter says. "What's the point of sending her if she's just going to die in the first five minutes?"

"Hey!" I say before I can help it. I mean yes, I was thinking the exact same thing, but somehow when Peter says it out loud it feels much more insulting.

"Cyn," Peter says, "there are lots of bad things in that prison, and not all of them are the prisoners."

"She'll be fine," Mr. Gabriel says. "Well, or she won't, but since she's the only one I know who can get in there at all . . . she'll have to figure it out." He turns to look at me. "Your roachness should be able to help you stay alive. Just try not to get into any physical altercations. Be, you know, sneaky and stuff."

I gape at him. "But . . . how will I even know where to go once I'm inside?"

"Oh, yes. Almost forgot. Come over here for a second."

"Uh . . ."

Mr. Gabriel gestures impatiently, and the cart-demon steps forward. I take several steps back before Mr. Crunchy's stealthy arm-claw stops me again, forcing me to remain still while the false facade of the monster that attacked me before comes toward me. My throat has not at all forgotten the feel of that tentacle wrapped tightly around it.

"Wait —"

"You'll need a little help to find your way to your objective," Mr. Gabriel says. "I'm going to give you a kind of compass."

"Sure, okay," I say. The cart-demon is standing right in front of me now. "Just hand it on over, then."

"It's more of an internal upgrade. Temporary, don't worry. Now come here."

"No," Ryan says. "Cyn, don't let him —"

"Cyn has to let me," Mr. Gabriel says. "If she wants to fulfill her end of the bargain and save you, Sweeney."

"I haven't even officially *agreed* to this bargain yet," I remind him.

"Well, agree if you're going to so we can get started," he says, clearly getting annoyed. "I've got other things to do, you know."

I suppose he's right. If I'm going to do this, I should get on with it. And I have to do it, because otherwise Ryan will die. He's getting closer to dying with every second we stand here.

"All right, then. I accept the terms as laid out earlier." I repeat them again, just in case: everything he said about not harming or commanding others to harm Ryan, Peter, Leticia, Diane, William, their families, Annie's family, or my family, in exchange for fetching the amulet piece for him. "Agreed."

"Agreed."

I feel the deal-induced tingly sensation again and hope very hard that I haven't made a terrible mistake.

"And now for that compass," Mr. Gabriel says, nodding toward me. Then cart-demon places a fake-humanish hand on my arm and I jerk away.

"Okay, fine! But call this guy off. I can walk over to you without his assistance, thanks."

He gestures again, and the cart-demon backs off about an inch. He follows me as I walk slowly over to where Mr. Gabriel flickers before his urn.

He seems to concentrate for a second, and then his right arm becomes noticeably more solid-seeming than the rest of him. He reaches toward me, and I want to step back, but the cart-demon is directly behind me now and I want to touch him even less than I want to let Mr. Gabriel touch me.

I force myself to stand still as Mr. Gabriel places his palm against the exposed area of skin between my collarbone and the V-neck of my shirt. The sensation is strange; his hand doesn't feel like an actual hand but also feels more *there* than I'd have expected his hologram body to feel. Although I guess I should have expected it, remembering the all-too-solid feeling of his holo-tongue against my ear earlier. I repress a shudder.

And then there's a surge of — *something* — from his hand, and I feel a sudden blooming of fire and fullness deep in my gut. Now I do step back, I can't help it, and I want to scream at the cold pressure of the cart-demon behind me and the simultaneous burning in the center of my soul.

"Calm down," Mr. Gabriel says. "It will fade in a moment."

Even as he says this, the feeling begins to become less intense. In another few seconds it's just the merest sense of awareness in the pit of my stomach.

"What did you do to me?"

"I told you. Internal compass. You'll know when it starts to work. Just follow where it wants you to go."

I step carefully around the cart-demon and walk back over to Ryan. Then I turn back to face Mr. Gabriel. "And so . . . then what? Assuming I reach this amulet-making demon without dying, he's just going to hand over the missing piece when I ask him?"

"You'd better hope so," Mr. Gabriel says. "If he seems reluctant, tell him I will owe him a favor once I've got my throne. As king, I'd be able to release him if I chose. That should be enough to bargain with."

This is all starting to seem even more impossible than it did before.

The darkness and the closeness of the rocky walls and the enormous presence of Mr. Crunchy distributed around the chamber all feels like suddenly way too much. I need to get out of this cave/hole/whatever the hell it is and out of this crazy demon-infested underworld and back to the world that makes sense, where my friends are, where there is school and pizza and musical theater, where most of the time monsters are not trying to kill you. It's true that some of them still get up there sometimes, but here they are *everywhere,* there are at least three in this room alone, and I need to get the hell out.

"It's okay, Cyn," Ryan says softly, taking my arm. "We'll figure something out. You're not going in there alone."

Mr. Gabriel chuckles and shakes his head.

"Run along now," he says, gesturing to Mr. Crunchy to escort us out. "Oh, and Cynthia?"

I wait for whatever parting shot he just can't resist taking.

He smiles his most winning smile. "Do try to get back in one piece. I still want to have the pleasure of killing you myself when this is over."

I force myself to smile winningly right back. "It's going to take more than a shiny new body to get you what you want, you evil piece of shit. I helped you die once, and I will do it again. And this time no one will be waiting in the shadows to save your sorry ass."

I wish I could make my own eyes burn like his do. My knees desperately want to give out right now so that I can curl up in a whimpering little ball on the floor, but I am *not* going to slink away from him in defeat. Especially since I probably *will* die before I get back, and this might be the last thing I ever get to say to him.

"Okay!" Ryan says as Mr. Gabriel's expression transforms into something far less happy. "Time to go!" He turns me quickly around, toward the opening leading back to the alley.

"Yes," Peter says. "Please lead the way, Mr. Crunchy!"

After a glance at Mr. Gabriel, who apparently grants permission, the insanely smiling Mr. Crunchy makes his jerky follow-me motions and squeezes back out through the doorway. We follow him. I wince at the pain in my arm as I brace myself against the wall. The cut stopped bleeding sometime during Mr. Gabriel's terrible poem — it wasn't actually all that deep, despite the pain — but it's clearly going to hurt for a while yet.

I notice that Ryan makes sure that he is walking between me and Peter.

I lean across him to ask, "So, how bad is this demon prison place, really? I mean . . . he must have a good expectation that I will be able to do this thing. It would be stupid to go to all this trouble if he really thought I was just going to die on the way. Because if that happens, then he won't get what he needs *and* he won't get to kill me personally."

Peter runs a hand over his face. "It's . . . it's pretty bad, Cyn. I mean I've never been there, I've only heard things."

"Is it like a regular prison with cells and guards and things?"

He shakes his head. "No. I think they just kind of shove the prisoners inside and lock the door behind them. There's an outer boundary that's freely accessible, and then the inner boundary is where those wards are, the ones you can get through but we can't."

Right.

"Okay, but we're going to figure that out somehow," Ryan says. "And so we'll all go in, and let's say we don't die and we make it through and we get this missing amulet piece. What then? We come back and then he regains his physical form and then he kills Cyn and takes Annie? I'm not sure I see the point of going on this errand if that's the way it's going to end."

"I assume," Peter says, "that Cyn is expecting to come up with a brilliant plan somewhere along the way."

"Don't act like you know her better than I do," Ryan snaps. "And just to be clear — that, back there, was the *last* time you are ever going to kiss my girlfriend."

"Let's not do this, please," I break in. "Peter is half right.

I mean I'm not *expecting* to come up with a brilliant plan, but I sure am hoping we do. At the very least we're buying some time to figure something out."

I turn to look at Peter.

"And," I continue, "Ryan was entirely right. That was the last time, Peter."

"Whatever," Peter says. "I'm not going to apologize for enjoying it."

We fall into an uneasy silence, following Mr. Crunchy. The streets/alleys/crevices seem to be getting more and more desolate the longer we walk. We don't see any other demons. Which, of course, I'm grateful for, because I think we've all had enough of demons trying to kill us, but it also seems strangely ominous. Like this is the part of town so sketchy that even the Really Bad Demons are afraid to lurk in it. The buildings around us all seem to be abandoned. The areas we were in earlier, where we first arrived and where Mr. Gabriel's hideout was, had seemed recently demolished — physical fallout from the infighting and chaos in the wake of Mr. Gabriel's escape and assault on the demon queen. This area seems like it's been falling apart for a very, very long time.

Eventually we turn one last corner and find ourselves facing an enormous black wrought-iron gate that has to be at least fifty feet tall. It's set in a circular stone wall standing alone in the center of a rubble-strewn square. The area enclosed by the walls is only about the size of a large in-ground swimming pool. There's certainly no prison right there behind the gate; it must be some kind of portal. Inside there's a swirling mass of what looks like black smoke. It doesn't extend even one wispy tendril beyond the boundary of the gate and the wall.

Mr. Crunchy stops and looks back and forth between us and the gate, smiling.

"Yes, we get it, thanks," I say. "Give us a minute." Because I totally need a minute.

Mr. Crunchy does not seem inclined to give us even a few seconds. He begins herding us toward the gate with his king crab legs. The gate, as if sensing our approach, swings wide open with a hideous metallic screech and waits. The gaping black space revealed is so like an open mouth that I can't help expecting a giant tongue to come sliding out toward us.

Mr. Crunchy gives us another push. I dig my feet into the ground, but they skid forward relentlessly. Ryan is struggling to resist the demon's shove beside me with similarly ineffective results.

"Hey!" Peter says in a very commanding sort of voice. Mr. Crunchy stops and looks down at him. "What were your instructions? To guide us to the gate, yes?"

Mr. Crunchy hesitates, then nods.

"Well, you have followed those instructions, haven't you? Here we are, successfully guided to the gate. Well done! You should probably return to your master to see if he will reward you for your excellent service." When Mr. Crunchy still hesitates, seeming confused, Peter adds, "Don't worry. I'll take it from here."

Mr. Crunchy's smile brightens. He nods once more and then turns and lumbers back in the direction from which we came.

The gate remains open, waiting. The black smoke seems to beckon us toward it, but still remains somehow contained within the circular space.

"Is this—this isn't the part yet where I have to go alone, is it?" I ask in a voice that comes out sounding much smaller than I would like. I know I *should* be doing this alone. I know it's my responsibility. But now that Ryan and Peter are here with me, I can't bear the idea of having them leave my side.

Peter shakes his head. "Not yet. The gate leads to the outer boundary. We'll be able to see the inner boundary once we go through. I think."

"You think?" Ryan asks.

"I told you I've never actually been inside. I only know what I've heard."

Ryan grumbles something sarcastic and unhelpful and Peter mutters something back, but I ignore them both because I am too busy staring at the swirling blackness that we are apparently just supposed to walk into. I step forward and tentatively reach out one finger to touch the place where the smoke stops. It's cool and slightly damp and . . . and it pulls at me. I edge closer, horribly fascinated. I watch my finger disappear, and then my hand up to the wrist. The pulling increases.

I swallow and pull my hand back, and it's harder than I am comfortable with. The smoke doesn't want to let go.

I take a careful step backward.

"Cyn!" someone hisses right behind me, and I almost stumble forward through the doorway all by myself. I whip hastily around.

It's Aaron. He's sort of crouching in place and wearing a hooded cloak-like thing that absolutely screams *I am trying not to be noticed.*

"Aaron!" we all shout.

"Shh!" He looks around. "Jesus, shut up, will you? I'm glad I caught you before you went through. I didn't dare approach until the big guy took off."

He's cleaned up slightly since the last time we saw him, but he still looks pretty bad. There are huge dark circles under his eyes, and his hair is completely flat and shapeless against his head. Clearly there hasn't been time for his usual hair-care rituals.

"You all have to go through together, or you might not end up in the same place."

We stare at him in confusion as he hurriedly gestures behind him.

And then we see Annie come running toward us from a dark alley on the other side of the square.

"Aaron." I grab his stupid cloak and pull him very close to me. "What is she *doing* here?"

He stares back at me in alarm. "She said . . . when I went back, to the library . . . you were gone, but she said I was supposed to . . ." He trails off at the expression on my face. "Oh, crap. I'm sorry, Cyn. I thought . . . she said . . ."

"Cyn!" Annie yells, throwing her arms around me.

I want to scream at her. I want to scream at her and then punch her in the face and then scream at her some more. Also, I want to kill Aaron for not only bringing her here but then *leaving her alone in a dark alley* where anything could have come along and snatched her away or killed her on the spot or a million other unspeakable things.

But mostly I want to send her safely back to where she belongs. Immediately.

"Aaron," I say, disentangling myself from Annie. "Take her back. Right now."

"But — but she said you needed her here. With you. For the plan —"

"What plan?"

Aaron is beginning to look very strange. "The plan to help my mistress. The one — she said you were —" He turns and stares incredulously at Annie. "You *lied* to me?"

Annie has the grace to look ashamed. "I had to! You wouldn't have helped me otherwise!"

"Well — no! Not if you're — oh, no, Cyn, you *can't* — I told you, you can't give him what he wants, you can't, don't you see? He'll be stronger than ever!"

"I have no choice," I tell him. "Now take Annie back."

"No," he says. "Not unless you swear to me that you'll stop this madness. We can make a deal —"

An impossibly loud roaring sound seems to burst out of the very air around us. The same horrible demon that briefly appeared in Peter's summoning circle in the library is now squeezing itself out of the alleyway — the same alleyway that Annie was hiding in just seconds ago, the realization of which makes my blood turn to ice inside me. Aaron yelps and vanishes. The demon screams, staring at the spot where Aaron had been standing, and then lifts its head(s) to stare at those of us still present.

And then it comes shrieking right for us.

"Everyone hold hands!" Peter shouts. "And *run!*"

The open gateway is right there in front of us but somehow it suddenly seems an impossible distance away. I have Ryan's hand on one side and Annie's on the other and am desperately screaming questions at everyone, trying to make sure someone has a hold of Peter.

"I'm good!" Peter shouts. "Go! Go, go, go!"

I throw myself into the swirling black smoke, holding as tight as I can to Ryan and Annie as I do. The blackness takes us in eagerly, sucking us forward into its cool, dark embrace. Just before the world vanishes I catch a glimpse of Peter grabbing the gate with his free hand and yanking it closed behind him.

And then everything is silence and smoke and my frantic, desperate thoughts of how the hell I'm supposed to keep all of these people I love alive and safe until I can get them back out of here again.

Chapter | 08

When the smoke clears, we are standing in a vast, open field.

Well, partly open.

There is grass under our feet but also a wall at our backs that seems to be made of some kind of shiny black stone. It is perfectly smooth and featureless, and it stretches up and up until it becomes lost in a hazy blur far above. I don't think that's really a sky up there, but it's not quite a ceiling, either.

The grass and the wall stretch endlessly to either side, but ahead, far off in the distance, I can see what looks like another kind of wall. The inner boundary, I am guessing. Which is where we have to go.

But first things first.

I turn to Annie, releasing my grip on her and Ryan's hands.

"What are you *doing* here? Did we not have an agreement? Do you not remember our agreement?"

She is trembling, and her eyes are shiny with tears, and she has obviously not yet recovered from the near-demon experience we all briefly shared before leaping through the gateway into the hungry black smoke. I should be sympathetic. I should try to comfort her; I should try to give her a minute to pull herself together. But I'm not and I don't. I'm glad she's afraid. She's probably still not afraid enough. She shouldn't even *be* here.

"Well?"

"Cyn—" Ryan starts, but I shoot him a *stay the hell out of this* look and his mouth closes with an almost audible snap. He goes to stand quietly beside Peter.

"Cyn, don't . . . don't be mad," Annie says.

"Um, too late!"

"I know I agreed to stay behind. But it wasn't right—I should be here with you. At least for this part, after—after you were done talking to him. I want to help!"

"But you can't help. All you can do is make this harder. Why can't you see that?"

Her expression begins to harden, her mouth set in a firm little line. "How do you know I can't help until you let me try?"

I wave my hands around, trying to indicate all of the horror and danger that surrounds us, although the effect is probably weakened by the soft expanse of cheerful green grass and the current lack of things trying to kill us. "Why does everyone seem to keep forgetting that this is the demon world? Do you remember what happened the last time you were here? Do you remember how helpful you were then?"

Annie flinches, and I take a breath, trying to calm down,

because I don't really want to have a big fight with her right before I go off to probably die. "Annie, I'm not trying to be mean, but — what were you *thinking*? I had to come or else Mr. Gabriel would kill Ryan. And Ryan had to come because of the curse. And Peter is a demon! He knows how to survive here. But you . . . you don't have to be here and I don't see what you can do other than scare me to death by putting yourself in unnecessary danger." I'm getting angry again. Because I don't have time for this. "Also, didn't we already have this same goddamn conversation in the library? Ryan is *dead* if I don't get this thing done and I still have to figure out how to do it without actually letting Mr. Gabriel win and instead of getting on with it I'm standing here explaining to you *again* why you need to go the hell back to school where you belong!"

Her face has been getting redder and angrier with every word I say. Now she shouts back at me, "Who are you to decide where I belong? When are you going to get it through your stupid head that you do not get to tell me what to do?"

"Argh! I'm not — that's not what this is about! I'm not trying to tell you what to do. I'm trying to keep you from dying!"

"By telling me what to do!"

"Ladies —" Peter steps forward, trying to get between us.

"What?" I shout at him, swinging the full force of my frustration over to his direction. "Can you not let us finish this conversation, please?"

"Um . . . no. Sorry, but no. We need to keep moving."

I sigh theatrically. "Fine. Please just send Annie back up and then —"

Annie growls "Don't you dare" just as Peter leans forward

and says, "Cyn, *listen*, we have to —" and I want to smack them both. Why won't anyone just do what I tell them? Ryan drops to the ground, apparently deciding to get comfortable while waiting for us to sort this out. The grass around him seems oddly taller than it did a minute ago. Peter notices me noticing this and then stretches a hand toward Ryan, his eyes wide.

"Ryan, no! Get up!"

"What —" Ryan starts, and then he shouts in pain and leaps to his feet. Or tries to. Some of the grass has wrapped itself around his leg, and he's yanked back down before he can get all the way up. His shouts get a little panicky as he swipes frantically at the grass, trying to rip it away. Peter yanks on Ryan's arm, trying to pull him up.

I rush to help, too, and together we get him back to his feet. The grass is even taller now.

Peter plucks a blade of it and holds it up in front of my eyes.

"See?" he says. "*See?*"

The blade of grass has a mouth. A mouth filled with tiny sharp teeth. It whips forward, trying to get free of Peter's grasp and bite me in the face.

Ryan's jeans are torn and his leg is bleeding. All of the grass is moving now, trying to get at us. Peter drops the piece he was holding and wipes at a bloody mark on his wrist. Annie is making unhappy noises as she starts jumping around, trying to keep the eager little grass-mouths from getting a taste of her, too.

I put a hand to my forehead. "Peter, please —"

"I can't!" he shouts at me. "I can't send her back. Not from here. And not without going up myself. She has to stay with us for now, Cyn, I'm sorry."

Annie looks torn between triumph and sudden, dawning doubt as she continues to dance around in the monster grass.

"Come on!" Peter says. "We have to move!"

He starts running toward that faraway second wall, and we all follow suit.

"Did you know the grass was going to try to eat us?" I demand, pulling up alongside him.

"No. But I knew this place wasn't designed to be a nice picnic spot. Anyone who comes here is supposed to just do what they came to do and get the hell out. I figured something would start urging us along if we didn't get moving. Which is what I tried to *tell* you, but —"

"Yeah, yeah."

We keep running.

The wall is getting closer. I glance down and notice that the grass has gotten shorter again, or at least we've moved past the section that decided to take violent manducatory action against us. I look back up and see a very large shape moving toward us from up ahead.

The others see it, too. In simultaneous unspoken agreement, we all come to a stop.

"Peter?" I ask. "What's that?"

"I have no idea," he says. "There shouldn't be anyone else here, unless another demon was just locked up. But . . . but that happens very rarely. I mean, like hardly ever. Maybe once every several thousand years or something. It would be a pretty big coincidence for our visit to overlap with one of those events."

We watch as it gets closer. I see Ryan spare an anxious glance down at the grass.

I really hate this place.

We start running again, trying to angle away from the thing up ahead, but it only changes course to intercept our new path. I stop again, panting, and everyone else stops, too. Then they turn to me as though I will have some solution for what is happening.

I look around, rather desperately. But there's no place to go. The thing is clearly able to move more quickly than we are, and it's going to catch us no matter what we try to do. There doesn't seem to be much choice except to wait. No one wants to run back to the carnivorous-plant-life area, or into the teeth and tentacles of the demon who is probably still waiting for us outside the gate on the other side of the smoke. Plus, some of us are kind of winded from the running and could use a breather.

Pretty soon, I am able to make out some unquestionably spiderlike features on the approaching figure. My stomach clenches into a tight queasy little ball.

"Um, Cyn?" Ryan asks. "Isn't — isn't that —"

Annie gasps beside me, and Peter stares in open disbelief.

"Yeah," I say. "Yeah, I'm pretty sure it is."

The figure finally gets close enough for us to see it clearly, and I am very sad to confirm that we are correct.

It's Mr. Gabriel's little brother.

I hear my friends shouting in alarmed voices around me, and I think someone is pulling rather urgently on my arm, but it's hard to focus on anything other than the approaching monster's horrible beetle face and waving spider legs. I don't understand. Was all of this . . . the deal, the prison, everything . . . was it all some kind of very elaborate double cross?

That doesn't make any sense. But neither does this sudden appearance of our old familiar B-list enemy. I realize that it somehow never actually occurred to me to wonder what had happened to him after Aaron took him away over the summer. Clearly it should have.

"Cyn!" Ryan's voice finally breaks into my temporary mental paralysis. "Shouldn't we be running away?"

I shake my head. There's nowhere to run to. He's nearly upon us.

"Get behind me," I tell Annie. It's a sign of how terrified she is that she does so without complaint. I speak next to Peter, without turning my head. "Is there anything you can do to fight him?"

"No," he says, but instead of fear in his voice, I hear something else. Frustration. And fury.

Of course; this thing is the monster that killed poor Hector.

We stand there, the four of us. Waiting.

The spider-demon closes the remaining distance and then stops a few feet away. I brace myself, but the anticipated attack doesn't come.

He seems to be waiting, too.

Several long seconds pass in silence. I hear someone shifting restlessly behind me. Ryan's hand is still clamped around my upper arm. The demon just stands there, perfectly motionless, like the most horrible statue ever.

Finally I can't take it anymore.

"What are you *doing* here?" I demand. I'm attempting to bury my fear under my annoyance. It works, at least a little.

"You," Little Brother says in his grating voice. "I have come to find you."

"Well . . . congrats. Here I am. Now what do you want? Did . . . did Mr. Gabriel send you?" Maybe he's here to deliver a message, I realize. Maybe he's not here to kill us.

The demon's insect face seems to darken and contract at the mention of Mr. Gabriel.

"No! *He* does not know I am here."

Oh, crap.

Oh, crappity crap crap.

Little Brother's gone rogue.

I back up slightly, closer to the others.

"Now . . . now think about this, uh, you," I manage, suddenly wishing I knew what the hell his actual name was. "Don't do anything hasty."

"Haaasty," he repeats, taking a step forward to follow me.

"Listen to her, you bastard," Peter says, stepping up on my non-Ryan side. "Remember what happens when your brother gets angry."

This line of argument had worked with him in the past, but this time it just seems to agitate him further.

"No!" he shouts. "You do not care if my brother is angry!"

Peter and I look at each other. "Well, no," I agree. "We don't care at all. But . . . don't you?"

"No," he says more quietly. "Not anymore."

Which means . . . he won't care if his brother made a deal with us. He won't care if killing us ruins his brother's plans. In fact . . . that might be exactly what he wants.

But he's still not attacking. He's still just standing there.

Annie leans forward and whispers to me, "Ask him again what he wants. Without mentioning you-know-who."

I clear my throat and address the demon again. "Uh . . . so what did you say you wanted again?"

"Find you," he says at once.

"Oh, right. Yes. But . . . why?"

"You fought us. Fought *him*."

"Yes. That's . . . that's true. He didn't give us any choice. We had to fight him."

"No," he says. "You could have served him. You chose to fight."

I concede the point. "Okay, yes. We could have given up, you're right. But we didn't want to serve him. We wanted him to leave us alone."

"Yes," he says, and now there is something different in his inflection. "You did not want to serve. So you fought."

He takes another step forward.

"I do not want to serve. I want to fight."

"Oh," I say. "Well, great. That's great. You should do that."

He moves his insect head slowly back and forth. Then he steps forward again. "I will fight with you."

"Um." I look around at the others, who are staring back

at me with equally bewildered expressions. "What?"

"I will fight with you," he repeats. "You do not fear my brother."

"Well, I *fear* him; I'm not an idiot. I just try not to let that stop me." I shake my head, trying to get back to the main thread of this conversation. "But . . . you tried to kill us. You *did* kill Hector, and you wanted to kill me —"

"Yes. Before. But not now."

Ryan speaks up beside me. "Are you saying that you no longer want to kill us? That you want to help us fight your brother?"

"Yes." It's hard to read the bug-face features, but I'd say he looks grateful that someone is finally understanding him.

"Just . . . just hold on a second, okay?" I ask him. Then I turn around and motion everyone into a football huddle.

"I can't even formulate a question," I say once we're all huddled in. "What? What the actual what?"

"Can we trust him?" Annie asks.

"No," the rest of us say back.

"But I kind of believe him," Ryan adds.

"Me, too," I admit. "And honestly, he just doesn't seem bright enough to come up with some elaborate plan of deception."

"But, wait . . . what are we saying exactly?" Annie asks. "Are we letting him, like, join the team?"

I want to remind her that she is not, in fact, on the team herself, but now doesn't seem the time. Instead I peek over my shoulder at where Little Brother stands, apparently patiently, waiting for us to finish our discussion. He certainly seems to have undergone some enormous change of perspective since we last saw him. Maybe he finally got tired of his big brother pushing him around and yelling at him and trying to steal his body.

I glance at Peter. "You're pretty quiet. What do you think?"

"I . . . don't know. Mostly I just want to kill him for what he did to Hector. But I also kind of believe him. But it was not very long ago that I fought this guy almost to the death. He's really strong, Cyn. Last time I had all of that extra strength courtesy of the queen, but now, if he changes his mind about what side he's on . . ."

That is a valid concern, obviously.

"How did he even find us?" Annie asks. "If he's not on Mr. Gabriel's team anymore, how did he know we'd be here?"

Peter looks at her. "That's an excellent question." He turns around and addresses Little Brother. "How were you able to find us here?"

"Followed."

"Followed us . . . through the gate?"

"Yes. I knew he would make you come to him. I waited until he did. And then I followed."

"But if he came through the gate separately," I ask Peter, "he would have lost us, right? Ended up in some other section, or whatever? Isn't that what Aaron was saying?"

"I know this place," Little Brother answers, even though I *clearly* wasn't talking to him. "Easy to find you again."

"Really?" Peter seems genuinely surprised by this. "But

why? It's not safe here for anyone — not even a big tough guy like you."

"That's why I come. Because no one else comes. I can . . . hide."

He looks suddenly off to the side, pincers alert.

I follow his gaze with a sinking heart, wondering what's coming to kill us this time. It appears to be some kind of metallic tumbleweed.

Ryan, Peter, and Annie turn to look, too.

"Razor balls," Little Brother says calmly. He nods once as if to confirm this identification. "They will slice you."

"I guess we should be going, then," Peter says.

"All of us?" Ryan asks pointedly.

Everyone looks at me.

I hate making these kinds of decisions under pressure. Well, also at all. But especially under pressure.

I look at the monster, trying to figure out what to do.

What do we know about him? He doesn't exactly have a stellar track record. He was with the group of demons that chased Aaron and me the second time Ms. Královna summoned me to lend her my power. He followed me back to camp through the tunnel she'd created, and then ran off and joined his brother, believing he'd eventually get to share in the spoils of Mr. Gabriel's success. He killed Hector when Hector stupidly tried to protect me from him. The rest of us had witnessed his unhappy awakening when Mr. Gabriel forcibly took over his body and smushed him down somewhere inside himself where he had no agency or control. And then Mr. Gabriel (wearing his brother's body) fought Peter (who was using borrowed strength gifted by Ms. Královna and *still* had a very hard time coming out on top), and my ridiculous but still effective *Mikado* fan drove Mr. Gabriel's defeated essence into the trap that the demon queen had waiting. And then Aaron spirited the unconscious spider-demon body away and I kind of thought I'd never have to worry about him again.

But here he is, wanting to join our ragged little band of adventurers.

Or pretending to.

But I can't really see what point pretending would serve. If he wanted to kill us, he could easily have done it by now. I suppose he could be working undercover for Mr. Gabriel, but I just don't believe he's that good of an actor. And I can't see what the point of that would be, either. We're already doing what Mr. Gabriel wants us to do. Unless he's been sent to make sure we stay on task? But that brings us back to the acting thing. Little Brother doesn't seem like the pretending type. He seems very consistently and sincerely his horrible, disgusting self.

We absolutely cannot trust him; I know that. But on the other hand, if he really would help us fight Mr. Gabriel, that would be a huge advantage. Especially since I have not made any progress toward coming up with a brilliant plan for how we can defeat Mr. Gabriel. Again. For good this time.

Everyone is still waiting for me to say something.

Also, the razor balls are getting closer.

Annie leans close to me. "If it helps you decide, I have a feeling he would try to follow even if you said no. He seems pretty determined."

I suspect she's right about that.

I look up at Little Brother. "We have an errand to run, and then we're going to go back and deal with Mr. Gabriel. Do you want to come with us now?"

"Yes."

"Okay." I take a breath. "Okay. Great." As before, it's really pretty far from great — I mean, all of this is — but I don't have time to find the kinds of words that would be appropriate. Ryan, especially, does not have time. Whenever I catch a glimpse of his hand, the red line tracing its way up his inner arm seems to be just a little bit longer. "Let's keep moving, then."

We set out across the grass again, walking swiftly to stay ahead of the razor balls: me, my lovely boyfriend, my lovely best friend, and my lovely, um, Peter. And the unlovely giant spider-monster who falls silently into step behind us, thinking whatever passes for thoughts in that unfathomable bull-bug head.

Peter plucks another blade of grass, which begins to grow and change in his grip and starts whipping around, trying to reach him with its blind and hungry little mouth. He amuses himself with it for a while, then drops it with a quick shake of his hand once it finally manages to pierce his skin.

Annie shudders, and Ryan rolls his eyes.

I still can't really believe any of this is actually happening.

Chapter | 09

The wall that marks the inner boundary, once we reach it, appears to be made of a similar kind of black smoke to what we'd encountered at the gate. Similar but not the same; I can see the threads of red that I assume make up the demon-energy wards that will keep the others out. The smoke swirls restlessly within the confines of its wall-shape, but it remains impenetrable to the eye. Like the field of grass and the outer wall, it seems to stretch endlessly in both directions.

"So how do we get in?" Annie asks. "Is there a door?"

"Another excellent question," Peter says. "I do not believe there is a door. Generally, no one ever goes in. Or comes out."

But if Mr. Gabriel is correct, I should be able to walk right through the wall. I guess I should check first to see if that's the case. And then . . . and then what? Leave everyone else here to wait for me while I go off alone to find this amulet-making criminal? The thought makes me feel very cold and small. As much as I hate my friends being in danger, facing this place without them would be even more terrifying. More than terrifying. Impossible.

Ryan nudges me with his hip. "Whatcha thinking, girlfriend?"

I lean my head on his shoulder. "I'm thinking that Mr. Gabriel is a giant asshole."

"Yeah. We already know that, though. Time for some new, brilliant-plan type of ideas."

"Yeah." I take a breath, which fails to be at all calming. "Okay. Here goes. I think I should make sure I can actually get through the wall. If I can . . . maybe I can try bringing you guys in with me. If it's my resistance that lets me get through, then if I share it with you . . ."

"That makes sense!" Annie says excitedly. "Of course — then we can all go. That's perfect."

I'm not sure how she manages to sound so enthusiastic about being able to enter a demon prison. I try to resist letting her inexplicable good cheer raise my spirits, because she's not supposed to be here and I shouldn't be liking anything about having her in this horrible place. But I don't entirely succeed.

"Okay," I say again. "Okay. I'm going to step through. And come right back. If I don't come right back, um, that means something went wrong. And if that happens —"

"Don't let that happen," Ryan says.

I give him an exasperated look.

"Just go," he says. "I don't want to make a contingency plan. Go and come right back. Come *right* back."

Annie steps up beside him. She takes his arm. "We'll be right here, Cyn."

Okay, I say to myself, because I've said it out loud way too many times already. *Okay.* I walk up to the wall and step through the thick, black smoke.

There's a tingle against my skin as I pass through. Then I step out into a vast, shadowy corridor. Dark stone walls stretch up into infinity on either side of me, and the stone floor ahead disappears quickly into blackness. I realize suddenly that nothing has been shifty in that demon-world way since we went through the first gate to the outer boundary area of the prison. The walls were just walls; the grass was just grass. Carnivorous grass, yes, okay; but still, it didn't flicker between grass and various other things. It stayed grass.

Nothing is shifty in here, either. Maybe it has something to do with the fact that it's a prison. Someday, if we survive, I'll ask Peter about it. Or Aaron or Ms. Královna or whoever else might know.

But that's for later. I promised to come right back.

Before I can move, though, I become aware of a slight tugging kind of feeling in my gut. In the thing that Mr. Gabriel put there — the compass. It wants me to step deeper into the prison. *Yeah, I know,* I tell it silently. *Just hold your horses.* But I guess it's good to know it's working.

I turn around, relieved to find the smoke-wall still where I left it, because it suddenly and way too late just occurred to me that it might not be. Then I step back through.

Everyone else is right where I left them, too.

Ryan and Peter both look visibly relieved, and Annie lets

go of Ryan's arm so she can hug me. Mr. Gabriel's little brother doesn't show any reaction that I can recognize.

"It worked!" Annie says once she releases me.

"Yes," I agree. "So now let's try to all go through together."

Peter glances at the wall and then back at me. "What's it like in there?"

"Dark. Lots of stone and shadows. I didn't stay long enough to see more than that. Let's go in and you can see for yourself."

We get ourselves into a row. Well, the humans and Peter do, anyway. Little Brother hovers uncertainly behind us.

"Come on, LB!" Peter says, patting his thigh like he's calling a puppy. At the other demon's blank look, he explains, "That's what we're going to call you, I've just decided. Because these guys won't be able to pronounce your real name, whatever it is, and we have to call you something, and 'Little Brother' is kind of wearying, not to mention slightly insulting to you, I imagine. So . . . LB. Okay?" He turns back around without waiting for an answer.

"Why do you get to name everyone?" Ryan asks irritably.

"If you wanted to name him, you should have spoken up sooner."

"Please shut up, you two," I say. "Everyone needs to hold hands now." Then I pause, having thought of one potential problem. "Um, someone has to hold the — uh, LB's, uh, leg. It can't be Peter, because of demon poison stuff."

"And because I hate him," Peter adds, not quite under his breath.

We learned the hard way over the summer that the spider-demon exudes a kind of poison to which Peter is highly susceptible. It doesn't affect non-demons, though, so the rest of us should be okay.

Ryan and Annie both suddenly find interesting things to look at on the ground or up in the not-quite-a-sky.

Figures. "Oh, fine. I've touched him before. I guess I can do it again." I turn to face the demon in question. "Um, I'm going to hold on to your leg. So that I can share my special power with you that will let us all go through the wall. Okay?"

He looks at me, then steps forward and holds out a furry appendage in response.

I swallow hard and force myself to grasp it with my hand. It's just as horrible and bristly and disgusting as I remember. Ryan grabs my other hand, and Annie takes his other hand, and then Peter takes hers.

Trying to ignore the feel of spider between my fingers, I close my eyes and concentrate on the now-familiar process of sharing out my roachy protection. Once I'm sure I've got everyone, I open my eyes. "All right. Let's go. On three. One . . . two . . . *three.*"

We step forward into the smoke.

And then we all start screaming.

The pain is immediate, as soon as the smoke touches us. We all scramble backward, dropping hands (and leg) and trying to get away from what feels like liquid fire. The active pain vanishes as soon as we move away from the wall, but the memory of it seems to linger on my skin, prickly and hot.

"What happened?" Annie pants, rubbing at her arms frantically. "Did it hurt like that when you went through before?"

"No!"

Peter is staring thoughtfully at the smoke. "It must be something about the wards. You were able to go through without a problem, because of your resistance. When you tried to share it, though . . ."

"I must be spreading it too thin," I say. "I can't take everyone together."

"Can you take us in smaller batches?" Annie asks. "Maybe . . . maybe one at a time?"

I shake my head. "I'm not leaving anyone over there alone. Maybe . . . maybe we all could try again?"

Everyone else emphatically rejects this idea.

We then spend way too much time discussing who to bring over in what combinations. LB is the only one who doesn't participate in the conversation; he seems content to wait quietly for us to decide what to do next. Mr. Gabriel must have gotten all of the talking genes in the family. As well as the looks and brains.

"Take me over first," Peter says finally. "I'll be okay there on my own for a few minutes."

Ryan endorses this immediately, but I am not so sure.

"How do you know?"

Peter gives me a tiny smile. "I don't. But at least I won't smell like prey. Probably if there's anything wandering around nearby, it will leave me alone."

I stare at him. "We *smell* like *prey*?"

"Uh, yeah. Don't worry about it. Not something you can

help. And it's not unpleasant, really. Kind of . . . well, kind of delicious. It's different for each of you, of course — different, uh, flavors. For example, uh, you, Cyn . . ."

We're all staring at him now. "Please stop talking," I tell him.

We decide I'll take Peter, then Annie, then Ryan, then LB. I don't love the plan of leaving my boyfriend alone with my archenemy's demonic spider brother, but it will only be a minute, and if LB really does want to get his revenge on Mr. Gabriel, then hopefully he'll remember that he needs to keep playing nice in the meantime.

God, I hope so.

It still all feels like a terrible idea, but I just keep reminding myself that Ryan will definitely die if we don't get into the prison somehow.

"All right," I say, stepping back up to the wall. "Come on, Peter. Let's get this over with."

"Come right back, Cyn," Ryan says, not looking at Peter.

I meet his gaze. "I will," I say. "I promise."

Then I take Peter's hand, wrap him in my protection as fully as I can, and we step through.

I'm braced for the fiery pain, but it doesn't come. It stings a little, but that's all. It's so faint it could almost be my imagination.

We step out of the smoke into the dark prison interior.

"Cheery," Peter says.

I try to release his hand, but he doesn't let go. Instead he rubs his thumb lightly against my palm and raises an eyebrow. "Wanna make out real quick before you go back?"

"No," I say firmly, ignoring the traitorous electron of *yes* that still lurks elusively somewhere deep inside me. "Stay here. I'll be right back with Annie."

I jerk my hand away and leap back through the wall before he can say anything else.

The others are still where they should be. I realize I was once again half expecting that not to be the case. I keep waiting for this horrible place to deliver the next kick in the gut. I know it will; it's just a question of when.

"Ready, A?"

She steps forward bravely. Like this is nothing. Like she's not in the freaking demon world about to walk through a wall of smoke to go into a place where the very worst demons of all are sent to keep the other ones safe. Like her whole life and future and immortal soul aren't still absolutely and terribly at risk.

I wrap my arm around her waist and guide her back into the wall. I can feel her sharp intake of breath at the sting, but she doesn't cry out. And then we're through, the now-familiar dark stone walls greeting us with their dark and stony sameness.

But not everything is the same.

Something is wrong.

We both whirl around, eyes wide and searching.

Peter isn't there.

Oh, crap.

I know instantly that he's not just playing with us. Peter loves to push my buttons, but this isn't his kind of joke. Something is really, really wrong.

"Peter!" I yell, before I can think better of it. My voice echoes off into the blackness, and I'm suddenly very sorry to have announced our presence to whatever things might be hiding just beyond the edge of the light, sniffing around for things that smell like prey.

"Where is he?" Annie whispers beside me.

I shake my head. I have no idea where Peter could have gone. Or what could have happened to prevent him from waiting where he was supposed to.

"Let's go back," I say. "Come on."

Annie doesn't argue. We step back into the smoke and I try not to let myself think that the others won't still be there when we emerge.

But they are; they're right there, Ryan looking surprised and alarmed when he sees Annie coming back with me, and LB continuing to have unreadable demon expressions that I can't begin to decipher.

"What's wrong?" Ryan asks at once.

"Peter's gone," Annie says. "We don't know what happened."

"We have to get back over there," I say. "All of us this time. Come on."

But it's no good; it hurts almost as much as when I tried to take all five of us through. There is a split second when I almost think I could push through it, but I can't do that to Ryan and Annie. Not when they sound like they're burning to death beside me.

The awareness of time going by with Peter all alone in

there is suffocating my brain, making it hard to think straight. He's been kind of a jerk since we got down here, true, but he's still *Peter* and I can't bear the thought of him dying in this place that he hates and only came back to because he cares about me.

"Try just us," Annie says. "Me and Ryan. I think . . . I think LB is so big that he's stretching your power too far." She turns to look at him. "No offense."

"But . . . but what if you guys disappear like Peter did? No. No, no, no. I should bring LB through first; he can take care of himself if we get split up. Right, LB?"

His black eyes stare expressionlessly back at me. "Yes."

I kind of wish he'd jump in with some helpful demon advice right about now, but he doesn't say anything else.

I turn back to Annie and Ryan. They aren't looking at me, though. They are looking up and past me. Their expressions are mirror images of startled dismay.

"Oh, come on." The words come out almost as a whimper. My stomach sinks down to about my knees as I slowly turn around.

The carnivorous grass seems to have caught up with us. Except it's . . . grown . . . since we last saw it. What's coming toward us from across the field seems to be an enormous twisty mass of intertwined ropes of green. Thrashing appendages as thick as redwood trunks throw themselves forward, methodically and relentlessly dragging the rest of the demonic vegetation along behind.

I dart forward and grab Ryan's and Annie's hands.

"LB," I say, "I'm going to bring these guys through the wall. Can you hold that thing off until I can come back for you?"

He looks at me for a long second. I resist the urge to repeat the question; I suspect quick thinking is far from his strongest attribute. I wonder if he is trying to decide whether I'll really come back for him or not.

"Yes," he says finally. Then he turns around to face the monster grass.

I run at the wall, Ryan and Annie in tow, before he can change his mind.

The sting is worse this time, sharper and deeper, but Annie seems to have been right about LB being the one causing most of the problem. We all cry out at the feel of it, but then we're through and the pain vanishes.

Part of me has been desperately hoping that we would come through to find Peter waiting, but he's still nowhere to be seen.

Ryan and Annie look around with wide eyes, taking in the infinity walls and the dark shadows and all the very ominous black stone stretching off in various directions. There are sounds coming from some of those directions, sounds like big things moving slowly in the dark, and I cringe again thinking of how I shouted Peter's name before.

I take Annie's hand and place it firmly in Ryan's.

"Stay right here. *Right here.* Do not move even a centimeter. Do you understand me?"

They nod. They look terrified. But they nod and stand obediently still. Annie looks like she's trying not to even breathe.

I should turn around and go back through the wall now. I

should go and get LB, who stayed behind to fight the demon grass monstrosity.

LB, who killed Hector and tried to help Mr. Gabriel kill most of us at camp last summer.

LB, who was one hundred and ten percent on board to do terrible things to Annie once Mr. Gabriel succeeded in his plan to recapture her.

LB, who now wants to help us defeat Mr. Gabriel.

Probably. Maybe. If we can believe him.

"Cyn?" Annie asks.

I still haven't moved. My conscience says I can't leave LB out there. Of course I can't. Of course not. We made a deal. Not an official demon deal, but still. I said I'd go back to get him. And we need his help. I mean, seriously, we need all the help we can get since I still don't have the slightest idea how we're going to stop Mr. Gabriel this time. But even if we didn't . . . I can't just leave LB there when I said I'd go back for him.

But what if Annie and Ryan aren't here when I come back?

I look at them, find myself trying to burn their faces into my mind as though I'm never going to see them again, and force myself to stop. I'm going to see them again in like two seconds. They're going to be standing right here.

"We'll wait right here," Annie says. "Don't worry."

Ryan catches my eye. He doesn't say anything, but he pulls Annie closer to him and gives me the slightest of nods. My heart wants to climb out of my chest and snuggle up around him. He is all at once telling me that it will be okay and they will be right there when I get back but that also if they are not then he will take care of Annie until I can find them again. I love him so much for understanding and for telling me it's okay to go but also I hate him for telling me it's okay to go because what if they're not here? What if they're not? What if I come back and they're gone?

What if they're gone and I never find them again?

I tear my gaze away and throw myself back through the wall.

LB is ferociously attacking the grass monster, slicing off strands of toothy greenness with his long beetle-pincer things and doing some kind of spider-kickboxing move to keep the bulk of it at bay.

"LB! Come on!"

He turns and for a second some almost-recognizable emotion burns in his inhuman eyes, but I don't have time to try to figure out what it is because we have to get right back through the wall so that Annie and Ryan will still be there. I grab his closest leg and pull. He gives one final kick-snap at the grass monster and lurches after me. I envelop him in my protection and drag us both back through.

It hurts a lot this time. LB doesn't scream but his leg goes rigid in my grip and it's all I can do not to scream myself. There's no question of not pushing through it, though. Because Annie and Ryan.

So we push through and come back out of the smoke into the dark, stony prison interior.

Where Annie and Ryan should be waiting, but are not.

I yank my protection back from the spider-demon and wrap it around me like a blanket, like something that can somehow soften the horrible emptiness that rises up inside me, that might smother the regretful yet self-righteous voices that swell up to say they told me so, that I should never have left Annie and Ryan alone for even a second, not for LB, not for anyone. That I should never have let them come in the first place, but I did and now I have failed them, and that is what I get for not being strong enough to do this on my own.

I look around wildly but it's stupid and pointless and I know it.

Annie and Ryan are gone.

Chapter | 10

"No," I whisper. "No, no, no, no, no, no."

The word gets louder each time I say it, but not loud enough. Nothing could ever be loud enough to reflect the way I'm feeling right now. I try, though. I have to try or I'll explode right here in the featureless, dark demon-prison hallway. I throw my head back and scream, long and loud. As long and as loud as I can.

"You should not do that," LB says from beside me. His gravelly voice is low and urgent. "You should not make those sounds."

I'd almost forgotten he was there.

I stop screaming and look up at him. "You understand screaming, don't you? You've probably made lots of people or demons or whoever scream over the years, right?"

"Yes," he replies somewhat hesitantly. "But —"

"I don't know exactly how it works with demons," I go on, "but with humans, we scream when we are really scared or horrified or upset. I am all three of those things right now."

"But you will make the monsters come," LB explains.

I know I should care about that. A distant part of my brain recognizes that Monsters Coming is a bad thing, a thing I should try to avoid at all costs. But most of me is too scared and horrified and upset to think about anything but the fact that I've apparently lost all the people I care most about in the bowels of a demon prison that I should never have let them come to in the first place.

"My friends are gone," I say, not expecting him to actually understand. As Peter keeps reminding me, demons don't really understand the whole friends idea.

"Yes," LB agrees. "Because of the moving."

My eyes snap to his ugly bug-face, all of my heartsick exhaustion suddenly transforming into some other kind of feeling that I can't yet quite identify.

"The . . . the what?"

"The moving. Of the prison."

I know this place, he'd said. Oh, God. I close my eyes for a second so I can better focus on my extreme stupidity. It never occurred to us to ask him *what* he knows, exactly.

I open my eyes again. "Please explain about the moving."

He seems to think for a moment, maybe searching for the human words. "The prison . . . turns. Inside the boundary."

"Have you — have you been *inside* the prison before? Inside here, past the inner boundary?"

His eyes dart away and several leg joints move in what might be an evasive spidery shrug.

I try to make my voice patient and gentle. Which is hard, because I am so not feeling patient and gentle right now. "You're not in trouble. I'm . . . I'm not going to tell. I promise. I'm just trying to find out how this works so I can find my friends again."

"Yes. I have been inside."

I take a deep breath. *Patient and gentle. Patient and gentle.* "So . . . you could have walked through that wall without my help?"

He shakes his head. "No. It's . . . hard. I can only do it sometimes. When I am most strong. And only at certain places. Places with . . . holes. Not where we were before."

"Would the places with holes be easier for us to get through, too? My friends and me?"

"Oh, yes. Much easier."

My fists clench tight at my sides, my fingernails digging into my palms. But I keep my voice calm. "LB?"

"Yes?"

"When you know about things that we're trying to do, I need you to speak up and tell me. Okay? Can you do that? It . . . it will help us get back sooner to fight your brother."

"Yes."

"For example, right now . . . do you know how we can find my friends?"

"Yes."

I wait, trying so hard to give him the benefit of the doubt.

"LB?"

"Yes?"

"What did I just say? About speaking up?"

He thinks about this for a long moment. Then he straightens slightly. "You want me to tell you how to find the others."

"Yes! Yes, exactly. And anytime you see me trying to do something and you know things that might help, I want you to tell me. Got it?"

"Yes," he says, sounding rather pleased at having grasped a new concept.

"Okay. Great. That's super great. So . . . about finding my friends . . . ?"

He bobs up and down excitedly on his spider legs. "I will show you. I know how the prison moves."

"Excellent." I make myself reach out and pat him on his disgusting bristly abdomen. "And is there anything else you think it would be helpful for me to know about the prison? About the monsters, maybe?"

"Yes," he says at once. I suspect this is LB's first experience with the power of positive reinforcement. Mr. Gabriel was probably all stick and no carrot. And his stick was probably more like a mace or scythe or flamethrower or something. "The monsters will try to kill you."

"Okay," I tell him. "That's really helpful to know. Is there a way I can avoid being killed by them?"

This seems to be a more difficult question. He considers me doubtfully. "I don't know," he says at last. "You are small and weak. You have roach power but they can still kill you."

"How about you? Can they kill you?"

"They can try," he says fiercely. "But they will fail. I will crush them. I will fight them and kill them and rip their bones —"

"Great," I break in. "Awesome. So, maybe if we encounter any monsters, you can try to kill them before they kill me. How would that be?"

"Yes. That would be good."

I give him another quick pat and then wipe my hands on my jeans. "Great. Let's get moving, then. Show me how to find my friends."

LB sets off down the corridor, away from the smoke-wall behind us. I hurry to keep up. The cautious part of my brain keeps trying to tell me that it still might all be a trap, that the whole big-dumb-demon thing could be an elaborate deception, but I just don't believe it. No one's that good of an actor. And LB, in my personal experience, seems to be the type who wears his heart on his sleeve. In the past, his heart was all about joining Mr. Gabriel in carrying out his nefarious plans and getting to share in the spoils, but I believe him about no longer being in his brother's pocket. I mean, it's one thing to put up with verbal and physical abuse, which, in the demon world, is kind of just normal operating procedure, but I suspect it's quite another to find out your own brother was lying to you in really significant ways and meant to steal your body away and force you down so deep inside yourself that you would be nothing more than a spectator to the rest of your own life.

That's the kind of thing that can make you seriously want to switch sides.

The tugging inside me has returned, but I do my best to ignore it for the time being. Friends first; amulet guy second. We hurry along, and the passages begin to multiply and branch off in various directions. But LB doesn't hesitate; he moves forward with confidence, turning left or right without even stopping to think about it.

I follow with a similar lack of hesitation, hoping with everything I have that he can get us to the others before they get hurt. Peter might have ways to protect himself — even though he's not a fighter, he's survived for hundreds of years in the demon world and one would have to imagine he'd learned ways to avoid being killed — but of course Annie and Ryan have no such experience or expertise. I send them silent directives to stay small and silent and out of sight until we can get to them.

Please.

LB turns another corner and I race to catch up, but before I can reach him one of his giant spider legs flicks back to push me back against the passage wall. He's not gentle about it, and it takes me a second to regain my breath and balance. But by then I can see exactly why he did that, and I don't mind his lack of gentleness one bit.

We have discovered one of the monsters.

It looks like an enormous gelatinous blob of some kind. I am very briefly grateful for the lack of tentacles, but then I think of everything I have ever heard about gelatinous blob monsters (a small yet consistent sample set of movies and bad TV), and I immediately suspect that it will dissolve any body parts that are unlucky enough to come in contact with it.

That . . . that might be even worse than tentacles.

There are teeth and eyes floating within the blob parts, in no discernible order or logical placement that I can recognize. It turns slowly to face(?) LB, and the eyes all widen as it takes in the spider-demon brandishing his impressive forelegs and bug-pincers. Then it seems to see me, and its eyes widen even more.

"No!" it cries in a very un-monster-like voice. "Wait!"

I know that voice.

"LB, STOP!" I shout, and I am relieved to see him pause in midstrike.

He twists his head and upper parts to look at me. "I should not kill the monster before it kills you?"

"I don't think that's a monster."

We both turn back to look at the blob, and it's already beginning to change. It shrinks into itself, the slightly translucent gel parts solidifying as it grows smaller and denser and more familiar by the second. And then a somewhat disheveled Peter is standing there before us, still wide-eyed and looking terrified.

"Cyn?" he asks. "Is that really you?"

"Peter!" I run forward to embrace him in a possibly overenergetic hug. We slam into one of the stone walls. Peter hugs me back just as tightly.

"It is one of your friends," LB says from behind me. "Not a real monster."

I laugh against Peter's neck. "Yes, thank you, LB. Good catch."

I pull away before Peter can think to get handsy, but he

doesn't seem the least bit mischievous at the moment. Only profoundly relieved.

"When you didn't come back, I thought . . . I thought something must have happened." He lets out a shaky breath. "I thought I'd end up trapped in here forever." As though speaking the words brings the fear back, he puts his hands over his face and slides down to the ground.

"Hey," I say, kneeling beside him. "Hey, it's okay. I'm sorry that happened—it turns out the prison moves inside the boundary. We are all idiots and didn't think to interrogate our best source of information." I nod backward toward LB, who stands patiently in the passage behind us. "I lost Annie and Ryan, too. So please get up now so we can go and find them, okay?"

Peter takes his hands away from his face and stares at me. "Annie and Ryan are in here somewhere on their own?" The horror in his voice makes me want to start screaming again.

"Yes. So let's go. Come on, get up."

Peter lets me help him up, but he shakes his head regretfully. "Cyn, this place . . . if they . . ."

"Shut up, please," I tell him, only barely managing to keep my voice to a normal speaking level. "They're going to be fine. Don't you dare start telling me all the ways in which they might not be fine."

He swallows and nods. "Okay. Sure, okay. Let's . . . let's go find them."

I turn around to face LB. "You did great," I tell him, forcing myself to step forward and give him another friendly pat.

"Now we just have to find the other two. You can do that, right? Take us to where they would be?"

"Yes," LB says with a confidence that would make me want to kiss him if he weren't disgusting and evil.

I gesture toward the passage spanning out before us, and he steps purposefully past us and forward into the dark. Peter and I follow closely behind.

The walls continue to be the same black stone. I keep expecting to come across doors or something behind which the prisoner demons are locked away, but then I remember what Peter said about the prisoners just being shoved inside.

"So are the monsters the demons that were sent here?" I ask him quietly. "Or are they part of the prison?"

"Hard to say," he says. "Since they're roaming around pretty freely, I'm guessing they might be demons who committed lesser offenses? Who . . . changed, somehow, after so many years of being locked away? But I don't really know. Like I said, no one that comes in ever comes back out."

"LB does," I say.

"What?"

"He can get in and out. That's how he knew about the way the prison moves. It didn't occur to him to volunteer that information, but he was pretty forthcoming once the topic came up. I'm trying to get him to tell us things that we might need to know without being asked in the future."

Peter considers this, looking at the gigantic form of LB striding along before us. "All I can see when I look at him is Hector's dead body."

"I know. I'm sorry. But I think we need him. I think we're going to keep needing him."

Peter sighs. "I know. But don't forget what he is. He's not . . . he's not like me, Cyn. He's still evil. It's just that his goals align with ours right now."

"Well, be glad they do," I tell him. "I don't think I ever would have found you in here without him."

"We might not have ever needed to separate without him," Peter points out.

"But we also wouldn't be able to fight our way past the monsters in here without him."

"Hmm."

We fall silent, focusing on keeping up with LB as he continues moving through the prison corridors as though he knows exactly where he's going. We hear occasional ominous sounds coming from adjoining passages, but we don't see anything other than endless stone and shadows.

"So how long have you secretly been a blob monster?" I ask.

He stumbles and then catches himself, shooting me a dirty look. "I'm not! That was just an illusion. I was trying to stop any of the real monsters from coming after me."

"I didn't know you could do that."

He shrugs, looking away. "It hadn't really come up."

"Is that how you survived down here all that time? Pretending to be worse than you are?"

"It's one of the ways," he admits. "Those of us who aren't the fiercest and strongest develop various coping mechanisms to stay alive. But don't ask me what the others are because I'm not about to start spilling all my secrets. I need to keep some of the mystery alive."

LB comes to an abrupt stop before us. We only barely avoid walking straight into his bristly abdomen.

"What?" I ask. "What is it? Did you find them?"

Before he can answer, several huge ropey things fling themselves around the corner and begin trying to stab him. They look like giant thorny plant stalks. He hesitates, trying to fend them off with a few of his legs while turning to look back at me.

"These are . . . real monsters? Or more friends?"

Two of the plant stalks twist past him and take swings at Peter and me.

"Real monsters!" I shriek, trying to press back into the wall beyond their reach. "Real monsters! Please kill them as previously discussed!"

LB springs into action. The thorn monster, from the bits I can see, seems to be a lot bigger than he is, but LB makes up for his smaller size with pure ferocity. I can see flashes of something else, paler and — bonier? — also attempting to attack, though the thorn monster seems to be taking up most of the available room in the passage. Peter watches LB with reluctant appreciation while I suddenly remember that I can help.

The next time one of the plant-stalk things comes close to us, I reach out and *push* — with my hands and my power — like I did when that other demon was trying to kill Ryan. It jerks back, and the stalks suddenly seem to decide to focus on LB instead of bothering with us.

Peter watches me for a moment. "Do you have to be touching the demon to use your power on it? Can you try doing it from a distance?"

"I — I don't know. I can try, I guess. I don't want to hurt LB by accident, though."

I creep forward, watching the battle and waiting for a piece of enemy demon to place itself far enough away from LB that I can aim at it without having to worry about hitting the spider-demon instead. Then I realize I have no idea how to even attempt this. I've gotten pretty good at channeling the power through my hands when I'm trying to share my protection with my friends, and the touch-and-push thing I've done so far with the demons seems to be a variation on that theme. Actually pushing my protection-power out beyond my body on its own is a completely different animal.

Peter seems to see the problem. "You have to visualize it," he says. "Think of . . . think of trying to create a ball of energy in your hand. Just like when you share your protection by sending it through your hand to someone else, only this time you're pushing it just past yourself into the air, like you're holding it in your palm."

It's a little hard to concentrate with the sights and sounds of giant demons fighting right beside us, but I do my best. I stare at my hand and try to picture my roachy power as a sphere of shining white energy. But nothing happens.

"Close your eyes," Peter says. "Just try to see it in your mind."

"I know what visualize means!" I snap at him, but I close my eyes as instructed. It does seem a little easier this way. I try to re-create the feeling of sharing my protection with Annie, only instead of Annie it's the air in the middle of my cupped palm that I'm trying to share with. And instead of protection, I try to think about the feeling of pushing my energy out as a weapon.

I think it's working. In my mind I can see it: a swirling ball of white light, centered in my palm. I open my eyes again, not looking at my hand, trying to find a target. I'm afraid if I see my empty hand I'll lose it; I need to keep seeing the image of the energy in my mind. Feel it coiled there, waiting to strike.

I find one of the plant stalks that isn't too close to LB and focus on it, picking a spot to aim for. Then I throw the sphere of energy like it's a softball, hurling it forward through the air. I can almost see it, arcing toward the demon, flying fast and true to its target. It collides with the thorny appendage in a silent explosion of light.

The demon jerks slightly, but nothing like when I was actually touching it. My euphoria evaporates.

"It worked!" Peter shouts jubilantly.

I am already shaking my head. "It was too weak. The demon barely felt it."

Peter rolls his eyes at me. "Hello? It was your first try? Come on, that was great! You proved you can use your power as a weapon without touching your target! That's awesome! All you have to do now is practice."

I open my mouth to tell him that we don't have *time* for me to practice, that we're already in the middle of the place that I should have been practicing for long before now, but before I can speak, something huge and hard slams into me and throws me facedown against the stone floor. I try to roll away but it has me pinned there, the enormous weight of it crushing my lungs against the ground and making it impossible to breathe. I can hear Peter shouting somewhere nearby but I can't make out what he's saying. I flail my arms, trying to get my hands on whatever is on top of me, but I can't reach, and I don't know how to send the energy up through my back and I can't concentrate enough to try the softball thing again and also I still can't breathe and things are starting to get a little fuzzy and dark and floaty.

And then something *else* slams into me and I think how unreasonable it is for anyone to expect me to be able to deal with two giant demons at once, especially when everything is so hard to focus on and I'm still facedown on the floor in the dark, and then suddenly I can breathe again.

After a few somewhat grimy-tasting but very welcome gulps of air, the sense starts to filter back into my brain and I can think clearly enough to try to get to my feet and away from whatever was just trying to kill me. But the getting to my feet idea proves to be a little overambitious, and instead I end up in a kind of pathetic half crawl toward where I can still hear Peter shouting. When I get close enough, I feel his hand grasp mine, and he pulls me up to a standing position. And then I stumble around to see what is actually happening.

The plant-stalk demon is dead, or at least motionless. The other demon, the paler one with sharper edges and white bony parts, is currently struggling underneath LB, just a few yards away from where Peter and I are huddling. LB is bloody and at least one of his legs seems to be damaged, but he practically radiates power and strength and joy as he strikes the bone demon again and again with his pincers and forelegs. I remember that he can feed on this kind of thing, the killing and the suffering of others. Which is normally repellent, but in this case I'm happy to have him eating his fill. *Bon appétit, you magnificent fucker.*

When the bone demon finally stops moving, LB gives it a final stab and then practically bounces off the corpse, turning to face me with unmistakable good cheer.

"I have killed the monsters!" he says proudly. "Before they killed you!"

"Yes," I agree. "Well done, LB." I shuffle forward and pat the least gory bit of him I can find. "Are you — are you hurt at all?"

"It is nothing," LB says. "Monsters cannot injure me."

Grateful all over again that he is on our side, at least for now, I force myself to nod and smile. "Great. Wonderful. Let's, um, let's keep going, then, okay?"

He skips forward around the corner, and Peter and I exchange a glance before hurrying after him. My chest hurts from the near crushing; otherwise I feel relatively okay. But I still let Peter help me as we move swiftly onward through the dark.

Chapter | 11

We catch up to the spider-demon before he can get too far ahead.

"LB?" I ask. "Do you think we're getting close?"

"Close?"

Oh for the love of God please don't tell me he's forgotten what he's supposed to be doing. I would have to kill him, and that would be both difficult and inconvenient.

Patient and gentle, dammit. I dig my fingernails into my wrist, and I manage to keep my voice calm. "Close to finding Annie and Ryan? My friends?"

He stands there, considering, and I infer that he is searching for the right words to answer my question. Peter sees what I'm doing to my wrist and captures my hands in his, stopping me from actually drawing blood.

"I only know which way to go to search. I do not know

exactly where they are. I cannot say how long it will be. Maybe very soon."

He's still on task. Thank God. "Okay, that's —"

"Or maybe never, if they are already killed by the monsters. It is hard to say."

Words fail me, and I can only stand there looking at him. After a minute, Peter clears his throat and says, "Great. Thanks, LB. Let's keep going, then, shall we?"

LB turns around and continues on his way. Peter puts his arm around my waist and guides me along after LB. "They'll be okay," he tells me quietly. "They're smartish for humans, and they've both proven to be pretty damn resilient in the past."

I blink at him gratefully. "Thanks, Peter."

"Plus, I feel like Ryan and I still have so much unfinished business. He can't just die in some dark hole without me even knowing what happened. It wouldn't be . . . it wouldn't have poetic resonance."

Now I am blinking less gratefully, but he's still sort of cheering me up, so I don't chastise him. Instead I ask, "Why *haven't* you ever tried to get Ryan out of the way?"

Peter flashes me a humorless smile. "Who says I haven't?"

"I believe that if you'd tried, you would have succeeded."

He's quiet a moment, and I'm not sure he's going to answer me. I wait, watching LB's spider legs propelling him onward with a horrible sort of grace.

"There's no way that would ever work," Peter says finally. "Despite what I suggested to him when we first got down here, if Ryan ever experienced an 'accident,' I know you'd suspect me. I can't . . . I wouldn't want you that way. Always doubting, never knowing if you could trust me. Besides, if . . . I'd want you to choose me of your own accord. Not because Ryan was suddenly no longer available."

Now it's my turn to be quiet. I don't know how to respond to that.

We walk in silence for a while before I manage, "I love him, Peter. I love you, too, but not like that."

"A *little* like that," he says, not looking at me. "You kiss me like you love it. Like you don't ever want to stop."

Somewhere inside me, my traitorous electron swells with agreement.

"I can't pretend there isn't something there between us. It's like . . . it's like a chemical reaction. Powerful and automatic and not our fault. But I love Ryan. It's different with him. And he predates you. And . . . that's how it's going to stay, Peter. I need you to know that. I love you, and I want you to be my friend. I don't think I could stand it if you weren't my friend. But I don't want you to have any illusions. This is not a love triangle. I'm with Ryan. I'm staying with Ryan. You need to be able to make your peace with that."

More quiet. More walking through the dark, suffocating passageways. And then Peter looks at me with that mischievous grin that I hate and love and fear and I don't know what else. I look at him and I take in that grin and all the feelings it inspires and I don't say anything, I just wait.

"I know," he says. "But that doesn't mean I'm going to stop hoping. Or stop trying."

His arm is still around my waist, and he squeezes me, half

tickling, half grasping for dear life. I laugh, because I can't do anything else.

"I know."

Sometime during the next interminable interval of silently following LB, trying not to fear the worst for Annie and Ryan, and also trying to ignore the ever-more-insistent tugging of my newly installed internal GPS, I realize that I have once again been neglecting to take advantage of a primary source of information.

"Hey, so what do you know about this amulet guy?" I ask Peter. "I mean, other than that he made the amulet and is locked up down here somewhere." Just as I say this, my demon-compass tries to get me to turn around and walk in the opposite direction. *You have to wait,* I tell it silently for what must be the hundredth time. I'm sure it's my imagination, but the tugging is beginning to feel somehow sulky and annoyed.

"Not a lot, unfortunately. He's super powerful, but I'm sure that much was clear already. They called him — well, in your tongue, he's called the Craftsman. Making powerful items was sort of a . . . a hobby of his, I guess. An addictive one. And eventually he started making things that drew too much interest from the wrong demons — or, well, the right demons, depending on your perspective — and they locked him up for it."

I scrape one finger along the endless stone wall. "He doesn't sound that scary." I find myself picturing a kind of gremlin-like Geppetto, tinkering away in his little demon workshop.

"He's going to be terrifying, Cyn." Peter reaches over and grabs my arm to get my full attention. "Don't have any misconceptions about that, please. The amount of power it takes to create the things he does — it's more than I can even imagine. And to have found an outlet for that power, one that he *loved*, and to have been prevented from ever doing it again . . . he's surely lost his mind, locked away down here. He's going to be huge and powerful and angry and insane. I think there's more than one reason Mr. Gabriel didn't try to come down here himself."

My mental image of Geppetto has morphed into something monstrous and unrecognizable, and I quickly shove him out of my imagination.

"How long has he been here?"

"A long time. Thousands of years, maybe."

"Jesus."

"Yeah."

I pick up our pace a little, closing the distance between us and LB. "You almost sound like you feel sorry for him," I say after a minute.

"I do," Peter says. "It must be terrible, what they did to him. What they're still doing. It would have been kinder to kill him."

"Why didn't they?"

Peter gives me a condescending glance. "*Demons*, Cyn. Not so interested in the kindness, remember? Besides, the more horrible the punishment, the greater the deterrent. They didn't want anyone else to follow in his footsteps. And no one has, as far as I know. Which makes the things that he created all the more precious now." He pauses, shaking his head. "I don't know how Mr. Gabriel's friends got their hands on that amulet. He's going to be very, very powerful once he gets that missing piece back. And his physical form."

"Right, well . . . we're going to figure out a way to stop that part from happening. After he takes the curse off Ryan."

There's a tiny hesitation before Peter answers "Right" that I don't like one bit. But I pretend I didn't notice. Ryan will be fine, and Mr. Gabriel will un-curse him, and then . . . and then . . . we'll figure something out. We have to, so we will.

Up ahead, LB suddenly pauses at an intersection.

You would think I would learn not to get my hopes up every damn time.

"Is it our friends?" I ask eagerly, leaning forward to try to see.

"No," LB says, backing slowly in our direction.

"Um," Peter says. He is looking back the way we came. I follow his gaze. Some enormous shadows are growing on the wall. There are at least two. Maybe more.

The shadows are definitely too large to be Annie and Ryan.

LB has turned to face us. "There are monsters in our way. Too many for me to fight."

"Is that including or not including the monsters coming up behind us from the other direction?" Peter asks, gesturing toward the still-growing shadows.

LB looks at the shadows. "Not including," he says.

Unfortunately, we are, of course, currently in a long passage without apparent side exits of any kind. Our only options are to go on, toward monsters, or go back, toward also monsters.

Needless to say, I am not a fan of either of those choices.

"Cyn?" Peter begins.

"Shh," I tell him.

LB has adopted a stance that I have lately come to associate with him trying to have thoughts about something. Since I am one hundred percent sure that I don't have any ideas for how to get us out of this situation, and (judging from Peter's panicked expression) about ninety-eight percent sure that he also does not have any ideas, I feel very strongly that we should let LB keep digging around in his brain for whatever solution he might be able to come up with. I just hope he finishes thinking before the monsters reach us.

To my surprise, when LB shifts position (which I take as an indication that he has completed his mental exercises for the time being), he addresses himself to Peter.

"Can you protect against my poison?"

"Uh — no, I don't think so. Not with just my own strength to work with. Why?"

"You must cover your parts as much as you can," LB says. "I will try not to hurt you."

Then he turns to me. "I am speaking up about something I know. But there is not time to tell you. Only to show."

With that, he hooks me with one of his long forelegs and pulls me against him. I yelp as I find myself thrown up beside Peter, who is swearing and squirming and trying to tuck his hands and head inside his shirt. Then, holding us both tightly in place, LB begins to run back down the passageway on his remaining legs.

We come upon the shadow-casting monsters almost at once. There are two, and they both seem to be insect-based in their appearance. I can't get a very good look from my current position, but I catch glimpses of long multijointed legs and jagged green carapaces and incongruously pretty, feathery antennae.

LB doesn't break stride. He keeps running, lashing out at the monsters in passing with a couple of limbs and his pincer-things. For a moment it seems like he's going to make it through, just push past them down the corridor and keep on running. But then I see one of the insect monsters jab out one of its own long legs, and suddenly LB pitches forward, tumbling into nearly a somersault. I scream, burying my face in his furry, bad-smelling chest. He's still covered in mud and blood and various other substances, and then there's his own underlying scent that is fairly repulsive all on its own even without the added embellishments from his recent victims, but in this moment I don't care about any of that. His protective leg presses tighter against us as he struggles to right himself with the others and turns to face our attackers.

I have no idea how he hopes to fight them while still holding on to us. From the way he hesitates, I don't think LB does, either.

"Cyn!" Peter shouts. "You have to help him!"

At first I think he means sharing my protection, but as

soon as the idea surfaces, I know it won't work. The monsters in this place — LB included — don't seem to be fighting with their demon energy. It's all physical, and my protective energy can't help at all with that kind of thing. But then I realize he means I should try to help by using my power as a weapon.

"It's too weak! I can't hurt them enough that way!"

"It's better than nothing!"

Which is a good point.

LB is circling with one of the monsters now, three legs raised in an offensive stance, antennae and pincers spread wide. I can see the other monster out of the corner of my eye, clearly trying to find a way to sneak around and attack LB from behind while he's distracted by Monster #1.

I try the softball visualization again, which is hard to do when my brain keeps wanting to imagine how we are all about to die instead. Also I have never actually been any good at softball, and so the focus of my visualization fails to be especially compelling. Sports have never really been my thing in general, a shortcoming of which I am now deeply regretful. Would some other kind of ball be better? Baseball, basketball, Ping-Pong ball . . . no. My mind is going entirely in the wrong direction. I could try visualizing a gun or something, but I have even less experience with actual weapons than I do with sports equipment.

I mentally throw up my hands.

Screw this.

Instead of a ball, I picture a kind of spotlight — my own personal follow spot. Only instead of directing light, my imaginary lens focuses my roachy power. This immediately feels

much more *right;* my fingers curl instinctively to form the bar-
rel as I stretch my hands forward toward Monster #2, who still
thinks he is being stealthy and unseen. I concentrate on the
way I've come to imagine my resistance, as a sort of glowing
energy inside me. At some internal lighting console I am opening the faders, feeling the buzzing as I slide them all the way
up. And then I open my eyes and stare at my target. And I turn
on the light.

It hits Monster #2 square in the face. This is definitely
a more effective mode of attack than the dumb softball. His
face doesn't explode or anything immensely satisfying like
that, but he jerks backward in surprise and — I hope? — pain,
and manages to smack his own head against the wall behind
him.

Monster #1 is distracted by this sudden interference
from an unanticipated source, and LB takes advantage of the
moment by grabbing the monster's head in his pincers and
squeezing for all he is worth. Monster #1's face *does* explode,
and it *is* immensely satisfying, although it is also immensely
disgusting as wet pieces of bug-face fly outward and splatter
all three of us in insect gore.

Monster #2, the would-be sneaky bastard, takes in this
new development for one silent second and then turns and
runs away. Fortunately (for us), he runs in the direction we
had originally been headed before, and I smile at the thought
of him racing headfirst into the pack of other monsters who I
assume are still coming this way.

LB doesn't waste any time. He shifts Peter and me more
firmly against him and then continues his flight.

"That was awesome," Peter says. His voice comes out weak and shaky despite his enthusiasm, and I look at him in alarm.

"Peter! Are you okay? What's wrong?"

"The poison," he says. "I'm okay. It's mostly blocked by my clothes, but it's still . . . uh . . . there. Draining. But I'll . . . I'll be all right."

I can't tell if he's telling the truth.

There's nothing I can do, anyway. I'm inclined to trust LB if he thinks it's still necessary to carry us and run. I hope he's still trying to run in the right direction to find Annie and Ryan. I'm afraid to distract him by asking, though. Also the motion is starting to make me feel a little carsick. Demonsick. Whatever.

I close my eyes and think about not throwing up. Also I think about what just happened with Monster #2. Because Peter isn't wrong — it was awesome. I can actually fight these things. Well . . . I can actually hurt them, at least. Or . . . okay, surprise them and make them smack their heads into walls. But I bet I could do more than that, with practice.

For the millionth time, I wish I understood more about how it worked. My resistance power seems to be fairly steady-state in nature . . . I can share it, I can use it, and it doesn't get diminished over time. But sending it out that way, to use it as a weapon . . . that might be different. As with most demon-related things, I don't know what the rules are.

Eventually I feel LB come to a stop. I open my eyes to find we're in a roundish space between two passages. LB gently lowers Peter and me to the floor.

"Rest," LB pants, and then slides to the floor himself.

"Are you okay?" I ask him.

"Yes. But need rest." I guess any increase in energy he got from killing the bug demon wasn't enough to balance out the rest of the fighting and running. And physical and demon-energy strength levels only seem to overlap in certain ways that I don't really understand.

"How about you?" I ask, turning to Peter. But I can tell at a glance that he is not okay. He's shivering a little, and his face is pale and drawn. "Oh, no. Peter. What can I do?"

He gives me a tired almost-smile. "You don't happen to have Darleen and Celia from camp in your back pocket, do you?"

Right. Because the last time he was affected by LB's poison, a little interpersonal camper drama was exactly what he needed to recover. "Sorry," I say. "Could I — maybe I could do a monologue or something?"

Now he almost laughs. "I'm tempted to say yes just to watch you try," he says. "But no. I don't think that would be much help. I can feed on fictional drama, but — and please don't take this the wrong way, Cyn — it needs to be *good* drama. Powerful. A quality reenactment of *Dear Evan Hansen,* sure. Even a decent production of *Cats* might help a little, if the performances were good enough. Well, maybe. If it didn't include 'Skimbleshanks: The Railway Cat,' I guess. But you, here, trying to recite some lines from a play from memory, or even attempting to sing something . . . it wouldn't be quite the same."

I want to be offended, but of course he's right. I'm no performer, or even a halfway decent singer. I bet if Ryan were here, he could do something feeding-worthy. My heart twinges at the thought of him, and I have to tamp down the panic beetles that suddenly want to swarm up from where I've been keeping them locked deep inside myself.

No. No falling apart. I can't do anything to help Ryan right now. But maybe there's still a way I can help Peter.

"The poison," I say slowly. "Is it physical? Or, like, demon-energy based?"

Peter perks up slightly, considering this question. "You think your resistance can help?"

"Maybe? It seems worth a try anyway. Considering we don't really have a whole bunch of other options."

He agrees with this assessment. I scooch over to sit beside him and take his hand. And then I realize that I have no idea what to do. How can I target the poison?

Peter notices my hesitation and guesses the reason.

"Maybe if you try to share it with me, like when we were going through the wall before? I might be able to — to direct it, once you do."

I nod and do as he says. It ends up being a strange combination of the way it works when I share my power with my friends and the way it feels when the demoness takes it from me. I let it flow through my hand and into Peter's, but then I can feel him sort of take hold of it and draw it toward where he needs it to go. It's — weird. But not unpleasant. I do begin to lose track of time, though, as I kind of float inside my body, caught up in the movement of the energy between us.

At some point I become aware that Peter has released my hand. "Cyn? Can you hear me?"

I blink and he slowly comes into focus.

"You look much better," I murmur. He does. His color has returned and the smile he gives me now has no almost about it.

"I feel much better. Thank you. But how do you feel? You seem a little . . . tired?"

I nod. I am tired. And suddenly the panic beetles are back, and I look at Peter in alarm.

"Could—do you think I did too much? Gave too much away? Oh, God, Peter, what if . . . what if it doesn't come back?" The thought is terrifying. I never wanted this power in the first place, but knowing how . . . how *diminished* I feel when I don't have it . . . the idea of losing it forever makes it suddenly hard to breathe.

"Shh," he says. "I don't think it works that way. I suspect you just need to rest for a bit. Using it as a weapon and then using it to heal me . . . that's a lot more than you're used to, especially all at once."

"Okay." I try to feel reassured by his words. But then another thought strikes me. "Wait—no. I can't rest. We have to keep going! We have to find them!" I struggle to get to my feet, but it's really a struggle; whatever I did to Peter just now, it totally wiped me out.

"Cyn, stop! Just . . . just sit there for a second, okay?" Peter runs a hand through his hair and glances at LB, who is still sprawled on the floor a little ways away. "I promise, as soon as the big guy is ready, we'll start moving again. He can carry you if you're still resting then. I will walk, and keep my distance from the poison. But we can't go anywhere until he's ready, unless you want to leave him behind?"

171

"No," I say wearily. "No, of course not."

I see LB's massive bulk shift, and I wonder if he is listening. I thought he was asleep.

"All right, then. So you just sit there and close your eyes for now, okay? If you're still resting when LB is ready to go, he will give you another lift. Deal?"

"I'm not making any more deals with demons," I mutter, but my eyes are already falling closed of their own accord.

Peter laughs. "Understood."

"Also I'm mad at you," I add sleepily.

"What? Why?"

"I've got freaking 'Jellicle Cats' stuck in my head now, you jerk."

He laughs again, sounding relieved. I feel like there's something else I want to say, but before I can remember what it is, my head leans back against the wall and I float away again into oblivion.

Chapter 12

I wake up with LB's spider leg plastered against my chest.

The smell and the motion hit me all at once, and I struggle in his grip. "Let me down!" I shout, and then, remembering that he's probably just trying to be helpful, I add, "Please."

He stops and lets me down. Peter, who was walking a careful distance away, comes over immediately.

"Feeling better?" he asks.

"Yeah. How long—?"

He shrugs. "Not sure. Time is weird here. A couple of hours, maybe?"

And still no Annie and Ryan.

I look up at LB, who is standing patiently where he stopped to let me down.

"This isn't working. There has to be something else we can do."

He shifts uncertainly. "We follow the right paths to get to where they should be. But if they wandered far, or if the monsters—"

"Let's assume they are still alive," I break in, not willing to entertain the other idea. "Isn't there any way to try to track where they might have wandered?"

LB and Peter look at each other. "There are some demons who could track humans that way," Peter answers for them both. "But not, unfortunately, either of the demons currently present."

"What about the monsters in here? Can they track humans?"

"Maybe? It's their domain, after all—at the very least they'd be likely to notice anything out of place."

"Okay," I say, pacing the width of the passage. "So let's catch one and see if we can make it find them for us."

Peter stares at me. I think LB is staring, too, but as usual his bug expressions are tricky.

I stare back. "What? We have to try something. LB has killed several of those things; why can't he catch one instead? And then . . . and then make it do what he wants? Isn't that how demon stuff works? The stronger ones make the weaker ones do their bidding?"

"Well, kind of . . . I mean it's not exactly quite that simple. And I have no idea how things work in the prison, Cyn."

"It works that way," LB confirms in his gravelly voice. "Stronger always wins. Everywhere."

"Not *everywhere*," Peter objects. "I mean—"

"Stop," I say. "This is not the time to debate demon

sociology. We're going to try to catch a monster. By which I mean LB is going to try to catch a monster." I turn to face him. "Okay with you, big guy? Can you do it?"

He draws himself up proudly. "Yes."

"Excellent! Let's go find one."

LB turns and bounces off down the passage with renewed purpose. Peter and I follow more cautiously behind.

"If you have a better idea, you are absolutely encouraged to share it," I say, not looking at him.

"I don't. I wish I did."

"I wish you did, too."

It doesn't take long for LB to find a potential victim. He comes upon a lone, unsuspecting, flower-themed monster in a kind of small cavern and jumps mercilessly onto it from behind. The thing literally has a head like a gerbera daisy: perfect yellow circle face containing eyes and mouth with giant fuchsia petals extending like a lion's mane all around. Except more like a flower than a lion. Except for the face and teeth parts.

"Remember, don't kill it!" I shout at LB as the fight commences.

The flower monster is surprisingly feisty. (Well, I suppose I shouldn't be surprised, since we are in the demon prison and it's a monster, but the cute daisy aspects are so disarming and misleading.) But LB seems firmly in control of the situation. In relatively short order he has pinned the monster to the ground, leaf-arms twisted up awkwardly behind it, and is growling some kind of painful-to-listen-to demon-speak at it as it writhes and struggles beneath him.

"What's he saying?" I whisper to Peter.

"Mostly threats so far, and a few grandiose statements about how strong and mighty he is. I assume he's working up to the you-have-to-find-Cyn's-friends-now part."

He seems to get there eventually, because he allows the flower monster to climb to its feet. He appears to have tied its leaf-arms together with bits of spiderweb, which I have to remember to ask him about later because I had no idea he actually had functioning web-producing parts in his spider sections. But now is not the time for that. Now is the time that the captive flower monster leads us to Annie and Ryan. Who are surely only hiding somewhere very nearby, and are not at all dead.

We follow the monster out of the cavern and down a series of passages.

"Do you think we can trust it?" I ask Peter.

"No way. But I think we can trust that it's terrified of LB. Now it just remains to be seen if it can actually track humans like it claims."

"It said it could?"

"Yes, but don't get too excited. I'd say that, too, if LB had me pinned to the ground and was threatening to eat my face."

"Hmm."

The flower monster leads us down several more passages before finally coming to a halt. LB peers past it into a large chamber just off the edge of the passage we're in. I can't stand it; I push past them both and run forward, ignoring Peter's urgent whisper-shouts behind me.

Two figures sit huddled against the wall at the far side.

My breath catches in my throat. They're not moving. But . . . but they're sitting. They're not sprawled out on the floor with their limbs at odd angles. They're not covered in blood. They might still be fine, totally fine, totally and completely —

Annie slowly raises her head and sees me standing there in agonized uncertainty. She blinks, and then her face lights up like the Fourth of July.

"CYN? Oh, my God, is that — are you —"

And then she is suddenly in front of me, throwing her arms around me, laughing and crying and hugging me with all her not-inconsiderable strength.

After a second Ryan is there, too, and once Annie lets go he takes her place, hugging just as hard, harder, but without the laughing and crying. He's just there, solid, holding on. It's really hard to let him go.

"Hi," he says, once he finally pulls back. He brushes a few strands of hair from my forehead. "Nice to see you again."

"We're so sorry, Cyn," Annie says. "We tried to wait where you left us, but then you didn't come back, and we heard something else coming . . ."

I shake my head. "You don't have anything to be sorry for. The stupid prison *moves*. This place was built by psychopaths. And I was dumb and never thought to ask LB what he knows about the prison before we went through the wall."

Ryan looks past me at the flower monster still standing with LB in the entrance. "Uh . . . new team member?"

"Oh! No, that's a monster that LB caught to help us find

you." I turn to LB. "I guess you can let him go now, unless—would he be able to tell us anything useful about the Craftsman? That's"—I realize we never actually filled LB in on what we were doing in this terrible place—"that's the demon we need to see to complete our errand. He's locked up in here somewhere."

LB has another growly conversation with the flower monster.

"No," he says finally. "The monsters do not go near the deepest prisoner level. The demons there will hurt them for sport if they can. He knows nothing."

"Oh," I say, disappointed and not exactly cheered by the details included with that explanation. "Okay."

"I will kill him now," LB says.

"Wait, what? No!" I stare at him, appalled. "Didn't you promise to let him go if he helped us?" I look at Peter. "Didn't he?"

"Yes," LB says, casting a glance at Peter, who nods in agreement. "But only to make him help. We do not need him now."

"That's—that's not the point!"

"That is . . ." He seems to remember my words from before. "That is how demon stuff works."

I put my hands on my hips. "Well, that's not how we work. Are you on this team with us? The team that's going to go back and fight your brother?"

"Yes," LB says without hesitation.

"Well, then you have to let him go. You made a promise."

"But . . . a promise is not a deal."

I feel a chill, hearing the same line that Mr. Gabriel spoke earlier coming out of his little brother's mouth.

"No," I agree. "A promise is a promise. On this team, we honor our promises." Well, except if evil demons force you to break them and make you kiss people you promised you would never kiss again. But I see no reason to bring that up. When LB still doesn't move, I give him my best tech-director-chastising-lazy-minions glare. "LB? I'm waiting."

LB's bug features manage to convey a very clear sense of confusion and reluctance and disbelief as he slowly turns and releases the bindings on the flower monster's arms.

The flower monster looks just as confused and disbelieving to be so released.

"Tell him if he tries to hurt us in any way, or tells any other monsters where we are, then the promise is over and you totally will kill him after all," I add hastily.

LB growls this to the monster; or at least, he growls something, and I satisfy myself with hoping it's a relatively close translation of what I said. The monster glances at me, then looks back at LB and growls a final incomprehensible word or two before taking off down the passage into the dark.

"How did you avoid getting eaten by monsters until now?" I ask Annie and Ryan. "I'm not sure how we would have managed without LB."

"I think it's this room," said Annie. "We were trying to find somewhere good to hide, and we stumbled upon this place. Do you see all the markings on the walls and the floor? We thought maybe they could be protective symbols of some kind. To keep the monsters away."

Peter looks around with interest. "Huh," he says, studying the nearest drawings. "Some of them definitely are. I wonder who . . . I guess maybe we're not the first to sneak our way in here uninvited. And maybe you guys aren't even the first non-demons."

"Some of them?" I ask. "What about the others?"

"Not sure. I only recognize a few. The rest I could probably decipher, but that would take a little time. I think it's best we try to stay away from them, just in case. Stepping across the boundary of the wrong kind of symbol could be the last mistake you ever get to make."

Ryan huffs unnecessarily loudly. "Uh, I think Annie and I managed to do okay all this time without your advice, thanks."

Peter turns to stare at him, and I feel the temperature in the room suddenly drop.

"Guys," Annie begins hesitantly.

"What is your problem?" Peter demands, stepping closer to Ryan. "From the looks of things, you two just sat here comfortably, waiting for us to come rescue you. Do you have any idea what we were going through out there, looking for you?"

"From what Cyn said, it sounds like you were mostly hiding in LB's shadow, letting him fight the monsters for you. Because *you're* not that kind of demon, right? The kind that can actually fight and protect people?"

"You—"

"And how did you manage to hook up with Cyn again so quickly?" Ryan goes on, talking over him. "Why were we the ones sitting here alone while you two were together? Did you have something to do with all of us getting separated in the first place?"

"Hey!" I shout. "That was the prison, not Peter. I believe I already explained about that?"

Ryan rolls his eyes. "Yeah, but how do you know Peter didn't know all about it? He knew what the prison was, knew enough to be afraid of coming here . . . not a big jump to think he might have known about how the boundary worked."

"Trust me," Peter growls. "If I'd been able to orchestrate us getting separated, I damn well would have made sure you stayed lost."

"Oh, so you admit it?"

"I'm not admitting anything! I'm just saying if you're going to accuse me of treachery, then quit underestimating me. You have no idea what I'm capable of. But if you don't start showing some manners, I think you're going to find out."

"*Stop it!*" I shout, pushing my way between them. "Are you kidding me? Do you really think we have time for this kind of nonsense right now? How's your arm, Ryan? Have you even been checking to see how much time is left before you die?"

That shuts them up. We all glance involuntarily at Ryan's arm. The red line disappears under his T-shirt sleeve. No way to tell how far it goes beyond that. My hand twitches, aching to pull up Ryan's shirt to see, but I fight off the impulse. I'm not going to humiliate him in front of Peter. Not when he's clearly so raw on the subject already.

"Look. Let's just get to this Craftsman demon and get what we need and get the hell out of here, okay?" The tugging has returned, more fiercely than ever; it's almost like the demon-compass knows I'm ready to finally follow its guidance now.

"Okay," Ryan mutters, not looking at me.

I whirl to look at Peter. When he doesn't answer, I poke him in the ribs. "Ow! Okay!"

"Okay!" Annie calls supportively from where she's standing several steps away.

I smile despite myself. "I wasn't worried about *you*," I tell her. "But thanks, anyway."

"Okay," LB adds from the entranceway. He hasn't moved since releasing the flower monster.

"Great!" I say. "We're all in agreement, then. Excellent. The unpleasant but helpful compass thing Mr. Gabriel gave me is telling me to go . . . there."

I point directly at one of the walls.

Ryan looks at the wall, then walks over to peer at one of the side passages. "Well, we can't walk through the wall," he says. "So I guess—" He takes another step forward, trying to see out into the darkness.

"*Wait*," Peter says, grabbing for Ryan's arm.

Ryan shakes him off violently and pulls away, taking another step toward the passage. "Don't you dare—"

But whatever else he's going to say is lost in a sudden rush of air and sound.

The stone at the entrance to the passage is glowing a bright and frightening red.

"I *told* you not all of those symbols were protective!" Peter shouts at him.

A great wind seems to materialize from nowhere, knocking

all of us over onto the ground. And then a bright, shining hole made of light opens in the wall and begins sucking everything toward it.

Annie is closest. She shrieks as the force increases and suddenly she's being dragged helplessly toward it.

"No!" I scream.

Ryan moves fastest. He grabs her hand just as her feet are sucked into the hole. She's still shrieking.

Peter, bless him, lunges forward and clamps a hand around Ryan's ankle. The three of them are still sliding, though. Annie's calves have disappeared into the hungry light.

I throw myself forward and latch both hands around Peter's calf. The hole seems to give a mighty tug and we all slide another few feet toward it. Annie's pulled in to the waist now.

"Cyn!" she screams, her face contorted by fear.

"Hold on!" *Please. Oh, please.*

But the light keeps pulling and suddenly Ryan is panicking. "Annie, no! Hold on, I can't —"

And then with a final horrified scream she's gone.

We slide forward again, until I feel LB's spider legs wrap tightly around my waist.

Ryan is scraping at the ground, trying to find something to hold on to. I'm staring at the spot where Annie disappeared, unable to believe what just happened. We just found her. We just found her again and now —

"Cyn," Peter says urgently. He's speaking loudly over the rushing of the wind, but he sounds calm. In control. "Listen to me. Are you listening?"

"Annie —"

"No, just listen. I can see what's on the other side of that hole. It looks — well, it looks like your high school."

"What?"

"It's an ejection trap. I can see the design of it now. Something to send intruders back where they came from. It must be intended to prevent breakouts — there are probably more of them scattered throughout the prison. They'd eject anyone who didn't belong and leave the prisoners behind. And since we came from the library, I mean originally, I think that's where it's leading to. So I think she's okay."

Ryan slides another few feet forward, still failing to find anything to stop his progress.

"I don't think we're going to be able to fight it," Peter goes on. "I don't think it's going to close until we all go through."

"But we can't! We have to stay here! We have to —" But at the same time my mind is screaming for Annie, not sure whether to trust that she's really okay, that she's really just back at school and totally fine. Even if it looks like high school, it might not be. It could be a trick. It could be anything. It could be someplace even more terrible than this.

And wherever Annie is, she's alone. We can't just leave her there alone.

"Listen!" Peter shouts. "I don't think it wants LB. He was still in the entranceway when Ryan triggered the trap, and he didn't come with us from the school anyway. If LB stays here, I think I can get us back. We have to go through, but I think, if he lets me, I can fix this. Eventually."

It's very hard to think clearly while a giant hole in the wall of a demon prison is trying to suck you against your will back to your high-school library. If that's even really where it's leading. But I try. I twist around, trying to get a clear line of sight to LB's face.

"LB! Are you listening? Do you understand what Peter is saying?"

After a pause, which makes me want to kick him, because *can't he see that we are in kind of a hurry right now?*, he says, "I hear him, but I do not understand."

"That's okay, big guy," Peter says. "Just listen. You have to stay here. If you want us to be able to come back and fight with you against your brother, if you want Cyn to get to finish her errand and go with you, we need you to stay right here, in this room. Can you do that?"

"Stay . . . ?" His gravelly voice sounds uncertain.

"Yes," Peter says. "I'm going to attach something to you. You're going to be our anchor. As long as you're here, I'll be able to get us back. It might take us a little while to find a way, but then we'll be able to come right back here. Okay? Can you do that?"

LB seems to be trying to have thoughts, and there is simply no time for that right now. We're still sliding onward toward the light.

"LB," I say in as patient and gentle a voice as I can while still talking loud enough to be heard in the wind tunnel. "Please. *Please.* I promise we'll come back. I promise. It's so important — you have to stay right here in this room and let Peter do what he needs to do. And then we'll come back and finish this thing and go and kill the hell out of your big brother. Okay? Please?"

There is another long pause in which Ryan and Peter try not to get sucked into the hole and I fight the urge to slam both of my feet into LB's dim-witted beetle face.

"Okay," he says finally.

"Great!" Peter says, almost before LB has finished getting the word out. "Hold still."

I catch a glimpse of demon energy flying past me, a kind of rope shape that fastens itself around LB's foreleg and then disappears.

"Okay," Peter says. "Okay, LB, now let us go."

He does. The spider limbs unwrap themselves from around me and we go flying toward the hole of light. The last thing I see is LB's face, watching us expressionlessly from the quickly receding dark.

Chapter | 13

The comfortable reading chairs of the high-school library seem like alien constructions to me. I am lying on the carpet, staring at one, trying to make sense of it. What kind of material is that, anyway?

And then everything floods back into my brain at once and I sit up, my heart pounding.

Annie, Ryan, and Peter are sprawled around me, also in various stages of getting into a sitting position.

"Annie? Are you —"

"I'm okay," she says. "I don't understand anything that just happened, but I'm okay."

And then my eyes fall on Ryan, and in the bright fluorescent light of the library the line running from his palm is deep and red and awful. I can't help it; I scramble across to him and pull up his shirt.

"Cyn! What —"

"Quiet." It hasn't reached his chest yet. I'd been braced to see it millimeters from his heart. But it's still on his arm. Not quite halfway between his elbow and his shoulder. I trace my hand along it, wishing I could just make it go away. With all the monsters and everything, it was easy to lose sight of what the real danger is. This tiny red line, marching relentlessly toward my boyfriend's horrible death.

"Hey!" a voice says from behind us, sounding startled.

The library monitor is there, staring wide-eyed at me holding Ryan's shirt up with one hand and running my fingers along his skin with the other.

"You — you can't do that stuff in here. I'm — I have to —" He turns hastily around toward the desk and, I assume, Mrs. Davenforth.

Peter is on his feet before I even have to ask him.

"Hey, Leon, wasn't it?" He puts his arm around the kid's shoulders, and Leon turns to look at him with a suddenly entranced, nearly worshipful expression. "Listen, I need you to do me a *really* important favor . . ." They head off into one of the aisles between the shelves.

Trusting Peter to smooth everything out, I turn my attention back to Ryan and Annie.

"You guys are really okay? Really?"

"Yes," Annie says. "Are you? What the hell happened?"

I tell her Peter's ejection-trap theory. And fill her in on what happened after she got sucked through the hole before us. I also reluctantly allow Ryan to pull his shirt back down.

Ryan shakes his head. "So . . . we're really just back? At school?"

"Looks like," I tell him.

"Do we even know what day it is?"

"Tuesday," Peter says, reemerging from the shelves. Leon practically skips off toward the circulation desk behind him, not a care in the world.

I envy him so much.

"Wait — like Tuesday? Like the day after we left?"

"Yup. Tuesday morning. Just about time for homeroom."

Annie looks at Peter, and then at me and Ryan. "But we're not . . . we can't go to homeroom. Don't we have to try to get back?"

"Yes," Peter says. "But to do that I need to figure out how to reopen that hole. Without the one-way vacuum action. Or with one-way vacuum action in the other direction, at least. And for that I need a little time."

"But —" Annie seems to be having an especially hard time with this. "But you don't even *have* a homeroom. You don't even go to our school." She lowers her voice to a whisper. "You're not even really our *age*."

Peter raises an eyebrow at her and grins. "Well, I didn't mean me, actually. *I* don't have to go to homeroom. I have to go do a little research. I'll catch up with you guys at lunch."

I look at him. "So — are you suggesting we just go about our business in the meantime? Go to class, et cetera?"

"I have a voice lesson today," Ryan says quietly. He says it with amazement, like the very idea of a voice lesson is something completely outside of his current realm of understanding.

"I think that's best," Peter says. "Until I can get us back. I mean, ideally, we're going to get this all worked out and then you'll all be returning to your lives and wanting to not be too far behind on classes and homework and whatever, right?"

The rest of us mumble various words of agreement, but it all seems so weird. How are we supposed to care about school when Ryan is still approaching death-by-demon-curse and LB is (hopefully) waiting for us in the demon prison and Mr. Gabriel is waiting for us to bring him the thing he needs to make him fully strong and physically present again and then we somehow have to kill him before he can finish carrying out his evil plans?

Annie gets to her feet. "I guess . . . I'm going to go find William." We watch her walk toward the doors and out of sight.

I glance at Peter. "Can you make it so no one notices that we're all wearing the same clothes we wore yesterday? And that we're all filthy?"

"On it."

"Thanks."

We fall silent, and Peter seems to realize that this is his cue to leave. "Uh . . . yeah. I'm just going to go, uh . . . go. See you guys later?"

He turns and jogs out without waiting for an answer.

"This is so messed up," I tell Ryan.

"I know," he says, putting his arms around me.

I let myself relax into him, knowing it's only for a moment, but relishing the temporary feeling of safety and comfort. I breathe in the smell of him, which a day without showering has only made more noticeable, in a way that totally works for him. I doubt I smell as good, especially since I was fighting monsters and stuff and — ugh — being smushed up against LB and everything he was coated with.

"Oh, no, do I smell like demons? I do, don't I?" I try to pull away from him but he tugs me back into place.

"You're fine. Stay still."

"I bet I smell like demon spider and plant monster."

"Mmmm. Sounds delicious."

"It's not! It's gross! Ugh, maybe I can sneak into the gym showers and wash off."

"Will you be quiet? I'm trying to enjoy this no-doubt very brief time we have to spend together alone before the next round of crazy begins."

"Okay. Sorry." But I only last a few seconds before asking, "Ryan?"

He sighs. "Yes?"

"You need to stop fighting with Peter."

"Okay, I really don't want to talk about him right now."

"I know. But it's important. We're all on the same side, you know? And . . . well, this last argument didn't really turn out so well, did it?"

Ryan is quiet a moment. "No. It didn't. I'm sorry about that. But . . . but I still don't trust him, Cyn. And I kind of hate that you do."

I sit up and twist around to face him.

"Listen to me, Ryan Halsey. I love you. I only want to be with you. I told Peter this, just so you know. And . . . okay, this is awkward to say, but . . . well, he could have killed you a thousand times over by now if he were going to. I know you guys don't get along, but it's not because he's a bad guy. He's one of the good ones. He sacrificed a lot to try to help us, you know."

"To help *you*," Ryan mutters.

"Yes, fine, to help me. Because he cares about me. Because he's my friend. And part of caring about me is helping me to protect what I love, which is why he went back to the terrible demon world that he swore he'd never return to in order to help me try to save *you*. It's kind of a big deal. And you being a dick to him is not only supremely unhelpful but also kind of ridiculously ungrateful."

Ryan doesn't say anything. But after a moment he pulls me back into place against him.

"I'm not asking you to be his best friend," I say. "Just try to act like we're all on the same team, okay?"

"Team Cyn," he says, and it sounds like he's smiling a little. "If we get team jerseys, I totally get first pick of numbers."

"No way. If it's Team Cyn, then I totally get first pick. You can be next, though."

"Fine. But Peter chooses last."

I laugh. "Deal."

"Deal."

After that we reluctantly get up. Leon waves enthusiastically at us as we leave the library. Everything feels very surreal. And the fact that real life feels surreal because it's *not* the demon world is an entirely whole new level of screwed up.

We walk down the hall toward where we will need to part ways to head to our respective homerooms.

"Hey," I say, "at least you didn't have to miss a voice lesson."

Ryan laughs a bitter laugh that I don't like one bit. "Like it matters."

"Hey!" I stop and pull him around to face me. "It totally matters. What the hell?"

"Does it? Do you really think we're going to make it through this and everything's going to be all right?"

"Yes," I say fiercely. "Yes I do, goddammit. Otherwise what the hell are we doing? We might as well roll over and give up right now."

He doesn't look at me.

"Hey," I say again. I take his chin and gently turn his head toward mine. "Don't you give up on me. No giving up, remember? Especially not now, after all we've been through. This is the last of it! We're going to get that curse off you, and then we're going to kill Mr. Gabriel once and for all. And then we're going to come back here and you're going to be the best Javert ever in the history of *Les Misérables*."

He half smiles at that. "Not if I don't get some time to practice in between all the demon stuff."

"You *find* time, my love. Oh, my God — think about how terrible you'll feel if you give up too soon and then we win and you come back fully alive and fine but then freaking *Jeff* gets your part because you weren't preparing adequately for callbacks! Think about how much that would totally suck. Plus, your girlfriend would be super pissed at you if you let that happen, and *trust me,* that would not be something that made your life better."

We'd started walking again at some point, but now we stop

at the end of the hallway where we have to go our separate ways. Other kids are wandering through the halls now, too. It really is just a regular day for all of them. It's still so hard to get my head around that.

"You make some excellent points," Ryan concedes, kissing the back of my hand. "I will ponder them further while I go through the motions of this day while really waiting for my archrival to figure out how to get us back down to the demon prison so we can pick up where we left off in the underworld."

"Now you're talking," I tell him. "But don't cancel your voice lesson, in case we're still here after school."

"Yes, ma'am." He kisses my hand again, then pulls me closer and kisses my forehead, and then my lips. And then he's gone, before I've had nearly enough of him. But it's okay, because there will be time for all of that. Because Peter is going to get us back down there in time to save Ryan from the curse. And then we'll destroy Mr. Gabriel, somehow, before he has a chance to take Annie and kill me. It's all going to work out. Absolutely.

I decide to skip homeroom and sneak into the gym so I can get that quick shower and maybe change into whatever gym clothes are sitting in my locker. Now that I'm aware of how disgusting I am, I can't bear to spend one more second than I have to in this filth. As I do these things, I mentally run through my day and try to figure out whether Annie or I will see Leticia and Diane first and what the best way to succinctly fill them in will be, without unduly alarming them or making them feel like they should try to come back with us. And then

I try to remember if I have any quizzes or anything today that I obviously didn't study for. I imagine a calculus test interrupted by a giant flower monster bursting into the room and eating up all the test papers with its cute gerbera daisy face, and I smile despite myself. My life is insane.

Peter shows up again at lunch. We all sit down at an empty table together — Annie, Leticia, Diane, Ryan, Peter, William, and me. I suddenly realize I am starving, which makes sense given how long it's been since we last ate anything. Terror must have been suppressing my appetite until now.

I am in my gym T-shirt, a purple hoodie, and a pair of yoga pants, feeling much cleaner and less disgusting. Peter also looks a lot cleaner than he did. Annie and Ryan haven't changed their clothes, but Ryan is making his slightly scuffed-up look work for him, and Annie wasn't nearly as dirty as the rest of us to begin with.

Leticia, Diane, and William have already been brought up to speed individually, but now that we're all together, there seem to be a million more questions from all quarters. Peter has confirmed that he can make our teachers believe that we were all present and accounted for yesterday, which is one less thing to worry about, at least. Leticia and Diane already covered for Annie and me with our parents, having faked an emergency study-sleepover, and Jorge did the same for Ryan (possibly using some other excuse). But Peter's still working on the details of how we're going to get back down to the prison.

"So you're just, like, going to keep going about your day?" Leticia asks, not for the first time.

"I know," I say. "It's crazy. But . . . well, Peter's right. I mean if we survive all of this, we are going to want to be able to come back and start living our regular lives again, aren't we?"

"*When* you survive," Diane corrects me.

"Right. That's what I meant."

William hasn't said much throughout all of this; mostly he's just sat quietly, holding tight to Annie's hand. Now he asks, "But you still don't have a plan? I mean for how you're going to stop Mr. Gabriel once he gets his body back?"

"No," I admit. "Not yet."

"Look, I know I'm the new guy around here, but I gotta say . . . this all just seems like a disaster waiting to happen."

"It's a disaster already happening," Diane mutters.

"I know," I say again. "I know. I just . . . I'm working on it, okay? I'm going to come up with something, I swear."

Leticia looks like she's about to say something else, but just then I notice that Ryan is suddenly looking past me with a grim expression. Everyone else notices me noticing, and we all turn to see what he's looking at.

It's Jeff, wandering over to a table on the other side of the room.

"Who's that?" asks Peter.

"That's the guy trying to steal Ryan's part," Leticia says. "We hate him."

"Reallllly?" Peter purrs. And then he launches out of his seat and makes a beeline toward Jeff's table.

"Hey!" Ryan says in alarm. He stares at me pleadingly. "Cyn! Make him stop!"

"How? I can't just body slam him in the middle of the cafeteria!"

Ryan's face suggests that he would have liked me to try, but I would never have caught up to Peter in time anyway. That guy can move eerily fast when he wants to. He's already smiling and chatting with Jeff and the other kids at the table.

"How am I supposed to stop fighting with him when he keeps provoking me?"

"I'm trusting you to be the bigger man."

"I *am* the bigger man," Ryan mutters, sticking his fork rather aggressively into his cafeteria lasagna. Annie, Leticia, and Diane (and, okay, me, too) are all suppressing smiles with varying degrees of success. William looks sympathetic.

Peter doesn't come back until we're all leaving for our next classes. "Nice guy, that Jeff," he says. "Did you know he played Javert at his old school, too?"

"He's not *playing* Javert at this school," Ryan growls, dumping his trash in the bin.

"Oh, yeah. Callbacks aren't until Friday, right? Hmm. Well, good luck."

Ryan walks out without saying another word.

"Please stop trying to start trouble," I tell Peter. "Seriously. Do you think I need more trouble right now?"

"It's good for him," Peter says. "Anyway, at the very least it's probably distracting him a little from the curse slowly trying to kill him. Besides, I needed the boost."

"Please don't create drama for Ryan just because you need a snack," I tell him. "I'm sure we can find you some good old-fashioned high-school drama elsewhere if you really need some."

"Okay, okay," Peter says. But somehow I don't feel entirely reassured.

After school, Ryan goes home to get ready for his voice lesson. Peter went off again after lunch to try to consult with some "friends" about the prison thing. I have no idea who these friends might be; as far as I know, he hasn't found a new Hector, and a human assistant wouldn't be any help in this case anyway. Maybe he's going to summon that tiny demon again. Whatever it is, I assume he's still at it and head home.

Both my parents are still working when I get there, which allows me to sneak my demon-filth-encrusted clothes into the wash and change out of my gym clothes without having to field any awkward questions. Then I take a nice long hot shower, washing my hair twice this time. Then I try to read my book for English, wanting to believe that it's going to matter at some point, but mostly I sit there staring at the pages and trying to figure out how we're going to kill Mr. Gabriel after we help him get his body back.

It's close to seven when I hear the doorbell ring. I assume it's the delivery guy from whatever place we're getting dinner from tonight, but then my mom's voice calls up from the foot of the stairs. "Cyn! You have a . . . visitor."

I put my book down and glance at the hallway toward the stairs. A visitor? Who —? But then I know.

I run downstairs to find Peter sitting on the couch, smiling blindingly up at my mother. She turns and raises a very articulate eyebrow at me as I arrive, breathless, too late.

"So, this is Peter," she says. "Your . . . camp friend."

"Just in town visiting my uncle," Peter says brightly. "Hi, Cyn! I thought I'd surprise you."

"Well, you succeeded," I say, trying to shoot daggers at him from my eyes without letting my mother see. She's too distracted with work to pay much attention to my life most of the time, but when she *is* paying attention, she doesn't miss a thing. And there are so very many things I need her to miss right now. There's a limit to how much demon-magic-smoothing-over I really want Peter to do to my family.

"Come on upstairs," I tell him. My mom's other eyebrow goes up, and I roll my eyes at her. "I'll leave the door open, Mom. No sex or drugs, I promise."

Peter laughs charmingly, and after a second my mother joins in. "Would you like to stay for dinner, Peter? We're having chicken."

I stare at her. "You're *cooking*?"

"Yes, I do that sometimes. Not on weeknights, usually, I know, but oddly everything kind of wrapped itself up early tonight, so I thought I'd take advantage."

"I'd love to, Mrs. Rothschild," Peter says before I can recover enough from my surprise about the cooking to stop him.

"Wonderful. I'll call you kids down when it's ready." She turns and heads for the kitchen.

I grab Peter's hand and very ungently drag him up the stairs.

"What are you *doing* here?" I hiss at him once we're in my room.

"Aw, I missed you, too, Cyn."

"Peter . . ."

"Come on, where else was I going to go? Anyway, I wanted to tell you that I'll be ready to try to get us back tomorrow."

My annoyance evaporates at once. "Really?"

"Yup. There's a variation on a summoning procedure that I'd been hoping I could use when I left that marker with LB. I had to confirm a few things, but I think I know how to do it now. As long as our spidery companion is really still where we left him, I should be able to open a gateway right back there."

I sit heavily down on my bed. "I feel so odd right now. So relieved and so terrified all at the same time."

"Yeah," he says, sitting next to me. "So this is your room, hmm?" He looks around with interest. "It's more traditional than I'd imagined. I thought there'd be, like, hammers and half-deconstructed set pieces lying around, and maybe a mattress in a corner as an afterthought."

"Gee, thanks."

"What? It's a compliment! You're committed to your art."

"I'm committed to my art *and* I like to have a nice room to hang out in and a comfortable bed."

"I stand corrected." He bounces experimentally on the bed. "It does seem comfortable. And quiet. Not squeaky at all. I mean if you were doing anything on it that might . . ."

I get up hastily and cross to my desk chair.

"Cyn?" my mother's voice comes calling up to me again. "You, uh, have another visitor. Ryan's here. I'll just—um, send him up. Now. Okay?"

"Yes, of course!" I call back, darting out to meet him at the top of the stairs.

"*Another* visitor?" he asks.

"Peter's here. He thinks he knows how to get us back down to the prison." I say this all in one great rush, before Ryan has a chance to get mad.

He still gets kind of mad, though.

"He couldn't tell you tomorrow?"

"Don't be like that. Come on." I lead the way back to my room.

"That's why your mom was being so weird," he says behind me. "She thought you might be up here making out or something and didn't want to send me up unannounced."

"Oh, stop it," I say, even though I'm sure that's exactly what my mother was thinking.

Peter, of course, is sprawled out on my bed, carefully positioned to one side as though to indicate that just until recently I was lying there beside him.

"I was sitting in the desk chair!" I nearly shout, pointing to it as though somehow that will help make my assertion more believable. "Peter, can you please stop being an ass for one second maybe?"

"Doubtful," Ryan mutters. He walks over to the bed and sits down, pushing Peter's feet unceremoniously out of the way.

"How was the voice lesson?" I ask.

"Fine." He's clearly not in the mood to be chatty with Peter here.

"You know," Peter says, sitting up, "if you're really that worried, I'd be happy to —"

Ryan turns on him so quickly he's practically a blur.

"Don't you dare," he says. His voice is so tight and threatening that my mouth falls open. I've never heard him sound like that before. His finger is about an inch away from Peter's left eye. "If you interfere in *any* way, I swear to God, Peter —"

"He won't," I break in, not wanting to let Ryan finish that sentence. I lean over and pull his hand gently away from Peter's face. "He won't do a thing. Right, Peter?"

Peter begins one of his noncommittal shrugs and mischievous smiles, but I am having none of that. If I'd had any doubt how important winning this role is to Ryan — which I didn't — the utter seriousness in his every cell at this moment would have driven the message home with deadly force. It's not just about this part anymore for him. It's about his entire future. If he doesn't earn this role fair and square, he's never going to have faith in himself again. It's stupid, because there's really no such thing as fair and square when it comes to casting, but I know that's how he feels. If Ryan gets the part, he has to feel like he deserves it. I can't let Peter taint this victory for him. I can't.

I drag my desk chair over to the bed and sit down, facing Peter, and look him dead in the eye. "Stop it. Right now. This is off-limits, do you hear me? If you do anything to influence callbacks, I will have nothing to do with you ever again. Ever. I mean it."

"Come on, I was only—"

"I mean it, Peter. We'll be done. Forever."

I watch as he takes in how much I really mean this. His smile vanishes.

"Okay. Okay, sure."

"Swear to me."

"I swear, Cyn."

I believe him. I know how much our friendship means to him. And . . . how much he wants it to be more. I don't think he'd do anything to destroy whatever tiny chance he imagines might still be there.

I sit back, exhaling. "Okay, then."

"Cyn?" My dad's voice now, calling up the stairs. "Your mother wants to know if Ryan is staying for dinner, too?"

"Yes," I call back, not taking my eyes off the two of them. I hate how shaken Peter looks, but it's his own fault; he was totally asking for it. And the relief in Ryan's eyes more than makes up for it. I need him to keep believing in himself. And believing that I believe in him, too.

"Now," I continue. "We are going to go downstairs and have a perfectly normal dinner with my parents. Right?"

"Right," they answer in unison. They glance at each other, but neither of them says anything else.

"Great."

Of course, it's not normal at all. It's the most awkward family dinner ever. But only in the expected ways that having dinner with your parents and your boyfriend and your attractive, male "camp friend" would be, and Peter and Ryan both try really hard not to make it any worse, and so they both get points for that.

Afterward, I walk them both out to the sidewalk.

"Where are you sleeping, Peter?" I ask him.

"Not here," Ryan says at once. I jab him with my elbow in the universal gesture of *shut up, you jerk*.

Peter gives me a strained smile. "My uncle's place, of course." He winks at me, but he's not selling it. Then before I can say anything else, he gives Ryan a weird sort of half salute and walks off down the street.

"His uncle?" Ryan asks.

"It's what he told my mother he was doing in town. Visiting. I'm sure he'll end up at some nice hotel or something. Probably a penthouse suite with free champagne and stuff. I'm not worried."

I am a little worried, though. Peter looked so sad in that last second before he turned away.

"Well, you know I'm not worried, either," Ryan says, putting an arm around me. "Thanks, for before."

"Of course. Peter takes things too far sometimes, but not when he really knows better. I just made sure he knows better now." I look up at Ryan. "How did the voice lesson go, really?"

"It was great. I'm going to kick Jeff's vocal ass."

"Of course you are," I agree. I squeeze him and then lean up for a kiss.

Ryan's not selling it, either. But I pretend that he is.

Chapter | 14

In the morning, we all go to school like it's a normal day. I make Ryan let me check his arm first thing; the red line is at his shoulder now. He swears it still doesn't hurt, but I'm not sure I believe him. And whether it hurts or not, it's definitely getting way too close to his heart.

We are running out of time.

I notice that everyone decided to wear comfortable clothing and shoes. Even Diane, which is extremely suspicious, since she is renowned for her impractical shoe choices. (William is dressed comfortably, too, but he usually is, and also he is way too reasonable to try to force his way into a trip to the demon world.)

"You guys are still not coming," I tell Leticia and Diane as we make our way to the library.

They exchange disgruntled glances. "Told you," Diane says.

Leticia shrugs and hands Diane a dollar. "It was worth a try."

They don't argue, but I see how unhappy they are with this situation. It makes me a little mad. "Have you guys not been listening to how horrible everything has been down there? Why would you possibly want to come with us?"

Diane stops abruptly and puts her hands on her hips. "Do you really not get it, Cyn? Are you that clueless?"

I stop, too, shocked at her tone. Diane is always the calm one among us. The one who remains unruffled no matter what. But she's definitely ruffled now.

"Do you really not see how hard it is to have to stay behind, knowing what's happening to all of you, knowing that you're fighting for your lives, making deals for *our* lives, and we're just here sitting in class and going through the day like nothing is wrong? When *everything is wrong*?"

"D, come on—" Leticia begins, touching her arm, but Diane shakes her off.

"No. I hate this. I hate us being stuck here not knowing whether the rest of you are alive or dead. It sucks."

"I—I'm sorry," I say. "I wasn't thinking. Of course it sucks. I hate that any of this is happening. You know that. But please believe me when I say that you guys being in danger too is not the answer."

"I know that!" Diane snaps. "I know, okay? But I can't stand this." This time when Leticia reaches for her she lets herself be reached. Leticia wraps her in a tight hug and gives me a hard-to-read look over her girlfriend's head. Sort of half apology and half agreement. With a sprinkling of also hating that any of this is happening.

"Come on, Diane," Leticia says now, walking Diane forward, her voice forcibly lighter. "If they all die, we're going to have to be the ones to carry on their legacy and keep their memories alive. And if they don't, we're going to have to let them copy our notes from math and history so they don't flunk out of their senior year. Our job is very important either way."

"Stop trying to make me feel better," Diane mutters, but she sounds less mad. "I don't want to feel better."

"Too bad," Leticia says. "That's what I do. And that's why you love me, so shut up."

"You shut up."

They slow down and I take the hint and keep moving, giving them some space for the rest of the walk to the library.

I'd hoped to convince Annie to stay behind this time, too, but as soon as I quietly mentioned the idea to Peter, he shook his head. All four of us have to go back through for what he's doing to work. Something about setting up a mirror aspect of the portal spell to reverse the polarity of the something or other. Usually I'm really interested in the technical aspects of things, but after his third attempt at explaining still left me totally confused, I decided I didn't really need to understand all the details, as long as it does the trick.

Leon greets us warmly at the library doors, then shows Peter where Mrs. Davenforth is so that he can convince her that she needs to stay quietly in her office for the next hour. Leon then goes back and mans the door, ready to turn away any potential visitors.

Peter's demonic powers of persuasion are really very handy.

The rest of us go back to the reading area and pull the chairs out of the way. Peter starts sketching something complicated on the carpet with lines of demonic energy. I am both terribly impatient for and absolutely dreading the moment when he finishes. Since then, of course, the next step will be the four of us returning to the demon prison and all of the monsters and everything else. And then getting the thing from the Craftsman and then going back to Mr. Gabriel and *then* —

"Hey," Ryan says, nudging me gently. "I can see that you are standing there thinking unhelpful thoughts. Cut it out."

"How can you see that?"

"Your face is exactly like the tragic drama-mask symbol right now."

"Oh."

"Cheer up. I hear you're missing a really boring lab in chem today."

"Oh, good. I'd hate to be bored when I can be terrified instead."

"Right on."

Too soon, but also not soon enough, Peter steps back from his creation. "All right," he says. "Everyone say your good-byes and then those of you staying behind should go back over there by the wall."

There is some hugging and murmuring and one extremely lengthy and passionate kiss between Annie and William that we all pretend not to notice, and then Ryan, Annie, and I all stand in a line beside Peter at the edge of the diagram. Only Peter and I can actually see it, but he has placed some books along the closest edge to show Ryan and Annie where it begins.

"So," Peter says. "Here's what's going to happen. We will all hold hands. On my mark, we will all step over the threshold of the gateway at the same time. Almost immediately, we will get sucked down into a kind of tunnel that will bring us back to the prison. It will be scary and probably also very loud. Do not let go of each other. No matter what." He looks around at us. "Any questions?"

"Will it hurt?" asks Annie.

Peter looks at her for a long second. "Let's say no."

Since I haven't yet had a trip to the demon world that didn't feel like knives or ice or fire, I was expecting it to be unpleasant. But I still really wish Peter was more convincing a liar.

"Okay, hold hands."

We do as instructed. Ryan is on one side of me and Peter is on the other. Annie is on the other side of Peter.

"Everyone is really, really clear on the not-letting-go part, right?"

We all nod.

"Okay. I'm going to count to three. On three, we all step forward. *On* three. Got it?"

We all nod again.

"One . . . two . . . *three.*"

We all step forward.

It feels like something has punched through my stomach to grab hold of my spine. And then the something yanks me down and forward into a tunnel of light and pain. Everyone is screaming. I now understand why Peter kept repeating the not-letting-go thing. It's hard to think about anything but the pain. But I try. I try to focus on my hands grasping Ryan's and Peter's. I try to feel secure in the knowledge that Peter is holding tight to Annie. I try to believe that this can't possibly last very long, that surely it's already almost over, that any second we'll arrive back in the room where we left LB and everything will be . . . well, not *fine* — ha-ha, that's funny — but at least less painful. Less painful would be really, really welcome right now.

It's lasting way longer than I thought it would and I want to ask Peter if it's almost over because I don't think I can stand much more of this but of course there's no way to ask because that would require not screaming and I definitely can't stop screaming because *oh my God it hurts so much.* I grip Ryan's and Peter's hands even tighter, as tight as I can, so tight that I'm not sure I'll ever be able to let go but that's okay, we can just hold hands forever, that would be fine as long as the pain would stop.

And then suddenly I smack into a hard surface and for a moment the world just goes away, all of it, even the pain, which is nice, *really* nice, but then I start to panic about not being able to feel anything because I need to make sure I'm still holding everyone's hands and I can't tell, I can't, I need to look and see but I can't find my eyes, I don't remember how to use them.

"Cyn! Cyn, it's okay! Stop — you can let go."

"No, no, I can't, Peter said —"

"This is Peter. Open your eyes, Cyn."

And now I can remember where my eyes are, and I open them. And it is Peter, and he has let go of Annie's hand, and she seems okay, and so that must mean it really is time to let go. Still, it takes me a second to force my fingers to release their grip.

Once Annie assures herself that I'm okay, she rounds on Peter and starts hitting him anywhere she can reach with tiny little Annie punches. "You liar!" she shouts. "You said it wouldn't hurt!"

Ryan, able to move about freely now that I have unclenched my hand from his, gently takes hold of Annie and pulls her away from Peter, who has not attempted to defend himself. "Annie, that doesn't count as a lie," he tells her. "Come on. It was too obvious. We weren't supposed to believe it."

Now Annie turns on Ryan. "Well, I did believe it! And that was — it was —" She goes limp in Ryan's arms and starts to cry.

I get to my feet and go to her. A small, petty part of me wants to point out that this is exactly why she should never have come here in the first place. But the rest of me just hates that she's so upset, and wants to try to make her feel better. "It's okay," I tell her. "It's okay. It's over now."

"It's not over," she whimpers into Ryan's shirt. "We're still here. We still have so much to do. And William is starting to feel like this is all too much, he's totally going to break up with me soon, I can tell."

"What? No, Annie —"

"Yes. I can see it. He wants a normal girlfriend who doesn't have a demonic stalker. I don't blame him. This is all so crazy and awful. And we still might not even win. It might all be for nothing and then Mr. Gabriel — he'll get me and I'll — I'll have

211

to stay here forever. *Forever,* Cyn, with *him,* oh, God, I can't, I *can't* —"

"Shh." I place one hand softly against her sweet, soft, curly-haired head. "He's not going to win. Are you kidding me? We'd never let him have you. Don't you dare worry about that."

I'm impressed with how calm and sure I sound. I almost believe me myself. Even though inside I know it's all bullshit, and I'm terrified that she might be right, and he *will* win, and all of the worst things ever will come true.

"He will not win," a gravelly voice says from behind me.

LB is — well, sitting is maybe not the right word. He's crouching on his spider legs in the corner, watching us. I'd nearly forgotten to worry that he hadn't stayed here as instructed. But of course he did, because here we are. And here he is. I could kiss him. Except still not really, because ew.

"LB!" I say. I go over to place my hand carefully on his mud- and blood-encrusted body. "Thank you. Thank you for staying here like we asked."

"You have returned," he says. He doesn't seem to quite believe it.

"Of course we returned. I promised, didn't I?"

"Yes. But . . ." He pauses, and I wait for the thinking to happen. "A promise is still not a deal."

"No, it's not. A promise is never going to be a deal. It's its own thing. A promise is a promise. Deals . . . deals you have no choice but to honor, right? But a promise . . . a promise you have to try really hard to keep. It's not always easy, but it's really important."

He looks blankly at me for a long moment. "I do not understand."

I give him another pat. "I know. It's okay. People stuff probably seems as messed up to you as demon stuff does to me. Anyway, it doesn't matter, does it? We're all together again, and now we can get back on track."

I focus on my internal compass, which was quiet the whole time we were back in the regular world. It now seems to sense my attention, however, and tugs especially eagerly toward the same wall as before.

"Peter," I say, beckoning him over. "Can you get us out of this room without triggering another trap? Because I really don't want to have to make that return trip ever, ever again."

"Yes," he says. "But everyone needs to do exactly as I say and *step only where I tell them to*." He glares pointedly at Ryan while he says this last part.

"Yeah, yeah," Ryan says. "Lesson learned, okay? Lead on, O demon guide."

Peter studies the stone walls for a minute and then the markings along the ground near each passage. He picks the one on the right for no clear reason that I can see, but I am more than ready to trust his judgment on this. And then he successfully guides us all carefully out of the room. Even LB, who I must admit I was pretty worried about with all those extra legs.

The tugging gets more intense the farther we go. I point where it seems to be leading, and Peter walks beside me, watching to make sure we don't run into any more sneaky traps or anything else. Ryan and Annie walk behind us, and

LB brings up the rear. The passages we're following all slope undeniably downward, and I don't love the feeling that we're sinking deeper and deeper into a hole we might not be able to climb out of. But it's not like we have a choice; the whole point of coming here was to find this guy. So I swallow my misgivings, and I keep walking. And my friends keep walking with me.

The compass seems to be getting a lot more detailed about its directions. More than once it nudges me to the right or left just before Peter points out something suspicious he wants us to step carefully around. Another time it yanks me backward abruptly, and the feeling is so full of warning and intent that I throw out my hand to stop Peter and the others as well.

Everyone instinctually goes quiet and waits. After a second, a large black shadow crosses our passageway up ahead and continues into an adjoining corridor.

Where were you when we were trying to avoid the monsters earlier? I ask it silently. But I think I know. I wasn't listening to it before, so it wasn't trying to help me. Now that I'm going where it wants, it's trying to make sure I actually get there. Maybe this is why Mr. Gabriel thought I had a shot at making it through alive on my own.

After another moment, the compass tugs me forward again. I consider telling Peter he can stop looking for danger, that my GPS has it covered, but decide against it. Just in case. Seeing as how the demon-compass was a gift from Mr. Gabriel, I can't quite bring myself to trust it all the way.

Suddenly we come around a corner into a large chamber,

larger than anyplace we've seen inside the prison so far. We stop, staring. The chamber is filled with prison cells. Or what look like prison cells, anyway. Everywhere we look, there are circles of vertical iron bars that stretch up and up until they disappear into the not-ceiling above us.

"I thought you said this wasn't like a regular prison," I whisper to Peter.

"Are you seriously calling this a 'regular prison'?" he whispers back.

"You know what I mean! I thought there weren't any cells."

"Well, apparently there are. Sorry. I told you I've never actually been in here."

Inside each circle is a demon.

This must be the deepest prisoner level that the flower monster was talking about.

And these must be the deepest prisoners.

Almost as one, they turn to stare at us. The entire chamber is deathly silent. The demons aren't moving, they aren't making a sound, they're just staring out at us from within their iron cages. They're all different — all different shapes and sizes and sporting various elements of animals and plants and I-can't-even-tell-what-else — but there's a similarity to them, too. It's something about the coiled tension in each of their stances, the sense of unrestrained danger that emanates from each one. All demons are dangerous, of course; nearly any demon would kill any one of us without hesitation, feeding off our pain and terror and eventual death. But these . . . these demons are worse somehow. There's an almost palpable layer of insanity coming from each one. Insanity and malice and . . . hunger.

I swallow hard and swing my arm to follow the direction of my inner compass. It points unwaveringly toward a cell at the farthest end of the chamber.

The demon inside looks kind of like Jabba the Hutt, if Jabba had a messed up fox head and several long arms resembling tree branches, each of which extended into delicate stick-like fingers. Except not really like branches and sticks, because as I watch they bend with a supple elasticity that makes me think of rubber bands. Except rubber bands that are alive and can grab you and do horrible things to you.

Ryan steps up beside me. "Is that him?" he whispers.

"Apparently," I whisper back.

I start walking toward the Jabba-fox-tree demon, keeping a careful distance from the other cells. Everyone else follows closely behind me. It's still eerily silent; all of the demons continue to stand still, watching us. They turn to follow us with whatever passes for their eyes as we go past. And straight ahead the Craftsman waits, what looks like a smile on his misshapen fox-like lips.

I stop a few feet away from his cell, afraid to go any closer, even though the compass inside me is pulsing impatiently, urging me forward so it can be *exactly* where its quarry is waiting, just ahead.

"Are you the Craftsman?" I ask him.

He is definitely smiling now. His fox head tilts slightly sideways as he considers me.

"Some have called me by that name," he says at last. His

voice is deep and unpleasant and heavily demon-accented, but at least he speaks words that I can understand.

"We were sent here by the demon who calls himself John Gabriel. He said — he said you have an object that he requires. The missing piece of the amulet you created."

His eyes seem to flare at the mention of the amulet, but his smile never changes.

"Come closer," he says after a minute. "Come here to where I can see you properly."

"Don't you dare," Ryan stage-whispers at me. I feel his hand grip the back of my shirt, bunching the fabric into a tight little ball.

"I'm not coming any closer," I tell the demon.

He shrugs his Jabba-like bulk expansively, but his eyes never leave mine. "Then I suppose you will not get what you came for."

Dammit.

I turn around to face the others, freeing my shirt from Ryan's hand. "This is ridiculous. We didn't come all this way only to fail because I won't walk over there. I'm going to do it."

"No!" Ryan, Annie, and Peter say in unison.

I raise my eyes to look at LB.

"He will not kill you right away," LB says slowly. "He will want to keep you here to entertain him as long as possible. It is . . . boring . . . in prison. Usually."

"Right," I say. "Okay."

I turn back around and walk over to the cell, ignoring my friends' unhappy noises behind me.

"Can you see me now?"

The fox-head smile stretches impossibly wide. "Yesssss," he says. With lightning speed, he reaches between the bars with his rubber-band twig-hands. One wraps itself tightly around my wrist, jerking me forward against the cell.

"Cyn!" Ryan shouts, and I glance back to see Peter restraining him from racing over to me.

"It's okay!" I call to him, my voice shaking uncontrollably.

It's *so* not okay. But Ryan coming over to join me would not help matters.

I look up into the crazy eyes of the Craftsman. He's even more horrible this close up. There's something very wrong about his fox parts. Normally I *like* foxes, I think they're majestic and pretty, but he's like . . . he's like someone's idea of a fox after hearing the description via a drunken, late-night game of telephone.

He grins at me for an uncomfortably long time, and I feel like he's looking right through my skin. For a moment my demon-compass is a hot, frantic engine inside me, burning up in its own ecstasy at reaching its intended goal, and then it's gone.

"Ah, yessss," he says. "I know what you seek." He turns and seems to dig around in the folds of his own disgusting Jabba-like hide for a few seconds. Then one of his other twig-hands pulls out what looks like a small bloodred stone.

"John Gabriel wants this. The final piece of my greatest creation."

"Yes," I say, relieved that he seems to understand the situation. "So if you could just hand it over . . ."

He laughs. He throws his head back and laughs exactly the deep, evil laugh that you would expect from a demon that sort of looks like Jabba the Hutt.

"Something's funny?" I ask, trying and failing to wrench my wrist free of his grip.

"You think I will give this to you. You think you will just ask me and I will give it to you and you will go along on your way."

"Not exactly," I say, trying to sound confident. "I assume you will want something in return." Hopefully Mr. Gabriel's suggestion of future favors will be enough; I don't have anything else to offer.

He laughs again. "No."

"No?"

"No. I will not give it to you. I see how desperately you want it. You have come here, to where no one comes. You have been injured, you have been in pain. This is very important to you. You have braved so much, come so far. And here it is" — he holds the stone up in front of my face — "here is the thing that you have come so far to find. I have it here, right here. You can almost touch it. And I could give it to you. I could give it to you and you could take it and try to find whatever reward you are thinking you will find."

"Yes," I say, or try to say, but it only comes out as the barest whisper. His fingers are hurting my wrist, but I don't want to let him know that.

"But what pleasure would that give me? No. No, *this* is pleasure. To see how badly you want this. To see how you are even now thinking of what you can offer me, whether it would be better to beg, or to demand, or to bargain. You will have time to try all of those things. We will stay here, you and I, just like this. For so many hours. For days. For years, maybe. We will see how many different ways you can try to get it from me. And I will still say no. Always. Just because I can."

"But . . . but Mr. Gabriel said when he is king, he could set you free—"

"When. If. A time that may never come. But this time, this moment, is happening now. And I like this time, this now. I like it very much. I will not trade it for an uncertain future. I will keep it. For as long as I desire."

He seems to have forgotten everyone else. I have almost forgotten them myself, lost in the malicious madness of those not-quite-fox-like eyes. He's right; it's torture to see the glinting stone right there, inches away from me, and know I can't have it. It begins to glow, as if it, too, is taunting me. He's holding Ryan's life right there in his hand. He's holding all of our lives, really. He's holding everything, every tiny lingering thread of possibility we still have. I feel the tightness of his grip around my wrist, feel how the bark-like edges of his fingers are even now tearing at my skin, and I see how he will never get tired of this, never— that he really could keep me here forever, baiting me, wanting to keep me begging for as long as any tiny sliver of hope remains inside my weary heart, and it's all I can do not to slide into despair right now.

"Yessss," he says, looking deep into my eyes. "You understand. You see how it will be. You will resist, but eventually you will begin to beg me. You will think that maybe, someday, I will relent. But I will not. I will —"

And then he jerks suddenly backward, crying out and staring wildly around as Annie darts away from the cage with the glowing stone tucked firmly into her hand.

Chapter | 15

The shriek of pure rage that the Craftsman lets out is the scariest thing I have ever heard in my entire life.

He expands, roaring, filling the confines of his cell and pressing his brown-gray flesh against the bars until I am afraid they may burst apart. The other demons begin to scream along with him, whether in sympathy or derision or just for the joy of screaming I have no way to know.

The one upside of this terrifying development is that, in his fury, he has loosened his grip on my wrist.

I yank myself away and race toward where the others are standing, wide-eyed and frantic. *"Run!"* I scream at them, and they do, thank God, except LB, who waits for me to reach him first.

I tear past him, catching up with the others, and he falls into line behind me. The other demons snatch at us as we pass their cages, but Peter — who has ended up in front — manages to lead us through the widest places, keeping us just out of reach.

"No!" the Craftsman thunders from behind us. "You will *not*! You —" His words dissolve, unraveling into a fresh burst of screaming accompanied by a horrible wet crackling sound. I can't help it; I glance behind me.

The demon has stretched some of his tree-like arms through the bars. At first I think he is just reaching toward us in his madness and frustration, but then I see that his long, stick-fingered hands are breaking apart from the rest of him. They fly forward, racing toward us on what are now flexible twig-like legs. As they run, eyes blink open in their centers, in what is left of the flesh that binds the legs together. The eyes are dark and senseless. They are followed very quickly by gashes of red wounds that open into mouths.

"He's coming!" I scream. "He's coming!"

Peter turns to see what I can possibly mean and nearly stumbles into the arms of a demon reaching out from one of the nearest cells.

"The ejection trap!" I shout at Peter. "We have to go back to the trap!"

He nods and takes off again, urging the others to greater speed alongside him.

I don't dare look back to see if those things are gaining on us. I just run, with everything that I have. I watch Ryan ahead of me, reaching out to Annie and trying to help her forward. Ryan could have outrun all of us by now if he were really going full speed. Part of me wants to tell him to leave us and go, save himself, but of course he'd never. And besides, if the rest of us died here, he wouldn't have a way to get the amulet stone back to Mr. Gabriel, and so he'd die anyway.

We follow Peter down passage after passage, trusting him to lead us back, trusting that we'll avoid the dangerous marks on the ground, trusting that there's even a tiny chance we might get away. LB is still behind me, still running, which has to mean that the hand-things haven't quite caught up yet. I have a stitch in my side like a knife and I can't breathe but I can't stop, none of us can stop, and so I keep going. I try to remember how much worse the pain was in Peter's tunnel, how much worse it will be if those things catch up to us. What would happen if they caught us and dragged us back to the Craftsman, all rage and madness waiting to be unleashed.

Suddenly Peter stumbles to a halt and stretches his arms out to stop us as well.

"Together!" he shouts. "We all have to go in together. To be sure."

"Wait!" I've just thought of something terrible. "Will it take LB? He didn't come with us last time —"

Peter hesitates for the tiniest second. "Yes! Just — we just have to all hold on to each other!"

Everyone grabs someone else. I reach back for LB's leg without hesitation and pull him forward, closer to me. And then I feel him jerk behind me, and I turn to see that one of the hand-things has launched itself at his back. He swipes it off with one of his free legs, knocking it into the others coming up fast behind it.

"Now, Peter! Now!"

He doesn't bother to count to three this time. We throw

ourselves into the chamber with the markings, racing toward the one that sent us back before. I have a single moment to worry that it won't work a second time, that we'll be stuck here and the things will get us, all of us, drag us away screaming to a fate I can't even imagine, but then the familiar glowing light opens in the wall, and I have never been so happy to see a demon portal in all of my life.

"LB!" Peter shouts. "Grab all of us and take us through together! Right now!"

LB acts immediately, wrapping spider legs around each of us, even Peter, and hurls us all as one into the shining hole.

The library reading area materializes once again around us. LB drops us, seeming disoriented. He takes a wobbly step sideways and immediately knocks over an entire shelf of books.

"What in the world—" Mrs. Davenforth's alarmed voice reaches us from the other side of the library.

Peter waves a hand and the school fire alarm suddenly begins pealing out its this-is-not-a-drill pattern, and then we hear the main library doors open and Mrs. Davenforth calmly instructing students to file out to the emergency exits. She's certain to check for stragglers before leaving herself, however. Soothing her after she gets a glimpse of LB standing in the middle of her library might be more than Peter's demon abilities are up for.

"Everyone stand completely still and don't make a sound," Peter whispers urgently. He makes another motion, and I see a hint of demon energy flash around us.

We freeze, waiting. The librarian's footsteps come toward

us, her heels clacking against the floor tiles until they reach the carpet that marks the beginning of the reading area.

She finds the toppled bookshelf and *tsks* in annoyance, seeming ready to start picking up the spilled books at once, before she apparently remembers the fire alarm. She straightens as if to leave, but then pauses again, looking around to see what could have caused this to happen.

"And who moved the damn chairs . . . ?" she mutters to herself. Her eyes pass right over us, several times, as she continues scanning the room for clues about the guilty parties.

With a final irritated shake of her head, she turns and clacks purposefully to the doors, closing them behind her.

We wait a few more seconds to be sure she's not coming back, then everyone seems to exhale at once. Peter waves his hand, and I assume his glamour is undone. While LB still appears distracted, trying to get his bearings, I move closer to Peter and whisper, "Did you know for sure? About LB?"

He looks at me. "No. I hoped, but I wasn't sure. Since he wasn't a prisoner, I didn't think the prison would care about keeping him in there, but . . ." He waits, probably expecting a reprimand, but I only nod my head wearily. There was no time. He had to make a call. A discussion would probably have left us all dead.

"Cyn," Ryan says suddenly, his voice sounding strange. I turn around just as he sinks into one of the reading chairs. His face is . . . gray.

Oh, no.

I'm at his side immediately. "What's wrong? Is it — where's the line?"

He doesn't even try to fight me as I pull up his shirt. I hear Annie gasp behind me. The line has started its journey across his chest. I'm no expert on human anatomy, but I know roughly where the heart is, and the line has clearly almost reached its destination.

I turn to Peter. "We have to go, now. We have to get that thing to Mr. Gabriel."

Which suddenly reminds me of how we even have that thing.

I whip around to face Annie, who is watching me warily. Part of me wants to murder her for putting herself in danger like that. But it's a pretty small part. Mostly I am just profoundly grateful. And really, really proud.

I pull her into a hug and squeeze her tight against me. She relaxes into it, hugging me back.

"Thank you," I tell her. "You're a crazy lunatic and I can't believe you did that, but — thank you. I think you saved all of our lives back there."

"Well, I owed you at least one life-saving," she says, pulling back. She's smiling, happy and more than a little proud herself, I think. "It was only fair."

"We are going to talk more about this later," I say. "But right now —"

"I know. We have to take Ryan back to get the curse removed."

I take a deep breath. "Annie, you have to stay here this time."

Her smile fades at once, replaced by that hard little line that I hate. "Cyn, after what —"

"I know. After what you just did, how I can possibly expect you to stay behind now? Because you have to. Because now we are going directly to Mr. Gabriel. The guy who *abducted* you and *brainwashed* you and wants to *steal you away for all eternity*. We cannot just parade you around in front of him, Annie. Come on."

"She's right, Annie," Peter says. "You know she is."

"I don't care," Annie says fiercely. "I am not being left behind. I can stand up to him. I'm not — I'm not going to keep being afraid all the time. I have to face him."

"No," says LB, who has been standing very still in the corner, apparently trying very hard not to knock over anything else. "You must not face him. I know exactly what he plans for you. You must not let him have you. If you go to him . . . you will not be able to fight. Not enough. He is too strong. He will win." He glances at me, half apologetic, half something else. "I am speaking up about what I know."

"Thank you," I say, meaning it.

Ryan groans behind me, and we all turn to look at him. One of his hands is resting on his heart.

"Annie, please," I say. "We have to go. There's no time to argue. Please. Give me the stone and let us go."

"Okay," she whispers. Her face is pale again, and the proud confidence that was shining there before has vanished without a trace.

"You were amazing back there," I tell her, hating to see her wilting this way. "But this fight . . . this one is not for you."

"It's absolutely for me," she says back, not meeting my eyes. "I'm the one he wants."

"Annie—"

She holds out her hand, the amulet stone in her palm. "Take it. I know you have to go. And I know . . . I know it would be stupid to go with you." Now she meets my eyes, and I can see she's struggling not to cry. "But I still wish I could. I hate this. I want to be there to see it end."

"I know."

"Please kill him for good this time, Cyn. Okay?"

"Oh, Annie. I promise." And I so want that to be a promise I can keep. But we didn't have time to make a plan. I have no idea what we're going to do once we give the stone to him and he un-curses Ryan.

She hugs me again and then presses the stone into my hand. It's no longer glowing, but I can feel the electricity of it, the pent-up power. Waiting.

"All right," Peter says. "Portal time."

For the first time I notice that he's not looking quite a hundred percent himself. "Hey, are you okay? Did—did you take in more of LB's poison?"

"Just a little. It's okay."

"I can try to heal you again—"

"No. You're going to need every bit of your strength down there. I'm fine. Now hurry up before your boyfriend dies right here in the comfy reading chair."

With that, he starts sketching out another symbol on the floor. I go back to Ryan and help him to his feet. Annie goes back against the wall, watching us sorrowfully.

"Where are you going to take us?" I ask Peter.

"Outside the prison gate," he says, still sketching. He has

to make a much larger shape this time to be able to include LB. "I think Mr. Crunchy will be waiting there to escort us back. Which is probably safer than trying to make our own way around unprotected."

"We can't just go directly back to where Mr. Gabriel is?"

Peter shakes his head. "I don't know exactly how to get back there from here. And . . . it might be good to keep LB a secret from him as long as we can. LB is pretty much our one advantage, and he'll be more so if his appearance is a surprise."

With everything else to worry about, I'd completely forgotten about the unpleasantness of the journey ahead of us. When LB, Peter, and I, supporting Ryan between us, step into the diagram, the cold and noise hit me like a truck. I focus on Ryan, who seems barely conscious. *Hold on,* I tell him, pressing my forehead tightly against his, willing the words to penetrate into his brain.

As before, the cold vanishes when we arrive, only to be replaced with the appalling blast of fiery heat.

"Where is he?" I ask Peter, looking around for our expected escort.

But it appears he was indeed waiting nearby. Just after I ask the question, Mr. Crunchy comes strolling around the corner, smiling at us brightly. But once his eyes fall on the spidery presence of LB, Mr. Crunchy's smile somehow becomes, while still *technically* a smile, much less happy. His head swoops down and forward to directly in front of LB's beetle face-parts. They begin to have what is clearly a very heated conversation in the ear-damaging strings of syllables that make up the demon language.

"Hey!" I shout up at them. "We don't have time for this!" I indicate the ailing Ryan beside me, then glare up at Mr. Crunchy's angrily inquisitive face. "If Ryan dies before we get back to your master, he's never getting what he wants from us."

Mr. C dips his head in still-technically-smiling acknowledgment and begins to lead the way back from the gate, but not without many suspicious glances over his shoulder at LB.

After a few awkward steps, it becomes clear that Ryan is never going to manage the trip back to Mr. Gabriel's hideout under his own power. I ask LB to give him a lift; Ryan is too weak to object, and I'd have overruled him if he tried.

This walk seems somehow both shorter and longer than the walk to the gate had been, what seems like years ago now, but which I guess was only two days past. I am still painfully aware that we don't have any kind of plan. I realize that some part of me had been hoping that the queen would show up at the last minute, once more our ally against our common enemy. But from what Aaron has indicated, the queen is down for the count. Maybe forever. Which means no more stupid-but-powerful magic items, no more advice, no chance of her materializing in the eleventh hour with a plan or an attack or even a distraction.

This time it has to be just us. I glance at LB, thankful that "us" now includes his significant addition of strength and experience, if not exactly brains. Whatever we attempt, we're going to need LB to be a part of it.

I try to think about what we know. We know Mr. Gabriel has that amulet that is making him super strong, even in its incomplete state. We know he has at least two demon minions, in the form of Mr. Crunchy and that terrifying cart-guy. We know Mr. Gabriel wants to re-create his body. Will *be* re-creating his body, very shortly, if we actually give him the missing piece of the amulet, which we have to do because Ryan is about to die. But until he creates his body, that amulet is — I'm pretty sure — sitting in the urn. The cart-demon certainly reacted like there was something important in there to protect, anyway. Although I guess if Mr. Gabriel's true essence is in there, that would be important enough.

Could we get the urn somehow before he manages to make a new body? Smash it, destroy whatever is left of him before it's too late?

I edge closer to Peter. "We need to try to destroy that urn. After Mr. Gabriel un-curses Ryan, but before he's able to re-create his body. If we get even the slightest chance . . ."

But Peter's already shaking his head. "Destroying the urn wouldn't be enough. We'd have to destroy Mr. Gabriel's essence, too. The urn is just a container; if we break it, his essence will just dissipate into the air. It might weaken him temporarily, but he'd be able to re-collect himself fairly quickly."

I drop my voice even lower. "*Can* we destroy his essence? Maybe . . . maybe if I used my power somehow, like I did against the monsters in the prison? Now that I don't actually have to touch him to use my power, I might be able to target his essence in the air. Or — hmm. Assuming I can see it."

Peter seems to consider this. "*I'd* be able to see it, even if you can't. Maybe I can direct you somehow."

"But what about the amulet? We should try to get that, too."

"How? If he's still got that other demon guarding it . . ."

The memory of the tentacle around my throat and the tiny, hateful eyes glaring into mine makes me shudder. "Maybe LB . . . ?"

Peter glances back at the spider-demon. "Maybe. But I still think we have to keep him in reserve until the last possible second. If we just let him march right in with us, Mr. Gabriel might be able to stop him."

He's right. But I really hate the idea of marching right in without him. I look hopelessly at Peter. "You realize this is more of a wish list than an actual plan, right?"

He gives me a heartbreaking smile. "Yeah. We'll just . . . we'll just have to do the best we can. We'll watch for an opportunity to smash that urn and snatch the amulet. And we'll make sure LB is ready to come in as soon as we call for him."

"God, this is terrible. It's never going to work. Is this really all we've got?"

"Yup. Unless one of us gets some other really brilliant idea very, very soon."

But just then I see the familiar building with the hole in the side that we now know is Mr. Gabriel's hideout up ahead. And then we're there, right beside it, and Mr. Crunchy performs his astonishing feat of contortion/contraction and goes in through the hole. And then there is nothing left to do but follow him inside.

It seems that our time for thinking of brilliant ideas has just finally run out for good.

Chapter 16

"LB," I whisper hurriedly. "Stay here until we call for you, okay?"

He seems confused as he gently sets Ryan on his feet. "But it is time to fight my brother."

"Not . . . not quite yet. Please. Just trust me. Do you trust me?"

He blinks his expressionless eyes. "Yes."

"Okay, then. Stay right here. And when we call you, come right away. *Right away*, okay?" I give him a few extra pats on the abdomen. I take Ryan's hand and pull him toward the opening. And then I take a deep breath and go back into the dark.

"The travelers return!" Mr. Gabriel calls out jovially as we climb back inside the interior ruins of the building. I'm the first to set foot on the rocky/rubbly ground, and then Peter and I help Ryan through the hole. Ryan looks awful. My heart hurts to see it.

Mr. Gabriel smiles at each of us. "Your mission was successful, I presume?" He's pretending to sit on his cart, next to his urn. Pretending, since, as a hologram, he can't actually sit on anything. But he can't resist striking this casual pose, flaunting how completely he's at his ease. How confident he is that he's already won.

We don't bother to answer. He has clearly prepared a monologue for this occasion. He beams out at us from his flickery projection, taking in our no doubt palpable sense of defeat. "But then why the long faces? Oh! Of course. Because you are about to hand over the very means of your own undoing!"

"You're ridiculous, you know that?" I ask him. "Seriously. Do you lie awake at night making up those kinds of lines?"

His smile doesn't falter, even as he places his hands over his heart in pretended pain. "Ah, even your barbed and hurtful words, dear Cynthia, cannot diminish my current good mood. Kindly hand over the item I requested, and we can get on with the rest of my to-do list."

For a second I am torn between competing impulses. I want to demand whether Mr. Gabriel knew that the Craftsman would not part with the stone willingly. I want to run to his stupid urn and smash the shit out of it, despite knowing the cart-demon would stop me before I got close. But nothing is as urgent as getting him to un-curse Ryan. Even if that means giving him what he wants. I console myself with the idea of LB, waiting outside to be our secret weapon. Surely he will be so unexpected, his presence so, dare I hope — upsetting? — to

Mr. Gabriel, once he discovers that his formerly spineless little brother has turned against him . . . surely that will give us some kind of advantage, some window of opportunity that we can't quite see right now but will immediately recognize when it presents itself?

But then Mr. Crunchy steps forward, and I realize he is about to reveal our secret right now.

"Whatever it is can wait," Mr. Gabriel tells him, gesturing for his giant minion to go back to his place along the wall. Mr. Crunchy widens his eyes in annoyance and frustration, smiling extra aggressively, but Mr. Gabriel is obviously intent upon his preplanned script for this moment, and does not mean to be diverted.

Peter gives Mr. Crunchy a *what can you do?* kind of shrug and smiles grimly.

"Now," Mr. Gabriel continues. "Cynthia, please step forward."

This is it, the moment when I have to actually give him the thing that is going to make him strong enough to kill me and go after Annie and all the rest. Which . . . I have to do, I *have* to, because otherwise Ryan will die, and then later Leticia and Diane and William and Peter will die. At least now they will get to live, no matter what else happens. I'll give him the stone and fulfill my part of the deal and my friends will get to be okay.

But not all of them, the panic beetles whisper from where they writhe beneath my skin. *Not Annie. Annie will be his forever. You couldn't save her. Even after all of this, you couldn't save her.*

Shut up, I tell them fiercely. *It's not over yet, you stupid beetles.*

It's not, I tell myself more quietly.

The beetles hear me, though, and laugh.

I look back once more at Ryan and Peter in case they have any last-minute helpful hints, but Peter only stares back at me with the same hopeless expression I'm sure adorns my own face, and Ryan seems to be focusing all of his energy on simply standing up. Then I step forward and hold out the stone in my palm. It begins to glow again, perhaps sensing the rest of the amulet nearby. Or perhaps it just likes to show off.

Mr. Gabriel gestures, and the cart-demon shuffles toward me. I stand perfectly still, not wanting to give him any reason to explode into that much larger and scarier version of himself. Once he is close enough, he plucks the glowing stone out of my hand. He carries it over to the urn and drops it unceremoniously inside. It falls with a small clank to the bottom.

"Ahh," Mr. Gabriel says with disheartening satisfaction. "Now, I will need a bit of privacy, so if you don't mind . . ."

"Fix Ryan first!" I demand, stepping forward. The cart-demon snarls threateningly in my direction, but I ignore him. "The deal was for delivering your stupid stone, not waiting around for you to use it."

"I wasn't —"

"He's about to die! If he does, the deal is forfeit, isn't it? I did my part; you have to do yours!"

Mr. Gabriel sighs and rolls his eyes theatrically. "You're so very irritating sometimes, you know that? I was *about* to say, if you'd have let me finish" — he gives me an exasperated glare — "that I would therefore remove the curse and you could be off along your way. For now."

"Wait, what?"

"Creating a new body takes a little time, Cynthia. Even with the help of my amulet at its full strength. What, did you think I was just going to pop offstage for a minute and then return to wreak my revenge right away?" He chuckles and shakes his head.

Then he turns toward Ryan and makes a quick pulling gesture in the air with one hand. Ryan gasps and falls to the ground.

I run over to him. "Are you all right?" I grab his palm and turn it toward me, looking for the mark, and the line. I pull up his shirt again and search his chest, run my hand gently over his heart.

It's all gone.

He's safe now. Forever.

I could weep, both with relief and with the guilty knowledge that Annie has no such protection. But I don't. Because I am still going to find a way to save her. Somehow.

"I'm okay," Ryan confirms. "Much . . . much better."

"Now," Mr. Gabriel says, "please go away." He turns to Mr. Crunchy. "Stay here and keep watch. Kill anyone who approaches. Well, unless it's one of these" — he gestures lazily at Ryan, Peter, and me — "or my Annie. They should merely be . . . detained."

"Wait!" I say, no idea what I'm supposed to follow this with. But we have to take our shot before it's too late. I step toward him, arm outstretched, and the cart-demon is before me at once, tentacles and teeth exploding from his human facade.

I fall back, screaming. I can't help it. My legs give way and I'm suddenly on the ground, still screaming, staring up into all of those terrible demon features and curling back into myself, desperate not to have that thing touch me ever, ever again.

"Patience, Cynthia," Mr. Gabriel says, smirking down at me. "Don't worry, we'll see each other again very soon."

Mr. Crunchy tries again to alert Mr. Gabriel to the fact that he has Very Important Information to share, but Mr. Gabriel ignores him, swirling into a sparkly cloud and funneling himself melodramatically back into his container. Even Peter rolls his eyes. The cart-demon, still snarling, backs away from us with the cart, but his tiny, horrible eyes stay fixed on me until the shadows swallow him completely.

I watch them go, hot, furious tears pricking at my vision. That was our chance, our chance to try to take the amulet and destroy Mr. Gabriel before he got his body back. And we missed it.

"You can bet you're still going to get in trouble later," Peter tells Mr. Crunchy once the others have vanished. "Even though you tried to warn him."

Mr. Crunchy smiles angrily at Peter and then looks pointedly away.

"So—" Ryan looks around, slightly bewildered. "So now we just go home?"

"Yeah," I say, defeated. I'm still on the ground. I can't meet anyone's eyes. "We go home and wait for Mr. Gabriel to put himself back together and then come to kill me and take Annie."

Ryan comes over and makes me get up. "Come on, Cyn. It'll be okay. We'll . . . we'll figure something out."

I don't have the heart to point out to him how we keep saying that but never actually do figure anything out.

"Yes," Peter says. "Let's just . . . let's just go outside. The light in here isn't very good for drawing diagrams."

We go outside. Mr. Crunchy glares after us, but does nothing to interfere.

LB is still waiting where we left him.

"Now it is time to fight my brother?"

I look at him sadly. We never even tried to call for him. But the moment came and went so quickly. If it was really even there at all. There wasn't time.

"Well . . . no. We have to — we have to wait. More. For him to create his body again. And then we can fight him." I'm exercising a lot of dramatic license here, but I'm sure some of what I'm saying is at least technically true.

I must be getting better at reading LB's bug features, because his disappointment is crystal clear right now.

I sigh and turn to Peter. "We have to bring LB with us."

"What?"

"Mr. Crunchy saw him with us. We can't leave him here defenseless and alone."

Peter jabs a hand in LB's direction. "Have you *seen* him? In what possible sense is he defenseless?"

"He's on our team! We can't leave him behind!"

240

"Cyn," Ryan says, "how? We can't exactly bring him to school with us."

"We did before!"

"For like five minutes! And he half destroyed the library!"

I look at Peter. "Couldn't he take human form? Like you? Like all those other demons did when they came to our school?"

Peter runs a hand over his face. "I—maybe. That was different—those other demons weren't coming through with their full bodies like LB would be now. It's harder this way. But . . . I could help him, I think. To disguise himself."

LB has been watching this conversation silently, his face turning from one of us to the other like a three-way tennis match. I have no idea how much he understands. But I really am afraid to leave him behind. We need him. If we're still going to try to fight back, we need him. And . . . I made a promise. That we would fight together.

"LB, listen to me. We have to go back to the human world for a little while. We need to . . . to make a plan. And also to be somewhere safer than here. Do you want to come with us? You could stay here and hide if you want, instead. But it might be better for all of us to stay together."

He answers at once. "I will stay with you."

I nod. "Okay. Peter, take us up, please."

We manage to get back up to school and out of the library without any insurmountable problems. Peter elects to spirit himself and LB away to somewhere more private so they can work on pretending to be human together. It appears to be just about lunchtime, so Ryan and I head for the cafeteria to fill the others in on what's happened and what's happening now.

Which is . . . uncertain.

Mr. Gabriel is, as we speak, regaining his full physical form. And then I assume he will come after us, once he's ready. Which means we have to get ready, too. Except there's nothing we can do to get ready. Which I'm sure Mr. Gabriel knows, or else he wouldn't be so confidently arrogant. We have no allies, no resources, no weapons, no anything. Except LB. But even in my most hopeful moments, I know that he's not going to be enough to get us through this.

On the way to the cafeteria we pass Mr. Henry in the hall.

"Hey, you two! I feel like I haven't seen you around much this week. Although . . . I know you were in class . . ." He trails off, confused, then seems to shake it off. "I must need more coffee. Anyway. All ready for callbacks tomorrow, Ryan?"

"Tomorrow?"

Mr. Henry laughs. "Today's Thursday, right? Making tomorrow Friday?"

We look at each other.

"Uh, right! Ha. Of course."

"Looks like I'm not the only one who needs some coffee. Well, see you both there." He starts to walk away, then stops, resting his hand on Ryan's shoulder. "Break a leg, Ryan. Break two of them, okay?"

"You bet, Mr. H."

We watch him continue down the hall.

"How did we lose a whole day?" I ask.

"I don't know," Ryan says. He thinks for a minute. "I have another voice lesson tonight."

"Good! And, well—so here's an upside, anyway. We're back in time for that, and, um, as long as Mr. Gabriel doesn't show up again too quickly, we'll be here for callbacks, no problem! So you'll, you know, have your lesson, and . . . and get into top form, and then kick Jeff's ass, and get the part, and then we'll go fight Mr. Gabriel and then we can come back and start rehearsals and set construction and stuff."

Ryan looks at me. "There are so many questionable aspects to what you just said that I hardly know where to begin."

"Don't begin. Just . . . let's just go have lunch."

"If today's Thursday, that means I missed a lesson yesterday."

"Oh. Well . . . I'm sure Peter can smooth that out for you."

"Yeah, but . . . I still missed the lesson, Cyn. I haven't been singing nearly enough this week, I'm going to be rough . . ."

"Uh, you've been kind of busy?"

"You were the one telling me I still had to take this seriously!"

"Well, yes! But also you have to give yourself a break! I mean, sometimes there are just conflicts to voice lessons that can't be avoided. Like when you're *dying of a magical curse in the demon world*, for example."

He sighs. "You don't understand."

"I—what?"

He stops walking. "I don't think I'm hungry. I'll—I'll catch up with you later, okay?"

I just stand there, watching, as he turns and walks back down the hall and into the stairwell.

Somehow being told by Ryan that I don't understand feels like the most upsetting thing that has happened today. Which can't be true, obviously, and yet . . .

I shake my head and continue toward the cafeteria. If there was ever a time I wanted to curl up on my bed with a comfy blanket and a playlist of all my favorite Sondheim songs, it's right now. But that's not a remotely viable option, unfortunately. I have to find Annie and the others and let them know what happened. And what's still happening, and what we still don't seem to have any way to prevent happening.

Ryan texts me that night to tell me the lesson went well, but I can feel his lack of confidence radiating through the screen. But I also know that trying to talk to him about it now would be exactly the wrong thing. So I just tell him that I love him and that I know he's going to be amazing, and then I try to go to sleep.

But sleep, of course, has other ideas.

I should feel relieved to be in my own bed, granted this temporary reprieve from demons and monsters and pain tunnels and all the rest. But I know it's not over, and we're just waiting for Mr. Gabriel to raise the curtain on the final act.

And waiting has never been the easiest part for me.

I'm also starting to worry about how safe Ryan and Peter actually are. Mr. Gabriel isn't allowed to hurt or kill them, or to order other demons to do so . . . but if they come back down with me to face Mr. Gabriel, something could still go wrong.

Another demon could get them, or Mr. Gabriel could find some loophole I didn't think of. . . . The protection I thought was so ironclad begins to seem less and less so the later it gets.

I lie awake for a long time worrying about that. And then, once I finally start to feel like I can sleep, I worry that Mr. Gabriel is going to visit me in my dreams. And when I finally fall asleep, I do dream of him . . . but it's not the kind of dream I had at camp, where he was *there*, really there in the dream. These are just shadows of him, scary images coughed up by my agitated mind. And as soon as I realize that, I finally do feel relieved, because I think it means he's still too busy bodybuilding to waste time messing with my head. Which maybe means we still have a little more time.

The next morning Ryan is wound as tight as I have ever seen him. I pull him away from the others in the band wing and take him to sit at the bottom of his favorite brooding stairwell.

"Demons or callbacks?" I ask him.

He laughs, surprising me. "Callbacks. Ridiculously." He glances at me and then down at the dusty floor. "I keep thinking about what you said before — what if we don't die, and I didn't try hard enough, and that Jeff guy gets my part? God, that would suck so much."

"It totally would."

"I realize that if that were to happen that I should probably focus on just, I don't know, being happy we're alive. But . . ."

"I know."

He puts his arm around me and pulls me tight against him. "I know you know. You get it. You always do."

Damn straight, you jerk, I think but don't say. I just squeeze him back.

"You're going to be great. I know it."

"Yeah," he says. But he's still not selling it.

And I don't know how to help.

At the end of the day, all the *Les Misérables* hopefuls assemble in the auditorium. Mr. Henry gives his usual speech about how they're all amazing and he wishes he could cast all of them but that would be hard to stage, ha-ha, and so callbacks and cast lists, et cetera. He then calls the potential Jean Valjeans to the stage and sets everyone else free to wait their turn. Some people settle in to watch, some disperse to find places to do extra vocal warm-ups, some just wander out into the band wing to pace and worry.

We're in the third group. Ryan's already warmed up, and I know he doesn't want to overdo it. Annie and the others offered to come for moral support, but Ryan told them that would probably just make him more nervous, and so they are waiting at the diner and we'll meet them there later for celebratory post-callback feasting.

So it's rather a shock to see Peter come sauntering down the hall.

"What is he doing here?" Ryan asks me.

"I have no idea. Let me — let me just go make sure nothing went wrong with LB or something." But I'm sure that's not why he's here. Peter doesn't look the least bit worried. He looks . . . trickstery.

I hurry forward to intercept him before he can get close. "What are you doing here?" I hiss at him. "Where's LB?"

"LB's fine. Still, um, practicing his human disguise. It does *not* come naturally to that guy. If you saw —"

"Cut it out, Peter. If nothing's wrong, then you shouldn't have come. You should be there babysitting."

"Relax, Cyn." He peers past me to where Ryan is glowering suspiciously in our direction.

"Peter, please." I lower my voice. "I know how you love to make trouble, but please, *please,* don't screw with him right now. This is really important. Really, really important. To both of us, if that matters at all to you."

He actually manages to look hurt. "We're friends, aren't we, Cyn? I mean really friends."

"Yes. Of course."

"Then trust me." And then he winks and pushes past me.

Ryan's glower deepens as Peter approaches. I mouth *I'm sorry* and raise my hands helplessly as I follow behind.

"Ready for the big contest?" Peter asks, grinning insolently and leaning against a locker.

"Give it a rest, Peter. I'm not in the mood, okay?"

Peter looks him up and down. "Yeah, I can see that. Funny, that Jeff guy doesn't look nervous at all. I just passed him around the corner. He looks like he could do this in his sleep."

Ryan takes a step toward Peter. "I said, give it a *rest*, Peter. You do not want to mess with me right now."

"Well, I kinda do, though. It's so much fun."

"Peter, that's enough," I say, trying to pull him away. "I don't know what you're up to, but just cut it out."

"Leave him, Cyn," Ryan says. "I can handle this loser on my own."

"Oh, you think so?" Peter asks, stepping closer.

"Yeah," Ryan says, also stepping closer. "I'm not afraid of you."

"Maybe you should be."

Ryan laughs scornfully. "I have your number, Peter. You're a monster, just like the rest of them. But you can't let Cyn see that, and so you're never going to do anything to me. But I know what you are."

"Maybe," Peter says softly. "Maybe I am a monster. But Cyn knows what I am, too. And yet she hasn't sent me away, has she? She doesn't seem nearly as bothered by my demon nature as you are. Were you watching when she kissed me? Did you see how much she liked it?"

Ryan lunges forward and I throw myself between them. "Stop it!" I scream at Peter.

The auditorium door opens then, and the stage manager calls Ryan's name.

"You're lucky," Ryan snarls, reaching past me to jab his finger into Peter's chest. Then he storms off into the auditorium.

I give Peter my scathing-est glare and follow after Ryan.

Mr. Henry has one of the Jean Valjeans up on the stage still. "Ah! Ryan, good. I want to hear you do a bit of the suicide in a minute, but first I thought we'd start with 'Confrontation,' so I can see how you and Kevin sound together, okay?"

Ryan nods and hops up onto the stage. Both of us know

Kevin from previous shows and drama class, and I had a feeling he was going to be the Valjean front-runner. At Mr. Henry's go-ahead, Mr. Iverson begins the introduction, and then Ryan starts to sing.

From the first word, I can hear the pent-up anger and frustration in Ryan's voice, courtesy of Peter. I could *kill* Peter in that instant. I really could.

But then I keep listening, and I realize: somehow it's perfect. Ryan's using it, channeling everything he didn't get to say to Peter into the song, especially as it goes along and Valjean begins to plead and argue and threaten in response.

Kevin is good, really good; he's gained some confidence since last year, and there's something just right about his voice for this part. And it's clear to everyone — Kevin and Ryan included, I can tell — that the chemistry between them is amazing. They circle each other, getting into the feel of it, and I can see that the rest of us have disappeared for them; there is only the song and the music and the characters that they have each slipped into so effortlessly.

It's incredible.

By the time they're finished, I realize I'm clasping my hands together so hard that my fingers ache. Both boys are grinning, fully aware of how very, very well that just went.

"Excellent, excellent, really well done, both of you," Mr. Henry gushes. "Now, Ryan, I just want to hear you sing 'Javert's Suicide'; I'm assuming you know this one by heart, too?"

Ryan nods, still grinning. Mr. Henry gives Kevin a chance to leave the stage and Ryan a minute to regroup, and then he gestures again to Mr. Iverson.

Ryan is fully back in his element now, though. I'm not even nervous for him anymore. I'm just in awe. The anger at Peter and the joy at how well "Confrontation" went are almost visibly swirling inside him, and he controls each emotion perfectly, easing from anger to wonder to confused agony to rigid surrender and despair. In my mind I can't help but envision the stage setting I'm going to create for him, attempting to do justice to what I can see is going to be a show-stopping performance.

The parents are going to be bawling their eyes out.

Mr. Henry releases Ryan with a not-so-subtle wink, and he bounds off the stage and scoops me into his arms with all the leopard-like grace and energy and *rowr* I have come to expect in my boyfriend when he's on his game. I kiss him soundly right there in the aisle, until a loud throat-clearing from Mr. Iverson encourages us to make our way out to the hall so they can carry on with the rest of callbacks.

When Ryan and I arrive at the diner, there is a general cheer of welcome from our group at the back table — which includes Annie, William, Leticia, and Diane, as well as Jorge and several of Ryan's other friends — and we immediately plunk down into chairs so Ryan can tell them how it went. The table is crowded enough that it takes me a minute to notice Peter and a rather strange-looking boy I've never seen before sitting at the far end. I nearly choke on my water when I realize that the stranger is LB. As soon as I can do so unobtrusively, I get up and wander over, pulling up an extra chair to sit next to them.

"Hi," I say, studying LB's fake-human visage with interest.

It's . . . passable; I mean, he looks human, and no one else at the table seems to be giving him a second thought . . . but there's something very odd happening in his facial features. Like the shape of his nose seems to keep changing slightly, even though I can't exactly catch it in the act, and some of the longer hairs of his eyebrows seem to be very subtly waving around of their own volition.

"It is I. LB," he says. Then he adds, more quietly, "This is not my real face."

"Yes, I know," I say, struggling not to laugh. "But it's very convincing. Good job."

I glance at Peter, who is watching Ryan holding court at the other end of the table. "How did you know?" I ask him.

He shrugs. "I watched Jeff's callback just before you saw me. He was good, very good, but . . . too confident. Too smooth. No fire. I knew Ryan had fire. I thought it might be helpful if I just kind of . . . stirred it up for him." He looks at me then, suddenly anxious. "I swear, that's all I did. No demon magic involved."

I smirk at him. "It's okay. I know you are fully capable of pissing Ryan off without the help of magic. I have observed that phenomenon many times." I lean over and squeeze his arm. "Thanks. This was . . . I know maybe it's dumb, because we might still all die very soon, but . . . this was important."

"I know."

"We will not die very soon," LB puts in. "We will go to kill my brother. *He* is the one who will die."

"God, I hope so," I tell him. I give him a few pats on the shoulder for good measure. "I really do."

Chapter | 17

Saturday morning, I head over to Annie's house.

After wading through the countless small children running and screaming in all the hallways — Annie's siblings, and their friends, and possibly total stranger children from around the neighborhood — I let myself into her room.

"Hey, lady."

"Cyn!" She immediately scoots over on her unicorn bedspread to make room for me. Then her smile slips as she takes in my expression. "Is everything —"

"Everything's okay. Or, you know, nothing new is worse, anyway." I lean back against her pillows. "I just — I feel like we need to be doing something. We can't just wait for him to come for us."

"I know. I've been thinking the same thing. But what can we do?"

"I think we need to go down there. Soon. Now. Before he's ready. Remember how he set Mr. Crunchy to stand guard? Why would he need a guard unless —"

"Unless he's vulnerable!" Annie finishes.

"Right. The only problem is . . ."

"How the hell can we fight him when he's a powerful demon and we're just . . . us?"

I smile ruefully. "Yeah."

She tucks her legs underneath her and sits up straight. I recognize this as her night-before-exam study pose. "Okay. Let's think about this logically. What assets do we have? We have you, and your super-roach powers. We have LB, who is also a powerful demon but, we assume, not strong enough to take on Mr. Gabriel single-handedly, or else he wouldn't have been wanting to team up with us. We have Peter, who is a far less powerful demon, but who does have some useful abilities and is way nicer to look at than LB."

"All valid points."

"We have Ryan, who is also very nice to look at, but who, other than acting and singing, does not have any special talents."

My mouth twists up into a helpless grin before I can stop it. "None that are applicable to our current situation, no."

Annie raises her eyebrows at me. "I am going to need to ask some follow-up questions on that later."

"We have Leticia and Diane and William," I continue, "who absolutely are not allowed to put themselves in danger. The deal I made with Mr. Gabriel will protect them from him, but the demon world is too dangerous all on its own. There's like a thousand things that could kill them the second they set foot there."

"Agreed," Annie says. She looks at me, waiting.

"And—"

"I know. Me, too."

I sit up to face her. "You're really not going to fight with me about this anymore?"

She looks sad, but resigned. "I'm really not. Despite how incredibly helpful I turned out to be in the prison"—she gives me a sardonic look—"I am aware that, as you said, parading myself around in front of Mr. Gabriel would be . . . well, stupid."

"I didn't say stupid."

"No, but it would be. I kept thinking maybe there could be some way to use me as bait—no, just listen. I thought about it, but I'm sure he would know it was a trap. And he'd never be careless enough to come up here fully, which means we'd have to go down there to kill him completely anyway. And I can't—I can't see how me walking right into his lair would be anything but disastrous."

I reach out to take her hand. "Thank you for understanding."

She shrugs. "I did struggle with it for a while. Especially with the fact that Ryan still gets to go, despite his just being a regular normal human person like me, and now that the curse is lifted there's no actual reason for him to be there . . . but I get that you need Peter, and I know Ryan would *never* be okay with you going off with Peter alone. Plus, your deal protects both of them from Mr. Gabriel."

I hope. "I'm so sorry I couldn't protect you."

She shrugs again. "Well, that's the whole problem, isn't it? I'm the one thing he won't let go of."

"Why do you have to be so damn irresistible?"

"Can't help it." She waves her hand along her body and smiles. "There's just no way to turn this thing off."

I smile back, but it fades quickly. "I guess that's it for our list of assets. It's not very long."

"Aaron and the demon queen are definitely out of the picture?"

"Yes," I say, and then pause, considering. "Well, I mean . . . we've all been assuming that. Based on what Aaron had said about her injuries. But maybe we should find out for certain."

"How?"

"Remember Peter's tiny little demon friend?"

"Oh, yes! Of course! He seemed like he was good at finding things out."

I whip out my phone and call Peter.

He answers on the first ring. "I'm guessing you still haven't broken up."

"Nope. Now shut up and listen, please." I relate our idea about getting his demon friend to do some reconnaissance for us. Peter agrees that it's worth a try, and we decide to meet up in Annie's basement tonight.

By eight o'clock, Annie, Ryan, Peter, Diane, Leticia, LB, and I are all assembled in the basement of Annie's house. I invited Leticia and Diane partly as a peace offering and partly because . . . well, I guess it's finally starting to sink in that my friends are smart and have good ideas and maybe I should listen to them once in a while. I keep wanting to protect them from all of this, but as Annie keeps telling me, it's not up to me to decide what's okay for everyone else. And anyway, it's not like having them involved in *planning* is all that dangerous.

Annie decided not to invite William. She still thinks he's too freaked out by all the demon stuff and doesn't want to keep reminding him about it.

Usually this space, too, is filled with many screaming children, but Peter does something to convince them that they all want to be somewhere else. Annie grips his arm and stares up at him in wonder. "Oh, my God, Peter — can you do that for my room, too? Please?"

We settle in as Peter begins to draw his symbol. LB has never experienced a suburban basement before, especially not one that hasn't been redecorated since the seventies, and he seems to be studying the fake wood paneling with great interest.

Ryan and Peter seem to have, by mutual unspoken agreement, decided to pretend the argument in the hallway before callbacks never happened. I'm glad. They both said some things I wish they hadn't.

Peter resumes his partial-demon appearance like he had that first time in the library (we'd forewarned L and D about this part), and then does whatever invisible thing he does to summon the demon to the circle.

The same tiny reptilian fluffball from last time appears immediately before us.

"Great One!" it squeaks, cowering and trembling. "I have been eagerly awaiting your call!"

"I have been busy!" Peter intones. "What new information have you gathered for me?"

"The John Gabriel will soon regain his physical form! His supporters are confident and joyful, ready for him to finish slaying the queen and take his place as ruler of all."

"Is there any chance that the queen will defeat him?"

"Oh, no, Great One! She is still gravely injured. No one will assist her, because no one believes she can win."

We all exchange disappointed looks. So much for that last hope.

"Have you learned anything new about the amulet?" Peter asks.

"It is a very powerful item, Great One. It adds the strength of the captured souls to the wearer, but also amplifies the wearer's own strength. Now that the missing piece has been restored, I believe it will make John Gabriel nearly invincible once he regains his physical form and can wear it properly."

"How soon will he regain his physical form?"

The tiny demon throws itself down upon the orange shag carpet. "I do not know, Great One! I know only that he has not done so yet, and his supporters believe it will happen very soon!"

"You have pleased me once again," Peter says, although his face, like the rest of ours, looks anything but pleased. "Continue your efforts and you will be rewarded!"

"Yes, Great One! I live only to serve you!"

Peter waves a hand, and the tiny demon blinks out.

"We have to go now," Ryan says at once. "Now, before it's too late."

"And do what?" Peter asks, his demon aspects absorbing once more into his handsome human form. "Politely ask Mr. Crunchy to step aside and let us through to kill his master?"

"LB could totally take Mr. Crunchy!" Ryan says.

LB seems pleased by this assertion, although his fake-human expressions are almost as difficult to decipher as his demonic beetle-face ones.

"Let's say," I break in, before they can continue, "we do go down now, and somehow get past Mr. Crunchy. Then what? There's that other demon, the horrible cart one, and maybe more — Peter's friend mentioned supporters, plural. I have to believe that there are more than just the two we've seen."

"Then . . . we do whatever we have to, to kill Mr. Gabriel before he gets too strong," Ryan says.

Peter rolls his eyes. "That's not exactly a plan, is it?"

"Do you have a better idea, genius?"

"It seems to me," Leticia says, speaking a little more loudly than necessary and pointedly not looking at the boys, "that the thing you need to focus on is that amulet. Without that, he's just his regular strength again, right? He won't be this terrifying, all-powerful figure that the other demons are afraid to stand up to."

"Well," says Peter, "his regular strength is still pretty impressive. Plenty of demons were afraid of him before, too. But . . . you're right. Not all of them. He certainly wasn't invincible."

"LB," I say. "Do you think you could fight your brother's guardian demons? Distract them so we can try to get that amulet? Kill them, if you can?"

"And then . . . and then we will fight my brother?"

"Yes. Once we get the amulet away from him."

"Yes," LB confirms.

I look around at the others. "So that's . . . sort of a plan, right? The amulet must be in the urn — that's where the cart-demon put the missing piece, and Mr. Gabriel went in there to do whatever he's going to with it. It has to be in there with him. If LB can keep the minions occupied, we can get the urn and steal the amulet."

"I don't love it," Peter says. "But I guess it's the best we're going to do on short notice."

He's not the only one who doesn't love it. I doubt there's any plan I'm going to love that involves going back to the demon world and facing our terrible enemy. But it's the last time. That's what I keep focusing on. We just have to really, really kill him (somehow), and then we'll be done with him forever.

Diane crosses her arms angrily. "And you still don't think having more help down there would be, I don't know, *helpful*?"

"Not human help," I say. "I told you — just because you're safe from Mr. Gabriel, it doesn't mean you're actually safe. Any of the other hundreds or thousands or however many demons there are could kill you in a heartbeat. We told you what happened to Ryan the first time!"

"Then why does Ryan get to go again?" she demands. "He's still human, isn't he? Or did I miss something?"

"Diane," Annie says, "we talked about this!" She widens her eyes meaningfully in what I can pretty easily interpret as a *please don't make me repeat the Ryan and Peter thing in front of Ryan and Peter* look.

Diane sighs in exasperation and leans huffily back against the wall.

I wish she wasn't making me so aware of how weak our plan is. Although . . . she has also just given me an idea.

"But maybe we haven't exhausted our sources of non-human help," I say. "Should we try summoning Aaron again? I mean, just in case there's anything he can do? Maybe he'll at least have an idea we haven't thought of, or something."

"If he'll even help us," Ryan says. "He seemed pretty appalled the last time we saw him. He might tell us this is our own problem now."

"But it's in his own best interest to stop Mr. Gabriel from getting any stronger. . . . I think it's worth a try."

Peter shrugs and closes his eyes.

I half expect Peter not to be able to find him again, but Aaron appears after only a few seconds. His eyes lock on mine before any of us can say a word.

"Cyn, how could you do it? I warned you . . ."

"No, it will be okay, we're going to stop him!"

"It's too late. You can't stop him. Nothing can stop him now."

"Aaron, please. If there's anything you know, anything you can tell us —"

He laughs — it's a cold, bitter sound that seems to suck all of the warmth right out of the room. "There's nothing I can tell you. I told you before and you didn't listen, and now it's too late."

"No, it's not too late — he doesn't have his body back yet. We can still —"

"Give it up, Cyn. It's over. If you'd only left it alone, we might have had a chance. My mistress might have recovered in time, and then she could have destroyed him. But now the most I can hope for is that we can stay hidden and that she won't die. You . . . you don't have anything left to hope for at all. He's going to get everything he wanted, and it's your fault."

And with that, he vanishes, leaving the rest of us in unhappy silence.

"Yeah . . . on second thought, I think it would have been better not to contact Aaron," Annie says finally.

"He's wrong," I say. "It's not too late."

It's not. Because it can't be.

No giving up.

Peter quickly goes upstairs with Annie to magic her room against tiny intruders ("Just in case we die down there," he explains) and then we reassemble in the basement. We watch as Peter sketches a new symbol in the carpet. Annie hugs everyone, even LB. "Be careful down there, please," she tells us. "Kick his ass and come back safe."

Then she backs away, going to stand beside Leticia and Diane, and we go over the plan, such as it is, one more time. And then Ryan, Peter, LB, and I all hold hands and step through

Peter's gate and into the demon world. My last thought as the gateway envelops us is *Holy crap how do I keep forgetting the part about the horrible coldness?*

Peter has brought us to the space just outside Mr. Gabriel's hideout. (He explained earlier that he could do that now, since he'd brought us back from there on the last visit. I explained in return that I have given up on trying to understand demon-world logic.) The cold is replaced once again by the fiery heat and the shifty landscape and all the other unpleasant aspects of the demon world. Except the demons, who seem to be steering clear of this particular stretch of real estate.

LB immediately begins to expand back into his true form. Watching him makes me wonder something. "Peter, why don't you ever go back to demon form while you're down here?" I ask. "Wouldn't it be safer?"

"Not necessarily," he says. "The demons we're facing now are all way too strong for me to fight physically; it seems better to be small and able to move more easily."

"And to run away faster," Ryan mutters.

"Yes, that, too," Peter agrees. "You're welcome to take on all the demons you want, Ryan, if you think they're so easy to fight."

"Boys, *enough*," I groan. "Can't you guys ever, ever give it a rest?"

LB has finished transforming, and now faces the entrance to the lair eagerly, eyes alight. "It is time to begin!"

"I suppose it is," I say with far, far less enthusiasm.

Apparently taking that as my signal to go ahead, LB

smushes himself through the hole. The rest of us crawl after him in quick succession.

I stand still, letting my eyes adjust to the darkness. LB has no such need to hesitate, however. He strides forward to where Mr. Crunchy is lounging, looking bored. The bored expression vanishes as soon as he sees us, of course. He leaps to his feet as LB launches toward him, pincers spread.

We'd agreed that I would not share my protection with LB at this time. He's too big; sharing with him is like sharing with the queen, and it doesn't leave much for me. LB seemed pretty confident he wouldn't need my help in any case. But LB seems pretty confident about a lot of things sometimes, and so I don't know how much to trust that.

Mr. Crunchy is much taller than LB, but he doesn't have LB's bulk. I want to believe that makes it more of an even match than it seems. Mr. Crunchy's pointy crab legs look like they can do a lot more damage than LB's spider limbs or even his pincers. And Mr. Crunchy has so many of them . . .

"Come on," Ryan whispers, pulling me forward.

Right. We have our own job to do.

Quiet as mice, Ryan, Peter, and I sneak along the wall and back into the deeper shadows where Mr. Gabriel had disappeared the last time we were here, leaving the sound and fury of the demon battle behind us.

For a little while the blackness is almost complete, and then it begins to very slowly brighten. Far up ahead, I can see what looks like a shimmering curtain of light. We move toward it. The noises from the main chamber become more muted the farther back we go, and by the time we draw near the shimmering curtain, we can't hear them at all.

The curtain is somewhat translucent. There's a great swirling mass of something behind it, something that seems to keep changing shape just before I'm able to identify what it looks like, but in the center of all of that is something solid and stable and immediately recognizable.

It's Mr. Gabriel's golden urn.

And I'm sure now — totally and completely sure — that the amulet must be inside.

Still standing in the shadows, I scan the rest of the room, looking for the cart-demon. Surely he wouldn't have left his master here alone, defenseless . . . but maybe he's not defenseless. Maybe that shimmery curtain is all the protection he needs.

Except if it's made out of demon energy, which I'm betting it is, then it's not protection against me.

I lean close to Peter, so close that my lips are right against his ear, and then I whisper with the barest possible amount of sound, "That's demonic energy, isn't it? Not physical?"

I pull back, and he looks at me unhappily. And then he nods.

I turn to Ryan, who also looks unhappy, and I point first at him and then down at the ground where he's standing. I trust that it's a very clear message of *stay right there.* And if it's not clear enough for him, then I trust that Peter will hold him back if he tries to follow me.

I take a deep breath and step forward out of the shadows. When nothing leaps out to stop me, I take another step. I keep looking around, but there's nothing but the empty chamber and the shimmery curtain and whatever lies behind it. It doesn't take many more steps for me to reach it. And then I stretch out my hand and hold it just before the curtain's shimmery border.

My first impulse is to test it, to extend a finger through it, to make sure it's not going to hurt or anything else. But then I think that maybe putting any part of myself through that border will make my presence known, to whomever might be around to know it, and I can't take that chance.

So I just reach through and grab the neck of the urn. And then I turn to run.

And then the cart-demon's tentacle-wreathed body slams into me from nowhere, sending both of us sprawling down hard against the ground.

I don't have enough air to scream or cry out or shout the names of my accomplices in warning, so I just swing the urn forward along the ground with all the force I can muster, praying it will reach them and that they will be able to finish what I started.

Ryan and Peter both lunge for it, understanding immediately what the priority is, and I'm so proud of them in that moment. But it's all for nothing. The cart-demon has too many parts, he's everywhere, all at once, and he snatches the urn out of reach and thrusts both boys violently back into the shadows without once loosening his hold on me. I struggle to get loose anyway, and in my twisting I see with a sunken heart how the demon reverently and almost gently restores the urn to its original location.

And then he returns his attention to me.

He flips me roughly all the way over so that I'm lying flat on my back now, gazing in silent horror up at him. His tiny eyes are unmistakably full of malicious glee as he holds me there, smiling with all of his too-many teeth. Two of his tongues slide out and taste the exposed skin of my arm.

I can't scream, even now. I'm sure, I'm sure he remembers that he's not allowed to kill me, but I'm also sure that doesn't mean he's not allowed to *hurt* me, and he proves me right on this almost instantly, lowering his head almost casually and taking a bite out of my left shoulder.

Now I can scream, and I do, and I see him pull back again, watching me, drinking in my pain and terror, his mouth stained with my blood. Another tongue snakes out and smears the blood slowly across his own face. I hear one or both of my friends screaming from behind me; I can't tell who it is or what they're saying but it doesn't matter, because we've lost, we've lost completely, and there's nothing either of them can do now. I know we're not supposed to give up, I know not giving up is the rule, the first rule, the most important rule, but I can't help it. I have to give up because the cart-demon is eating my shoulder and the stars are black and cold and that was our last and final chance and now it's gone.

And then something enormous barrels overhead and slams into the cart-demon, throwing him back and away from me.

LB, bleeding and dirty and glorious, leaps enthusiastically onto his opponent, spider legs spread wide, and I swear his demonic beetle face has never looked so brightly and unambiguously full of joy.

The cart-demon immediately entangles LB in his tentacles, but LB only begins snapping them off with his pincers, causing thick, bruise-colored blood to come gushing out of the severed pieces of limbs. Someone grabs my arms and I scream again as my injured shoulder is jerked upward. I slide back along the ground, away from the fighting demons. Away from the amulet.

"No!" I shout, struggling to get away. "I need to get back! I need to get it —"

"Cyn, you're going to lose too much blood!" It's Ryan, peering down at me with terrified eyes.

"That doesn't matter! Nothing matters if we don't get that thing away from him!"

He knows that I'm right, because this time when I pull away he doesn't try to stop me. Instead he helps me to my feet and then helps me forward again, toward the curtain, circling around to avoid the flailing limbs of the battling demons. After a second, Peter appears beside us, limping and disheveled. He adds his support to Ryan's, and together the three of us reach the curtain again.

But this time when I reach through to grab the urn, something grabs me back from the other side.

Chapter | 18

I freeze, staring up at the swirling mass that has suddenly stopped swirling. Ryan and Peter stare with me. LB and the cart-demon are still too caught up in their fight to notice what is happening here.

Slowly, I try to draw my hand back. It comes, but not alone. An immaculate set of shiny black claws are locked around my forearm.

Then the claws abruptly let go as the shape behind the curtain grows and swells monstrously, the shimmering curtain dissolving as the thing behind it solidifies. We scramble backward, and the other demons have finally noticed that something is going on that they should maybe pay attention to.

Mr. Gabriel is standing before us. He's in his original full demon form as I first saw it during the melee battle for the demon throne: half enormous, upright bull's head and body, half monstrous black bird, with almost-human arms and not-at-all-human claw-hands. His sleek black horns curve up from his head, gleaming like new. Which makes sense, I guess, because they are.

Around his neck, tiny against his gigantic stature, a complicated piece of metalwork hangs from an incongruously delicate silver chain. The metal is dark and tarnished, and there are several milky-white stones set irregularly around the perimeter. And in the center, the familiar, final stone glows in nearly blinding bloodred triumph.

The amulet, complete at last.

Mr. Gabriel stretches luxuriously, enjoying our bleak enthrallment. "It's so *nice* to be really here again," he says. "And how lovely of you to be here waiting for me. Is it a welcome-back party? Will there be cake?"

I hate him so much in that moment. I mean, I always hate him, obviously, but right now, for him to have reappeared when we were so close to winning our advantage, for him to be standing there, really standing there, new and terrible and so goddamn smug — it's unbearable. If I could kill him with my hate he'd be dead right now. He'd be the absolute deadest thing in the entire universe. Dead a hundred thousand million times over.

But I can't, and so he continues to stand there, alive and aware of our powerlessness. Aware that his long-anticipated revenge is finally about to begin.

He smiles widely at me and then begins to sweep his gaze over to the cart-demon, no doubt to give him some unpleasant instruction regarding what to do with us, when his eyes snag on the bristly/furry arachnid-bovine-hexapod form of his brother.

There is a moment of uncomfortable silence.

"*You* are unexpected," Mr. Gabriel says finally. "But not at all unwelcome. I will deal with you shortly. And we will discuss just exactly where you have been all this time."

"No," LB says, standing up straighter on his many legs, some of which still have tentacle bits wrapped around them.

Mr. Gabriel stares as though he believes he must have misheard this statement. "No?"

"No. We will not discuss. You . . ." LB hesitates, then glances at me and continues, *"You are not the boss of me!"*

I have to bite the back of my hand to stop myself from exploding in sudden hysterical laughter. I remember shouting that in panicky anger at LB over the summer. I can't believe *that's* the line he's decided to borrow out of all the things I must have said to him or in his presence since we first met. At the same time, I am touched that he is quoting me in his emancipation speech. And my laughing now would totally ruin his moment.

"Oh. Oh, I see." Mr. Gabriel starts to laugh, having no such similar concerns about moment-ruining. "You're . . . you're on Team Cynthia, now, are you? Wow. I — okay, I will admit that I did not see that one coming. Well, once I kill her, you can decide whether you want to be next, or whether you would like to reconsider your position."

LB turns his head toward me, and I know he is asking whether this is the moment when he finally gets to attack his brother. For once, his expression is absolutely clear — I can see in his shiny beetle eyes all his imaginings of conquering this enemy that for all I know he has secretly been dreaming about murdering his entire life. But before I can give him any kind of indication, before I'm even sure myself whether this truly is the moment, there is a flash of light in the entryway to the chamber, and we all turn to look.

Aaron has appeared, looking even worse than when we last saw him. For a second, my heart leaps up, believing this must mean that the queen is going to help us after all, but Aaron's expression is ghastly — not at all the face of someone who has come to tell us good news. He shoots me one agonized glance of guilt and shame and possibly a hint of defiant anger, and then he reaches back and pulls Annie out of the shadows behind him.

There is a piece of gray duct tape stretched across her mouth, and her eyes are red and angry and terrified. Her hands are bound behind her. The sight of her standing there, standing *here*, feet away from the new and improved Mr. Gabriel, after everything, is like a cosmic punch in the gut, in the heart, in my very soul. I nearly double over with the shock of it.

But then I recover, because I have to, and also because suddenly the person in the room I am hating the most is Aaron.

Fucking Aaron.

"Aaron, what . . . what the hell?"

"I had to!" he shouts back defensively. "Mr. Gabriel's demons found us! They — they had the queen surrounded. This was the only deal they would accept to let her live."

My poor brain can't even begin to process this. It's like last fall all over again, when Aaron first tried to betray us, only a

271

thousand, thousand times worse. I walk toward him, slowly, forgetting to even wonder whether Mr. Gabriel and the cart-demon will allow this freedom of movement. "I don't care what reasons you thought you had," I tell him in a deceptively calm voice. "Get her back up to where it's safe. Right. Now."

He shakes his head, looking miserable but determined. "I'm only doing what I have to do. Just like you are. My mistress —"

I haul my arm back and punch him in the face as hard as I can.

He reels backward as I stumble back myself, shaking out my hand. That hurt a lot more than I was expecting. But it was so worth it. I want to do it again. I stride forward to do just that, but one of the cart-demon's still-intact tentacles curls abruptly around my waist and yanks me backward. I scream with frustration and with the fresh agony in my shoulder, struggling to get free, to get my hands around Aaron's hateful throat, but the cart-demon is entirely too strong. In my peripheral vision, I see that Ryan and Peter are being similarly detained.

"That's enough," Mr. Gabriel says, as though we are quarreling children assigned to his care. "If our friend Aaron made a deal with my associates, it would be shamefully impolite to allow him to be molested while fulfilling his part of the bargain." He turns to consider Aaron, who can't seem to meet anyone's gaze at this point. "Bring her forward, please."

Aaron takes one of Annie's arms and pulls her stumbling forward several steps. She jerks away from him and backs against the nearest wall, staring in horror at Mr. Gabriel.

"That will do," Mr. Gabriel says, looking at her with a terrible smile. He turns back to Aaron. "You may go."

Aaron vanishes at once, like the disgusting coward he is.

"Now," Mr. Gabriel says softly, turning his eyes again to Annie, who immediately shrinks back even harder against the wall. "*There* you are." He begins to walk slowly toward her.

"Don't you touch her," I say.

He stops, sighing in annoyance. "Your turn will come soon enough, Cynthia. Try to be patient. You're interrupting my reunion with my beloved."

"She is not your *anything*," I snap at him, and then, as some demented musical-minded part of me shouts *Now, Pippin, now!* in the back of my mind, I scream LB's name.

LB practically flies across the room, throwing himself, finally, at his brother.

Mr. Gabriel seems momentarily paralyzed with shock at this attack from a completely unexpected quarter. But not for long. His surprise quickly turns to outrage, and he begins to fight back, not just with his claws but also with the familiar red glow of demon energy that I remember from the demon battle for the throne so long ago.

It becomes clear very soon that LB is at a supreme disadvantage.

Disturbingly quickly, our secret weapon goes from enthusiastic offense to a sort of frantic scrabbling to get away. It's heartbreaking to see him realize how outmatched he is, to understand that there is no possible way he can win this fight. And—I suspect that Mr. Gabriel isn't even actually trying to kill him. He wouldn't want to kill LB now; he'd want to keep him alive, to punish at his leisure.

I have to help him. I know it won't be enough, but I can't just stand here and watch.

I've never shared my protection from a distance before, except when the demoness took it from me. But I've sent it out as a weapon, and so I must be able to send it out as a shield in the same way. I could try attacking Mr. Gabriel, but from the various prison experiments it seems clear that my power is much stronger as defense than as offense. I force myself to concentrate, staring at LB and willing my power to settle over and into him the way it did when Ms. Královna borrowed it those two other times before. I visualize my follow spot again, and then add several more, all at full intensity and bathing LB with a powerful, illuminating glow of protection.

I can tell when it happens. Both because of the immediate unpleasant weakness I feel and the way LB suddenly stops cowering. Mr. Gabriel lands a couple more energy blows on him before realizing the change. They both stop and look over at me.

Mr. Gabriel smiles. "I'd nearly forgotten you could do that," he says. "Unfortunately for you and my betraying brother, however, I have enough power in reserve to overcome even your roachy protection. Observe."

And with that, he backhands LB with a bone-shattering swing of his arm, fortified with an intensely bright-red burst of demon energy. LB flies backward across the length of the chamber and crumples against the wall. One outstretched spider leg twitches feebly and then goes still.

Mr. Gabriel now turns his back to all of us and focuses once again on Annie, who starts screaming behind her duct tape. I pull at my tentacle restraints, but I know it's hopeless. There is nothing I can do. Mr. Gabriel starts toward her again, slowly and deliberately, drawing out the experience. Annie is throwing herself backward against the wall so hard I'm afraid she's going to bash her own head in. But maybe that's her intention. It would certainly be better than being taken alive by Mr. Gabriel.

But those should not be the only choices, goddammit. I was supposed to save her from this. Hot tears squeeze relentlessly from my eyes, perhaps trying to burn the image before me out of my vision. I have to do something. I have to do something. I can't let this happen.

But there it is, continuing to happen. Mr. Gabriel looks down and watches Annie convulsing in mad terror for a few more seconds, then says "Shh" in a soft voice. She stands instantly still, frozen in place. Her eyes still burn with fear and hatred but it's clear she's no longer able to move anything below her head.

He gestures at the floor beneath her, and suddenly the stony surface erupts, sending the section of rock she's standing on shooting upward until she is abruptly perched on a newly formed ledge along the wall, at least ten feet from the ground below.

Mr. Gabriel reaches out with one claw-hand and traces a delicate caress down Annie's cheek. Even with her on the ledge, he still towers over her, and he has to crouch slightly to be closer to her level. She closes her eyes, tears now spilling freely down her face.

"I know," he says. "This is a very emotional moment for

me, too." He caresses the other side of her face, capturing a tear on the tip of his claw. "I have missed you so very, very much. But I knew that we would be together again, no matter how hard they try to keep us apart. You belong to me."

He moves his other claw-hand, and the duct tape rips from her mouth. Her eyes fly open again as she cries out in pain. I can see her force herself to meet his gaze. "I do not belong to you, you psycho bastard," she says.

He smiles indulgently. "Oh, yes, you do. You used to know that; you have only forgotten. But you will remember. In time." He runs a claw along the side of her body this time, and I can't stand it, he can't be *winning,* he can't have Annie, it's not . . . he can't . . .

Annie is still doing her best to be strong. "No, I don't," she says to him. "Let me go."

He doesn't bother to respond this time. He just keeps his eyes on hers and continues to drag the tip of his claw along the side of her body, her legs, and back up to her face. He presses just hard enough this time to draw a thin line of blood along her cheek. Then he brings the claw up to his mouth and slowly licks it off.

"Stop it," Annie says, and her voice begins to falter. "Please."

"There we go," he says, his smile stretching wider. "There's my polite girl."

Annie spits in his face.

He jerks back, and for a second his eyes flash with anger, but his pleasant mask is back in place a moment later. He wipes the spittle from his cheek and then licks that off his claw, too. "Don't worry," he says. "I will teach you how to behave appropriately. The king's consort is an important role. I know you'll want to do your very best to please me."

He stares into her eyes, and I see her features begin to slacken, the hate and fear beginning to dissolve into something else.

No, I think, new horror cascading over me. *No.* He is not going to take her mind again.

I yank my power back from LB and thrust it toward Annie, driving it as far into her as I can, imagining every single cell of her being coated in my protection. She blinks and shakes her head, and suddenly her face is her own again. Her body, too. She looks at me, realizing what I've done.

Unfortunately, Mr. Gabriel realizes it at the same time.

He whirls toward me, staring down in fury. "Release her!"

"Nope. Sorry. I may not be able to stop you from touching her body, but you can stay right the fuck out of her mind."

Mr. Gabriel strides over to me and jabs one of his claws into my wounded shoulder.

The pain is explosive, worse even than Peter's light-tunnel back to the demon prison, and for a moment I'm lost in my own screaming agony.

When I come back to the room, Mr. Gabriel is watching me expectantly. "Release her. Now."

"You know I won't," I say softly. My throat hurts from screaming. "You'll have to kill me."

For a second, I think he is considering it. The fire twining in his eyes flares red, and his claw-hands are shaking with rage. But then he regains control.

"Oh, no. You won't escape that easily. I will have my long,

slow revenge." He smiles then, and looks away. Away toward Ryan and Peter.

"You can't hurt them," I remind him. "Our deal."

"Yes. *About* that." His smile stretches hideously. "Remember that time when I died, and was thereby released from all of my former obligations? I have this strange feeling that the same thing applies when one gets a new body. For all practical purposes, I am now a new man. A brand-new man. With nothing to stop me from doing whatever I want."

That can't be true. I look at him, trying to see the lie in his eyes. He has to be lying. He has to be.

"I can see that you don't quite trust my analysis of the situation. Shall we test out my theory? Why don't I kill one of your friends, and then we'll know for sure." He points back and forth between Ryan and Peter, watching my reaction. "Which one should it be?"

Suddenly LB drags himself forward from his corner. I'm shocked that he's alive, then relieved, and then confused. I have no idea what he hopes to accomplish.

"You must stop," he says to Mr. Gabriel. "You must not hurt them."

"*You* must shut up and think about what you've done," Mr. Gabriel snaps. "If you keep annoying me, you're only going to make it worse for yourself."

"I do not," LB says, still dragging himself forward, "listen to you anymore." He begins struggling to get to his feet.

Mr. Gabriel rolls his eyes. Then he looks back at me. "Okay, why don't I just choose for you. How about this one?" He points at Ryan.

"Stop!" Annie shouts. "Stop it!"

She is standing on her ledge, fists clenched tightly at her sides. Mr. Gabriel turns to look at her, eyebrows raised.

"Don't hurt them," she says. "Any of them. Please." She looks down, takes a breath. "I'll do what you want. I — I won't fight you. Just let them go."

"Annie, *no!*" I stare at her, appalled.

She looks at me. "Cyn, he's going to win. There's nothing we can do. I — I'm going to have to go with him no matter what. If I can save you —"

"You can't save that one, sweetling," Mr. Gabriel breaks in. "Cynthia has to pay for what she's done."

"But the others?"

He gazes at her, considering.

"Annie, no, you can't —" It's Ryan who says it this time. Mr. Gabriel doesn't even look at him, just waves a hand in his direction, and Ryan's mouth snaps shut.

"Annie, please." I'm begging now. "Please don't do this. We'll — we'll find another way —"

Annie laughs a sad, heartbreaking little laugh. "Still trying to tell me what to do," she says, shaking her head. "When will you learn that you can't keep making everyone's decisions for them? I'm a big girl, and I can make my own choices." She looks me right in the eye. "Just like I did when we were in the prison."

My heart falters to a stop inside my chest. She can't mean what I think she means. She looks away again almost at once, turning her eyes to Mr. Gabriel instead. "Let me come to you of my own free will. Isn't that what you really want anyway?"

"Yes," Mr. Gabriel says. He takes a step toward her.

Something in his face is different — it's like all the layers of power and threats and sarcasm have been peeled away, and what's left is raw desire . . . the part of him that has always believed in their supposed "love," the part of him that wrote those horrible poems, the part that wants so desperately to think that she really would come to him now, at the last, because she wants to. "Yes. That is exactly what I want."

She's crying again now, and I think that's what convinces him. She looks terrified and miserable but resolved, like she really is giving herself up to save Ryan and Peter and maybe LB, too . . . and I suppose she might be, because if this goes wrong, Mr. Gabriel will punish her for all eternity.

"Show me," he says, moving close to her. "Come and kiss me, like you mean it."

He leans down, his mouth by her face, big enough to eat her, but he only waits, tilting his head slightly. Waits for her to press her lips against him by choice, unglamoured, uncompelled.

She reaches out, resting one hand gently against his furry shoulder. Then she leans forward and touches her mouth to the very edge of his.

And then she grabs the amulet in both hands and leaps from the ledge.

The force of her fall breaks the delicate chain, and Mr. Gabriel roars in surprise and dismay and something deeper, darker — he had believed her, in that moment, and she had fooled him. The realization of that trickery, of that betrayal, sends him over the edge with maniacal rage.

In the second that she jumps, in the second it takes Mr. Gabriel to realize what is happening, I yank my protection back again and grab the cart-demon's tentacle in both hands, slamming my power into it with every fiber of my being. The cart-demon jerks back in surprise and pain, releasing us as all of its tentacles fly up to protect it from whatever is hurting it, unable to recognize the source of the attack.

While I'm doing this, I am also aware of Annie screaming Ryan's name as she falls.

She throws him the amulet, her aim pretty wildly off, but Ryan — having apparently also understood what Annie had planned to do — is ready, and he dives for it, catching it neatly before it hits the ground. He turns immediately and throws it to Peter.

Peter stares at it for a second and then turns and races for LB, jumping up and fastening (with a small burst of what I assume is some kind of magical demonic adhesive) the chain around his bull-bug head.

"Now," Peter tells him. "Go show your asshole brother who's boss."

Mr. Gabriel is already lumbering across the chamber, his eyes darting between Annie and the amulet, clearly torn between these two desperately compelling targets. The cart-demon realizes what has happened and turns to LB, reaching with many limbs to grab the amulet back, but LB has regained his feet with a quiet, awed kind of composure, seeming nearly overcome by the level of power that must now be racing through his battered body. He reaches out almost lazily toward the cart-demon with his pincers, and I see the impossibly bright red energy gathered there just before he strikes.

The cart-demon explodes into ribbons of purplish-blue gore.

Now LB has Mr. Gabriel's full attention. "That is *mine!*" he screams, jumping onto his brother with arms and claws spread wide.

Ryan, Peter, and I all run to the other side of the chamber where Annie is crouched against the wall.

"Are you okay?" I ask her, scanning for damage. "Are your legs broken?"

She shakes her head. "I thought for sure I'd have broken something—"

"That was me," Peter says, panting a little from all the running. "Slowed your fall."

If it weren't forbidden to kiss Peter, I would totally do it now. Annie nearly tackles him with her thank-you hug. Satisfied that she's all right, I turn back to face the battle; we're not out of the woods yet. I send my power once more to LB so that his brother's magical blows, now at only regular Gabriel strength, fail to achieve the level of damage intended. Between the amulet and my protection, LB is now more than a match for his brother. And he is giving it all he's got, which is not an insignificant amount—fueled by who knows how many years of abuse and fear and desire for payback.

Despite his very close acquaintance with the power of the amulet, Mr. Gabriel seems horribly surprised by how much effort the fight is requiring of him.

LB has Mr. Gabriel fully on the defensive now, pummeling him with both body and demon energy. "You," he shouts in between blows, "are . . . a very . . . bad . . . brother!" After a few more seconds, he stops, rearing up on his hind legs and staring down at the cowering form of Mr. Gabriel beneath him. "You must be punished," he says calmly, and raises his pincers for a final, crushing blow.

I don't want to take any chances. Remembering what the tiny demon had told Peter about the amulet amplifying power, I use my spotlight visualization again and — repurposing the protection I'd granted to LB — focus my weaponized resistance through the amulet, adding my own energy to what LB is already providing. I don't know for sure if it will work, since I'm not actually wearing the amulet myself . . . but perhaps the amulet recognizes that my efforts are intended to help its new owner, and so allows my contribution. Or maybe LB himself is the one who allows it. In any case, together we let everything fly against our common enemy.

Mr. Gabriel screams as the blow hits him, and then lies still upon the floor.

Before we can fully take in this very welcome spectacle, Mr. Crunchy comes bursting into the room.

"What — I thought you killed him!" Peter shouts at LB.

"I thought —" LB begins, then shakes his head and raises a pincer in Mr. Crunchy's direction. A burst of energy flies out and hits Mr. Crunchy square in his horrible smiling face. He explodes, showering us with more demon blood and guts and crunchy bits.

When the dust — and everything else — settles, LB limps over to us. He seems a bit tired and in a lot of pain. But also exultant. "I defied my brother."

"You sure did," I tell him. "And now you won't ever have to worry about him again. None of us will." I try to let the truth of that wash over me. It's over. It's really over. It's —

"Um," Annie says, looking past LB.

We all follow her gaze.

Mr. Gabriel is not dead.

Being much stronger than either Mr. Crunchy or the cart-demon, he apparently wasn't quite as easy to kill even with the help of the amulet. He does look to be in supremely bad shape, however. His legs are visibly broken in multiple places, his wings are mangled — one appears to be only attached by a thread — and there is a great deal of blood pooling beneath him on the ground.

Cautiously, we walk toward him.

He looks up, but he only seems to see Annie.

"Beloved," he whispers, reaching one nonhuman arm in her direction. "Come to me. It's not too late. I will forgive you your trespasses. Just . . . just a little atonement and all will be well. You can still be mine."

"You really just can't give it up, can you?" I ask him.

Now Mr. Gabriel notices the rest of us. His expression hardens, and he looks at me with fire in his eyes. "Your time will come, you bitch. I will make you suffer as no one has suffered in millions of years." He begins to smile, imagining this happy scenario.

Then he lashes out with completely unexpected speed and grabs Annie. He pulls her down against him, holding her there with surprising strength. I lunge forward, but he puts the tip of one claw against Annie's throat, and I force myself to stop.

"That's right," he says. "Don't you see? I will always win. Because we are meant to be together. Nothing — nothing can keep us apart."

Annie had ceased struggling when she felt the claw at her throat, but suddenly she begins again, throwing herself violently backward and out of his grasp.

"No means no, you asshole!" she shrieks at him.

He reaches for her again, but weakly; he must have used the last of his strength for that one final grab. Annie looks down at him for another second, her face filled with hate and fear and revulsion. Then she picks up one of the pieces of Mr. Crunchy that landed nearby. With a fierce grunt of effort, she lifts the severed crab leg, point down, and stabs Mr. Gabriel in his furry chest.

He screams, and then she stabs him again.

Ryan, Peter, and I pick up tools of our own, and we all begin to help her.

By the time we're done, his head has been completely severed from his body, along with several other parts of him. We didn't want to stop until we could feel really, really certain that he was absolutely dead this time.

"He's really gone now, isn't he?" Annie asks, rather breathlessly. She was the most energetic participant in the stabbing and dismembering activity.

"Yes," LB says with reassuring certainty. "My brother is truly dead. Not even his spirit remains."

Annie drops her claw and collapses in a heap to the ground. "Good," she says. "That's good. I — I might just need a minute now, okay, you guys?"

"Sure," I say. "There's one more thing I have to do anyway." I have suddenly remembered a promise that I made. I go over to Mr. Gabriel's mutilated torso, my jagged bit of Mr. Crunchy's exoskeleton in my hand. I use it to carve away at his chest until I find his heart. My wounded shoulder protests loudly (I think it's stopped bleeding, but now that I'm less distracted, the pain is becoming rather difficult to ignore) but I keep going anyway. His heart is bigger than I expected, but the rest of it fits what I'd imagined perfectly. It's a blackened, bloated, sickly-looking thing, with misshapen edges and a faintly rotten smell.

I put down my cutting tool and reach into Mr. Gabriel with both hands.

And then I wrench his heart from his body.

I lean down to where his lifeless head is lying in the dirt. "I told you I'd rip your heart out if you ever touched her again, you bastard," I whisper.

Then I walk back over to the others.

"What are you going to do with that?" Ryan asks.

"You must eat it," LB says.

We all turn to stare at him.

"You would gain much strength. It is a thing that is done."

Okay, obviously *that* is not going to happen.

I offer LB the heart instead. "Do you want it? I, um, don't think it would agree with me."

His beetle eyes widen in surprise. "Truly?"

"Sure. You had to put up with him longer than any of us. And we never would have defeated him without you."

He reaches forward with his two good legs and takes it reverently. Then he begins tearing into it with his bug-pincers, stuffing bloody black chunks of it into his mouth, and we all have to look away.

Chapter | 19

After he's done eating his brother's disgusting heart, LB removes the amulet and holds it out to me.

"Are you sure?" I ask him, secretly and enormously relieved. I'd been a little worried that he'd want to keep it. Not everyone could experience that much power and willingly give it away.

"Yes. You are our leader. The spoils are yours." He hesitates, then adds, "Also you already let me eat the heart."

I take it, holding it tight in my hand. Inside the milky-white stones, I can see swirling shapes that I suppose are the captured souls of the demons Mr. Gabriel killed to power this thing. I wonder if they know where they are. The red stone is, for the moment, quiet and dark.

"Are you going to keep it?" Ryan asks.

"No. I think — I think I have a better idea. A safer idea." I turn to Peter. "Can your tiny demon friend find out where the queen is holed up?"

The answer turns out to be yes, sort of, eventually. First, though, once Peter has summoned his little friend, he directs him to do something about my shoulder. (Apparently, the tiny demon is good at healing minor physical injuries, which is one of the ways he makes himself valuable to larger demons who might be able to help him survive.)

"Oh, yes, Great One!" he says, coming over to peer at the wound through my torn shirt. "It is very important to take care of these things right away. Tentacle demons can leave such nasty infections." He puts his tiny reptile hands on the skin around the bite, and I feel a surprisingly gentle warmth flow through me. When he's finished, it's still a little sore, but most of the pain is gone.

Peter offers his friend's services to LB, but the spider-demon refuses. "My brother's heart is already making me stronger," he says. "I do not need tiny-demon help."

Peter shrugs and sets the tiny demon to the next task.

He can't find the queen's hideout directly, but he *can* find some of Mr. Gabriel's supporters who were with the group that found her and made the deal with Aaron.

It also turns out that Aaron, in his haste to save his mistress, didn't think to make it a condition of the deal that the demons who agreed to let her live would also refrain from telling other demons where she was.

This makes it somewhat easier for Peter's demon to find out where she is — at the center of a violent mass of demons ready to finish the job that the other demons started — but it also means there is a violent mass of demons standing between us and our current objective.

"I will fight them," LB assures me.

I really kind of wanted to be done with the fighting by this point.

"Wait," Annie says. "Maybe you won't have to. No one but us knows that Mr. Gabriel is dead yet, right? So if LB shows up pretending to be speaking for his brother—"

"No," LB says.

"But—"

"No. I will not pretend."

"That's okay," I say quickly. "We'll think of something else. Maybe . . . what if you show up and tell everyone that your brother is dead? That would probably give some of his former supporters second thoughts, at least, right?"

LB nods his head slowly. "Yes. Many will not support him once they know he is dead."

I want to ask about those remaining few who might still support a dead Mr. Gabriel, but then I decide it's probably better not to know. And then I take a moment to marvel again at the fact that he's really dead. Gone. For good. For real. And then I look back at his massacred corpse to show myself that it's really, really true.

Because it's still so hard to believe.

In the end, I give the amulet temporarily back to LB, and Peter makes himself look like the blob monster again, and together they give the general impression that the rest of us are under their control. Then we let the tiny demon guide us to where the demon queen's hideout is. LB flashes the amulet around and announces his brother's demise and only has to make a few argumentative demons explode before the rest of them decide to disperse.

And then we are standing alone at the entrance to another shifty abandoned building/deep, dark cave/hole among the roots of a monstrous tree. Peter dismisses his little demon, who winks out at once. I'd wondered about bringing him inside with us, but Peter thought the queen's injuries, if she's really close to death, must be far beyond what his friend could deal with. And anyway, it's better for our plan if I'm the one doing the dealing.

Everyone has asked me, several times, whether I am really sure I want to do this.

I am. Whoever has the amulet is going to have to worry constantly about other demons trying to take it away. I *really* don't want that person to be me. And Ms. Královna is still the closest thing we have to an ally down here. If this works, she'll be able to stay the queen. That seems far better than having some new horrible demon in power who doesn't share our semi-friendly and mutually beneficial relationship history.

And besides — it gives me one last chance to make something good come out of all this.

"Well, you're the boss," Annie says, after asking me if I'm sure one more time.

"Apparently not," I respond seriously. "Not the boss of you, anyway." I want to be mad at her for what she did, for how she risked everything, *again*, when maybe there could have been another way. But I'm not. How can I be mad when she ended up saving us all? She was amazing. Maybe I really can learn to let the people I love make their own decisions. Even when I hate those decisions. Maybe especially when I hate them.

She holds my gaze, smiling a little. "Well, team captain, then. We're totally getting T-shirts, you know."

"Jerseys," Ryan says at once. "And I already called first pick of numbers."

Annie puts her hands on her hips. "What? Why do you get first pick? And when did you even call it?"

"Stop," I groan. "Everyone shut up and get in the hole."

LB goes in first, and the rest of us follow. I hear a startled cry up ahead and emerge to find LB holding Aaron up against the wall, a pincer open at his throat. We seem now to be inside a pleasant manor house, although the walls shift in color and style and the decorations can't seem to decide what they want to be. Out of the corner of my eye, I almost get glimpses of stone-walled cave and giant tree-hole, but for the most part the manor house facade holds.

"You're—you're not dead!" Aaron says. He has a very satisfying black eye starting to form. I would like to give him a matching one on the other side.

"No thanks to you," I snarl at him. "Where's your mistress?"

His face goes white. "Cyn—please. She didn't know. I'm the one who made that deal. Don't—"

"Aaron," calls a weak but familiar voice through an open doorway. "Don't be rude. Invite our guests in."

LB steps back, and Aaron, swallowing nervously, leads us into the next room. The demon queen is sprawled out on an enormous circular bed. She's in full demon form, all fishy and eely, with her poisonous stingers — many of them broken or frayed — arranged artistically around her on tiny cushions. Her tentacles (she has those, too, although thankfully not very many) are also visibly damaged, and there are scary-looking wounds all along her body. Even her colors are dim and muted. She takes in our motley crew, noting LB with particular interest, and then settles her eyes on me.

"To what do I owe the pleasure?" she asks. "You'll have to forgive me for not getting up. I'm afraid I'm not quite at my best at the moment."

"I may be able to do something about that," I tell her.

I hold my hand out to LB, and he takes off the amulet and places it in my open palm.

The queen stares, captivated.

"So it's true," she whispers. "All of it. And you — you managed to take it from him?"

"He's dead. For real this time."

"I see."

She still hasn't taken her eyes off the amulet.

"I think," I go on, "that I may be able to use this to heal you."

Now she looks at me again, an unmistakable wariness in her eyes.

"If I wanted to kill you, I wouldn't have to be sneaky about it," I point out. "Trust me, I have no desire to be queen of the demons, or to help anyone else take your place. I just . . . I just want all of this to be over. Well, and I want a few other things, too."

Somehow, that last part makes her relax. I guess if there's one thing demons understand, it's making deals.

I thought a lot about what to ask for here. I'm sure there's plenty I could bargain for, with the amulet in my hand. I could make it so we all get into any schools we want and have our pick of all the top choices. I could bargain for money, for power, for all the best opportunities for all of us, for the rest of our lives. But I don't want those things that way. I don't want to know that everything good that happens to us is because of everything bad that happened down here.

I want to be done with deals. Done with demons. I want this to be my last trip ever and to not have to come back again as long as I live.

"I want you to fix it so that no more demons can come up uninvited to interfere in our lives ever again," I tell her. There's a slight cough behind me, and I roll my eyes. "Not counting Peter, who is, obviously, already interfering. And Peter can still summon his friends or associates or whatever if he wants to. But I want all of us to be safe from any of Mr. Gabriel's former followers seeking revenge, or anyone else coming after us for any reason whatsoever. 'All of us' to include Ryan, Annie, Peter, Leticia, Diane, William, and all of our families and friends and loved ones."

I'd wanted to include LB in that list, but he refused. He *wants* to fight any of his brother's supporters who dare to come after him. And I hate that idea, but I didn't argue. Much. See? I can learn. I am learning.

I did suggest one possible alternative, though, which he said would be okay.

"Also, LB—that's the big guy there—is allowed to come ask you for a favor if he ever needs one. Which you will grant, if it's within your power and doesn't directly threaten your goals and interests."

The queen nods, acquiescing.

There's a chorus of other slight coughs behind me.

"*Also,* none of us are ever to get any terrible diseases like cancer or syphilis or anything else, and none of us will die in tragic accidents. And we'll always be able to get really good deals on phone and cable and internet service. And shoes." I threw in that last one especially for Diane.

I wait, and then there's one more very quiet cough.

I manage to smother a smile. "And Ryan will have his lovely full head of hair for the rest of his life and not go bald like all the men on his mother's side have since the dawn of time."

"I believe all of that can be arranged," the queen says, smiling slightly.

"And — and I want to be able to get great theater tickets at ridiculous discounts wherever and whenever I want. Forever." Well, why not? Shut up.

"Done. In exchange for what exactly?"

"I am going to use my ability and this amulet to heal you. If I can. But I think I can. And then — and then I am going to give the amulet to you."

She blinks, the only outward sign of her surprise. I'm sure she thought it would be a lot harder to make me hand it over. If I would at all. I know I could have tried for a deal that was just a loan, so that we'd have to renegotiate for new things after so many years or whatever. But I really do want to be done down here. I don't want to have to think about seeing her again, about making new deals. Yeah, I know I might regret that down the line, and maybe I should be adding things about college funds for my potential future kids or whatever . . . but aside from a few small rewards that I think we've totally earned, I don't want demons controlling our lives. Not even in good ways.

She looks at me for a long moment, something I can't identify flickering just behind her eyes.

"Deal," she says at last, and I feel the tingly sensation of a deal made, and I exhale with enormous relief.

Then I step forward and sit beside her on the bed. I hold the amulet in one hand and place the other on her smooth, scaly skin. Closing my eyes, I visualize my protection channeling through the amulet and into the demoness. As with Peter in the prison, I only have to go halfway; she takes it from there, pulling my power toward her and using it to heal herself. I think that's part of why I couldn't remove the curse from Ryan in the same way — not being a demon, he wasn't able to direct the power on his side of things. Well, that, and possibly curses are different from other kinds of wounds. Peter seemed pretty sure that only the curse-placer could remove the curse, after all.

Or else it's just one more thing about how demon stuff works that I will never understand.

My thoughts start to float around, and I realize that I'm drifting away inside myself, as I did that first time with Peter. It's kind of nice, and I don't fight it. When I come back, Ryan is sitting beside me and my head is resting on his shoulder.

"Did it work?" I ask sleepily. I feel like I could take the world's longest nap, right here on this giant demon bed.

"Yes," says the queen in a far stronger voice than before. I turn to see her standing now, but I don't remember her actually getting up. "Thank you, dear Cynthia. That was . . . quite refreshing." She's switched to her partial human form, which makes it a lot easier to talk to her. She also looks much, much better.

"Excellent. It's been a pleasure doing business with you. Except not really."

"Of course, you realize this doesn't negate our previous deal."

I stare up at her, suddenly no longer sleepy.

"What?"

"Our previous deal. The lendings to me of your power? You've still got one more to go."

"No. Because remember? Three times? That, just now, was the third time. Deal over. I never have to come back here again."

"I'm afraid that's not the case, Cynthia."

I feel the familiar unpleasant sensation of hatching panic beetles, but I ignore them, because she is wrong about this and so there is nothing to panic about.

"No. No, no. Three times. Those were the terms. The first time, and then two more." I want to ask someone to back me up on this, but no one else was actually present and conscious when she and I made the original deal in the first place.

"Two more times *of my choosing*," she says. "I did not summon you this time."

"But —" I point at Aaron. "He . . . he came, and . . . and he said . . ."

"I was unconscious," she says calmly. "Aaron may have asked you to come, but it was not at my command. And while I greatly appreciate your generous offer just now to help me heal my very serious wounds, that was, in fact, your own generous offer. I didn't ask you to do it."

I keep staring at her. "You can't be serious."

She only smiles.

"I gave you the amulet! You're — you're like a million times stronger now. You won't even need me! Just . . . just let this be the third time." My voice gets very small. "Please."

"I'm sorry, Cynthia. I cannot change the terms of the deal any more than you can."

I am speechless. This is really, really not fair.

"But," Ryan says, "but . . . you could just promise not to summon her again, couldn't you? I mean, okay, you can't change the deal, but you don't have to act on the third time, right? You could just let it go."

"I could," she agrees. "And perhaps, as Cynthia has pointed out, I will not need her assistance again. But if I do . . ." She trails off and shrugs her almost-human shoulders.

Then she turns and moves toward a door that appears to lead farther inside her sanctuary.

"Aaron, please show our guests out." And with that, she disappears through the doorway.

Aaron silently leads us back out to the main entrance. LB once again goes first, then Ryan, Peter, and Annie. As I duck my head to go after them, Aaron puts a hand on my arm. He stands like that for a moment, seeming to be trying to think of something to say.

"I hate you," I tell him.

"I'm sorry," he says. "For all of it, really. I kind of like you guys, you know. I hope . . . I hope she decides never to call you again."

I shake him off and push my way out of the hole. I glance back only once, and see his shoulder fins waving in what might be farewell.

There is a gateway waiting for us outside the queen's hideout.

I turn to LB. "We have to go back now."

"Yes," he says.

"Are you . . . will you be okay? You did a lot of fighting today. I know you said your brother's heart will help, but . . ."

"I will be okay," he says in his calm, gravelly voice. "I will be more than okay."

"Well, good. That's good. I'm very glad to hear that," I say, meaning it. I reach up to place my hand on his abdomen, which no longer disgusts me nearly as much as it used to. "Thank you for all of your help. You were a very important member of our team."

LB looks down at me with his shiny, unreadable eyes. "If you need help again, I will help you. A promise. Not a deal."

"Thank you, LB," I say, surprised and pleased. "That is a very lovely promise."

"Maybe I'll give you a call sometime," Peter tells him. "Check in, see how things are going."

LB nods his bull-bug head, apparently finding this an acceptable proposal, and then begins lumbering away down the street/path/dried-up ravine. He does already seem stronger. He's also got a noticeable bounce in his step, although I'm not sure that has anything to do with his physical state of being.

The gateway brings us back to the library. It's dark outside, and I realize I have no idea how much time has passed this round.

"I think we've been gone at least another full day," Peter says, guessing our concern. "And one night."

"Can you do anything about that?" Ryan asks him. "Help us out? Jorge might have run out of excuses for me by now."

"Sure," Peter says. "I can help your families believe whatever you want to come up with. Overnight school bonding activity or something?"

I feel a little guilty letting Peter magically affect our parents' minds, but . . . in the end I accept, as does everyone else. One must be practical about these things.

With Peter's help, we get out of the school without setting off any alarms or anything. Ryan takes out his phone and walks a few feet away to call for a cab. Annie steps away too, to give Peter and me a chance to say good-bye.

He is smiling at me sadly. "I guess it might be a while," he says.

"Not too long, maybe," I say. "You could come see *Les Misérables* when it goes up."

"That's true. But that's not what I meant." He looks at Ryan.

"Do not sit around waiting for us to break up, Peter. It's not happening."

"I know," he says. Then his smile twists up a little and he gets that evil glint in his eye that I have learned to be wary of. "Not anytime soon, anyway. But I've got time."

The car arrives, and Peter walks us over to it.

"You're not coming?" Ryan asks.

"I've got my own way home," Peter says. "Is it okay if I kiss your girlfriend good-bye?"

"Nope," Ryan says, pulling me into the car beside him. But then he pauses, and leans over to offer Peter his hand. "Thanks, Peter. For everything. We owe you a lot. I — I owe you a lot."

Peter looks for a moment like he's trying to decide what to say. Then he just takes Ryan's hand and shakes it. "You're welcome. Try to stay out of trouble for a while this time, yeah?"

Then Annie gets in on the other side of me, and then we are all waving at Peter through the window. And then the car turns a corner, and he is out of sight.

Chapter | 20

The cast list goes up Monday morning.

Ryan's name is there, next to Javert, exactly where it should be.

Jeff ended up with Thénardier, which (we hear) he claims to be fine with, since he's already had the chance to play Javert at his old school. We don't care if he's fine with it or not, though, really.

Mr. Henry is overjoyed to have his anticipated dream cast, since everyone else also got the parts they had been expecting to. I am overjoyed to get to begin work on the barricade, as well as the runaway cart and the suicide bridge and everything else. My backstage minions are primed and ready.

I am also overjoyed to be back in the human world where I belong, surrounded by my friends, and not facing any immediate threats of death or destruction. I try not to think too much about the possibility of being called back once more to the demon world. The queen really is super strong with the aid of the amulet now. She should not need me. At least not anytime soon. And maybe not ever. Probably not ever. Really almost certainly not ever. So I am not going to worry about that. At all.

But I'm still going to keep practicing using my ability. I know Peter will help me if I ask. Hopefully I'll never need to use it. But I spent too much time over this last week kicking myself for not being prepared. I'm not going to be caught unprepared again.

Ryan has started talking about college applications again. And snacks. I am overjoyed about this, too.

Peter sends a letter a couple of weeks later, including not only news about himself but also of LB, whom he has taken to summoning every now and again for a little chat and check-in. LB has apparently gained some notoriety for his role in recent events, and now leads a small gang of demons who follow him as their leader. I'm really glad for him. I wonder if we can send them down some team jerseys.

Les Misérables rehearsals started the week after callbacks. It's mostly a ridiculous lovefest, because all of us are so excited to be a part of it. Mr. Henry has literally not stopped smiling once since the cast list went up. Jeff really does seem to be perfectly content being Thénardier (not that it matters, but whatever) and he's actually pretty funny in the bits I've gotten to see him do so far. Peter has offered to give him boils or something for our amusement, but really we don't mind him so much now that he's no longer a threat to the proper order of things in the universe.

Tonight is the first night Ryan is going to sing "Stars," and even though I have heard him sing this song about a hundred million times now, I sneak out to the audience to watch him. It's always different when he's onstage; he stops being Ryan and becomes whoever he's playing, and even though I've seen that happen a whole bunch of times, too, it doesn't stop being a magical thing to see.

The music begins and at first no one but me and Mr. Henry is paying much attention, but then Ryan begins to sing and everyone else stops what they're doing and turns toward the stage. He begins softly, taking his time, and as always I could just sit and listen to him forever. But I'm also listening to the words, and even though I know how the story goes and of course this is already the beginning of the end for poor Javert, setting up his inflexible stance that ultimately breaks him, right now all I can hear is the part about the stars all knowing their place in the sky, and that sense of everything being where it belongs washes over me again. I'm so profoundly relieved and grateful to be here, now, living this moment and doing what I love and being with the best people in the world.

When he finishes, everyone in the audience and several people who have been watching from the wings break into spontaneous applause and Mr. Henry beams and Ryan lifts his head and looks to where he knows I will be sitting, to share this moment with me, and I can tell that he, too, is so very grateful for right now.

Later, while Mr. Iverson is working with the chorus on "At the End of the Day," Ryan comes to find me backstage.

"Finish that barricade yet?" he asks, pulling me into a hug.

"Don't rush me unless you want technical difficulties during your suicide scene," I say into his chest. He smells good, like sanity and safety and clean, sexy teenage boy.

Everything is going really well, and I am so happy, and . . . I still can't quite relax. Not quite.

But I want to. I try to. I think happy thoughts and I force myself to smile.

"I can feel you smiling," Ryan says accusingly. I try not to mind that he can't tell a real smile from a forced one. But then, he's not actually looking at me. Just feeling the way my face moves against his chest. Feelings can be deceiving.

"That's because everything is good. And no one is trying to kill us. And Mr. Gabriel is really, finally dead." I say this like I believe it, hoping it might help.

And I do believe it. I do. Of course I do. I saw him.

But you saw him the last time, too, the panic beetles, still there, always there, whisper hatefully, their hooked beetle feet horribly pierced into the soft tissue of my guts.

"Yes," he agrees. "All of those things are very true. Also, this show is going to be amazing."

"That is also very true."

Out in the auditorium, the chorus is singing about being one day nearer to dying and how there's going to be hell to pay and I close my eyes and try to focus instead on the feel of Ryan's heart beating strongly and steadily inside his chest.

"It's really over, Cyn," he whispers. "He's gone. It's going to be okay."

"I know," I say.

But I am lying. I don't know if I'll ever be able to believe we're really safe.

After rehearsal, we meet up with a bunch of our friends at the diner. I pause in the doorway, just looking, once more just appreciating the way they are all, against all odds, *still* here and healthy and alive.

Annie and William went through a bit of a rough patch when we first got back—apparently Annie wasn't entirely wrong about William starting to wonder if all the crazy demon stuff was really something he was prepared to deal with. But Annie managed to talk him down, and at the moment they seem as blissfully in love with each other as they ever were. As I watch, Annie glances down to take a bite of her pie, and William's eyes on her face don't betray the slightest trace of doubt. He looks ready to follow her anywhere. Which shouldn't ever have to be anyplace too terrible ever again.

Diane and Leticia are sharing fries and making each other taste various concoctions of dipping substances and laughing hysterically. Diane and I had a bit of a rough patch of our own, because she was still mad at me for not understanding how much it sucked for them to have to stay behind while we kept going off to probably die. But last week she came and sat next to me on the floor of the band wing in the morning and reached over and borrowed my pencil out of my hand without asking, and I knew then that I was forgiven. Leticia walked in a moment later and saw what was happening and gave Diane a long and silent hug, and none of us ever spoke about it again.

Ryan has gone over to talk to Jorge and the other guys, and is already helping himself to whatever Jorge is eating, and so I head over to where my girls (and William) are and try to catch the waitress's eye. Annie manages to give me one of her thousand-watt smiles around a mouthful of pie, and Diane slides the plate of fries toward me, and then Leticia slides over a bowl of what looks like ketchup and mustard and coleslaw all mixed together, waggling her eyebrows suggestively, and I'm so happy and in love with all of them that I would totally sweep them into a giant group hug if it were physically possible to do so without all of us ending up covered in coleslaw and pie.

But underneath the happy I can still feel the panic beetles dragging around inside me with their trails of terror and despair, and I don't know what to do about that. I don't know how to make them stop. Because I still don't know how to believe it's really over.

That night, I have three dreams.

The first is one of the Peter dreams I still have every once in a while. I continue to try to not feel bad about these dreams, and tell myself they are manifestations of that single rogue electron that maintains the tiny secret Peter fan club in some undisclosed location deep inside of me. I tell myself that that electron is entitled to dream its dreams just like the rest of us. I tell myself that I can't help it, and so feeling bad would be pointless.

We are sitting backstage at camp, and the show being performed is something about giant demons shaped like flowers and insects and mud. At the moment, a blade of grass is singing a solo about the taste of human flesh.

Peter is stroking the inside of my arm. It leaves a trail of tiny sparks, and I can feel them travel all the way down to my toes.

"You know these dreams make me very uncomfortable," I tell him.

"You don't seem very uncomfortable," he says, grinning. He moves his fingers up to the side of my neck, and I shiver.

"But I will be. Later."

"Oh, well."

He pulls me close and kisses me, and I kiss him back, because it's only a dream and doesn't count.

The second dream is far less pleasant.

I'm running through the demon prison, giant hand-monster pieces of the Craftsman chasing me through the dark, stony landscape. I see a doorway ahead and I dive through it, but instead of leading to another part of the prison, it places me back in the chamber where we killed Mr. Gabriel. All the various demon body parts are still there, including Mr. Gabriel's severed head, which opens its eyes as I approach.

"You're dead," I tell him firmly. "You're really dead this time."

"Am I, though?" he asks, his human voice speaking clearly through his Minotaur mouth. "Will I ever really be dead? Maybe I will live on forever in your dreams."

"No," I say, because that is a horrible idea. "Anyway, my dreams don't count. Nothing that happens in dreams is real."

Mr. Gabriel raises an eyebrow at me and says nothing.

I turn and walk away, looking for the exit, but I can't find it. I stumble over something, and I look down to see a Frisbee-size version of Mr. Crunchy's smiling face. As I watch, it grows two long crab legs and rises up from the ground. I back away, and it comes smiling after me.

"You're dead, too!" I tell him, and he tilts his face inquisitively as if to silently echo Mr. Gabriel's "Am I, though?"

I feel around for the piece of him I used to stab Mr. Gabriel but I forgot to bring it, and I don't have any other kind of weapon, and Mr. Crunchy is getting closer. I turn around and run, still looking for a way out. Instead I find myself headed for a shimmery curtain of light. I push past it, and I see Mr. Gabriel's overturned cart and the golden urn lying shattered on the ground. I see the cart-demon caught between his two forms, sporting several truncated tentacles and oozing purplish-black blood onto the floor. He stretches some of those tentacles toward me, his eyes bright white in the otherwise dim and shadowy space.

I glance back to see where Mr. Crunchy is and I slam into something hard that scrapes my skin and clutches at me as soon as I try to pull away. I look up and the Craftsman's fox-like face gazes down at me, his eyes burning like coals. "You stole from me," he says. "I haven't forgotten that." His twig-fingers dig painfully into my arms.

"You'll never really be free," Mr. Gabriel says from behind

me, and I struggle to turn around. He is standing in his attractive human form, all in one piece again. Mr. Crunchy's head on its two crab legs stands to one side of him, bouncing slowly up and down in place, and behind him I see the prison flower monster, its leaf-hands clenching rhythmically around nothing. There are more demons behind him, countless more, so *many*, and the Craftsman's grip grows tighter and tighter until everything goes black and the shadows have swallowed me whole.

In the third dream, I am sitting across a table from the demon queen. The table is small and round and covered with a pretty pastel tablecloth. She is in her mostly human form, looking like the sexy replacement Italian teacher she had briefly impersonated last year, but her long and twisty horns stretch up and out from her gorgeous thick dark hair, and her hands extend into bright-red claw-nails that come to shiny points. The amulet rests snugly atop her impressive cleavage, hanging from a new silver chain. (The chain, I notice, is a lot tougher-looking than the delicate one Mr. Gabriel had. I can tell it's reinforced with a good deal of magical energy, too. Ms. Královna is no dummy.) The red stone glows with what seems like immense satisfaction. I guess it's happy with its new mistress. Aaron is serving us tea. He's wearing an apron that says DEPECHE MODE. His shoulder fins seem larger than I remember, and his striped eely tail lies in a long, lazy coil behind him.

"Aaron believes I owe you a debt," the queen says, wrapping her nail-claws around a floral teacup. Aaron pours again and the scent of jasmine now floats enticingly out of my own cup, which is adorned with tiny musical notes and green finches. I pick it up in my own normal human hands. It's pleasantly warm between my palms.

"I did help you when I didn't actually have to," I say. "Even after what Aaron did to Annie." He looks away, ashamed, but I don't care. I want to punch him again, but I don't want to put down my cup.

"True," she says, taking another sip of her tea. I take a sip of mine, and the taste is exquisite, more delicious than tea has any right to be. I wonder what's in it.

"I do not generally concern myself with repaying debts," she continues, "and it's possible Aaron only feels lingering human guilt for having betrayed you." She smiles at him, momentarily distracted. "His human feelings are so . . . peculiar. We will grind them out of him eventually, of course, but I find I am rather enjoying them for the time being."

Aaron blushes, seeming both embarrassed and pleased and also possibly slightly aroused, and I want to get this conversation back on track before they forget I'm there and start doing whatever unimaginable things they do together when they're alone.

"Wasn't it Aaron's fault that Mr. Gabriel got out in the first place?" I ask.

Aaron jerks his head up, glaring at me, but the queen only laughs.

"Yes, of course. But he has more than redeemed himself. And in the end, I seem to have come out even further ahead than if your Mr. Gabriel had never escaped at all." She caresses the amulet absently with one red claw-tip.

"Why does everyone always call him *my* Mr. Gabriel?" I demand. I really hate when they do that.

She only looks at me, still smiling.

"More tea?" Aaron asks her, and she holds out her cup for him to pour. I remember to take another sip of mine, and again I'm amazed by how good it is.

"In any case, I have decided to give you a small gift in return, Cynthia."

"Are you forfeiting the third visit?" I ask hopefully.

"No. But I am granting you some time. A guarantee that I will not call in that final favor anytime soon. Certainly not within the next few years, probably not for the next ten or fifteen." She looks at me, and her eyes seem to penetrate right down to my core. I don't know what she sees there, but it captures her attention for several long seconds before she continues. "Perhaps not for decades. I will grant you as much of a reprieve as I can. You . . . have spent enough time in the demon world for now, I think."

Yes, I say in response, not with my lips but with my entire being, and I can tell the demoness has heard it just as clearly as if I had spoken it aloud.

"That is all for now," she says. "You should probably be getting back. Finish your tea."

I drink the rest of what is in my cup, wanting to remember the way it tastes, the way it embodies so much more than what it should, and then Aaron is gesturing for me to follow him.

"Thank you," I whisper to the queen.

She nods once, slowly. I rise, placing my cloth napkin on the table, and follow Aaron to the door.

"Thank you, too," I tell him. "I guess I don't really hate you."

"It's okay," he says. "I get it if you do. I've done some pretty terrible things to get what I want. But I know you understand what it's like to want things."

I reach for the door, which is glowing softly, but before I can go through he calls my name and I turn back.

"The panic beetles are all dead now," he says. "Relax already."

I step through the door and wake up in my own bed.

There is just the faintest hint of morning light beginning to filter through the window shades. I lie there quietly, still tasting the tea on my tongue, feeling lighter and more hopeful than I have in a very long time. Distantly, I think I hear something, and then I laugh out loud as I realize it is my own brain, playing "Any Dream Will Do" from *Joseph and the Amazing Technicolor Dreamcoat* as what it seems to feel is appropriate accompaniment to this glorious new morning. I'm not sure if it's the line about the breaking dawn or the obvious dream connection or if that's just what coincidentally decided to come up via shuffle on my internal playlist at that moment.

My good mood falters slightly as I contemplate whether the last dream being real — which I have no doubt it truly was — means all the dreams were real. Maybe not; maybe my brain was just running the full spectrum: one nice dream, one nightmare, and one that wasn't really a dream at all. That seems possible. It's not like everything always has to be all or nothing.

I've never really liked that about the world; mostly I *want* things to be all or nothing. I want up and down, good and bad, right and wrong all to be clearly defined with solid boundaries and no leaking of goodness into badness and wrongness into rightness or any other disharmony of concepts. But I think about LB, and Peter, and even Aaron, and I don't know how to reconcile what I want with the realities of who they are and what they've done. And I think about Ryan, and Annie, and how I don't always love their choices but how that won't ever stop me from loving them. And I think about me, and how my own right-and-wrong boundaries have gotten more than a little muddy and how maybe in the big scheme of things it's not really the very worst thing that can happen.

I mean seriously, have I learned nothing from *Les Misérables*? Try too hard to hold on to all of your rigid ideas about black and white and the next thing you know you're jumping off a bridge because you let a good man who did some questionable things go save another good man instead of dragging him off to jail where you've been sure he belongs for seventeen years and you just can't handle all of those contradictions. I mean the lesson is really pretty clear.

I do know that real life is not *always* exactly the same as musical theater. (More's the pity.)

I also know that it's probably always going to be a lot messier than I want it be. But maybe I can learn to be okay with that.

I decide that I don't have to figure all of this out right

this second. Maybe I'll tell Ryan about the dreams and ask him what he thinks. Well, I'll certainly tell him about the Ms. Královna dream, because I know it will put his mind at ease as well. Probably I will not mention the Peter dream. Because there wouldn't be any point, and because a girl's subconscious is her own business, and so almost entirely no more secrets means still some very tiny secrets, sometimes.

My tiny electron of Peter-fandom twinges knowingly somewhere inside me.

But then it is drowned out by all the other electrons that are in love with Ryan, and I smile thinking about getting to see him in a few hours, and of all the many hours after that. Years' worth of hours. With no demons. And no more trips to the demon world.

At least not for a very, very long time.

Acknowledgments

As usual, writing this novel was not a solo journey. So much gratefulness goes out to awesome draft readers Brent Felker, Bridey Flynn, and Jenny Weiss, who provided crucial notes and reassurance, and to Jaz Ellis for sharing his stage-lighting savvy and his heart and for generally making my life better in every conceivable way. Thanks also to everyone who answered my random questions about things like school schedules and personal injury experiences; to Kristin Cartee for sentence-wording opinions, punctuation discussions, and occasional panic management; and to all my friends for their abundant support and encouragement when I needed it, which was often this time around. And of course, none of this would be possible without my agent, Jodi Reamer, and my editor, Sarah Ketchersid, who remain amazing and wonderful and for whom I am still so grateful, always.